Also By Brenda Hasse

<u>An Afterlife Journey Trilogy</u>
On The Third Day
From Beyond The Grave
Until We Meet Again

<u>Adult</u>
Haunted Fenton
The Haunted Tours Of Fenton
A Victim Of Desperation

<u>Young Adult</u>
The Freelancer
A Lady's Destiny
The Moment Of Trust
Wilkinshire

<u>Picture Books For Children</u>
My Horsy And Me, What Can We Be?
A Unicorn For My Birthday
Yes, I Am Loved

The Healer's Apprentice

~

Brenda Hasse

The Healer's Apprentice

Copyright © 2024 Brenda Hasse

All rights reserved. No part of the book may be used or reproduced by any means, graphic, electronic, or mechanical, including photocopying, recording, taping, or by any storage information retrieving system without the permission of the publisher except in the case of brief quotations embodied in critical articles or reviews.

The characters in this novel are based on several people in history, while others are fictional. The names, incidences, organizations, and dialogue, in part, are either the products of the author's imagination or used fictitiously.

Because of the dynamic nature of the Internet and Web, addresses and links may have changed since publication and may no longer be valid.
Cover background photo by Mark Carline.

979-8-9864383-5-1 (HC)
979-8-9864383-6-8 (PB)
979-8-9864383-7-5 (EBK)

To my husband, Chuck

Chapter 1

Edinburgh, Scotland – February 1786

Haggadah leaned out of the room's only window and snatched the damp clothing from the rope that spanned the width of the narrow cobblestone lane. She stared at the chaos of people that resembled scrambling ants in the crowded passageway several stories below. A steady drizzle of rain dampened her face, forcing her back inside to help her mother, Freya, pack what little they had. "It's starting to rain."

A young woman of ten and six, Haggadah watched her mother shove a nub of a candle, a stale half-loaf of bread, a jar of preserves they received as a gift, and a small tin containing two coins into the carpetbag.

The satchel had been a gift from Frey's wealthy employer, or so Haggadah had been told. Even though her mother tried to shield her from the harsh realities of life, Freya confided the truth of her pregnancy. As a maid, she had been raped by her employer. Once the growing child within her became apparent, the man's uncompassionate wife fired Freya from her job to save the wealthy family from social embarrassment or perhaps continue the masquerade of her marriage. Cast out into the street, Freya was left to struggle on her own. With a few coins to her name, the expectant mother became a tenant in a crowded room on Niddry's Wynd, giving her a roof over her head.

When it came time for the baby to be born, Freya's labor was long and laborious. Concerned, one of the women fetched the town healer to help with the difficult birth. As the infant was placed in her arms, she stared at her daughter's innocent, cherub face. Even though her pregnancy had cost her dearly, she considered the baby a blessing.

Haggadah knew she was loved, for her mother often told her so. Together, the pair found a way to survive. After all, they had no other choice.

Six months ago, they watched from a distance on the first day of August as the Grand Master Mason, Lord Haddo, laid the cornerstone for the construction of the

South Bridge and announced the demolition of the tenement building to make way. Now that the construction contract was awarded, word spread throughout the building for the occupants' immediate eviction. The crew would begin tearing down the tenements by day's end.

Haggadah handed the damp, tattered garments to her mother.

Three resounding knocks from a strong fist sounded upon the door, warning the pair that their time in the tiny apartment had ended.

Panic sparked within Haggadah's heart as she looked at the closed apartment door and then at her mother. "Mum?"

Freya frantically glanced around the room as footfalls echoed from the staircase. She looked at her daughter and nodded toward the superstitious herb hanging on the wall. "Grab the bay leaves. We must hurry." After placing the wadded clothing in the center of their threadbare blanket, she tied the opposite corners together, forming a makeshift knapsack. The mild exertion caused Freya to cough. She paused to inhale a wheezing, deep breath and gather her strength.

Haggadah pulled the bay leaves from the nail where they hung. Even though she and her mother attended Mass every Sunday, always praying for a better life, they believed in the silly wives' tale of the herb warding off any witches or evil doers. Haggadah gave her mother the dried and dusty herb before scanning the dirty, bare walls and room. It was odd to see it empty of the twenty people usually huddled together and sleeping on the floor. She watched her mother place the talisman in the carpetbag.

Heavy footfalls echoed on the stairs as the tenants from the upper two floors evacuated the building. Haggadah was thankful she would never climb the twelve flights of stairs to get to their apartment again, but where would she and her mother live now? The four walls were the only home she had ever known.

"Put on your cloak." Freya ordered as she took both garments from the peg on the wall and handed Haggadah her overcoat. "Then slip your arms through the ties," she gave the makeshift knapsack to her daughter, "and carry this on your back." A cough rattled deep within her chest once again.

Concern masked Haggadah's face as she adjusted the knapsack on her back and waited with her hand on the doorknob for her mother to catch her breath. She took one last look at the room. Even though their home was often cold during the winter, reeked from the excrement in the bucket used as a chamber pot, and the air was filled with smoke from the small fireplace, at least it protected them from the weather. No longer would they have that luxury.

"We must go." Freya picked up the carpetbag, jingling the two coins in a small tin at its bottom.

Haggadah opened the door, stepped forward, and nearly collided with a barrel-chested man rushing down the stairs.

Freya stepped forward and turned to grasp the doorknob. She saw the nearly full bucket in the corner of the room. No one had thrown its contents to the street below at the stroke of ten the previous night. It was of no concern to her now. The single mother left the room, closing the door.

Looking over her shoulder to ensure her mother was behind her, Haggadah descended the stairs at a slow pace, hoping her matriarch could do so without becoming winded. As she stepped onto the cobblestone pavement of Niddry's Wynd, she looked heavenward at the gray morning sky. Its continued drizzle reflected the sorrow in her heart. Haggadah pulled her hood onto her head and turned, expecting her mother. Instead, a nicely dressed family stepped onto the narrow, cobbled street. She assumed they had lived on a floor in the center of the building where the more well-off families resided. Haggadah was thankful to have lived on the upper floors rather than the lowest, where the poorest of the poor resided. The stench from the dumped chamber pots permeated their walls, making it unbearable to open windows for a reprieve from the stench.

When Freya joined her, they followed the parade of former residents through the narrow passage. Haggadah envied the wealthy who could afford a room at boarding houses, that is, if they could find one. Like many others, she and her mother's future looked bleak. Echoes of fussy babies, inquisitive children, and footfalls droned like a marching garrison as people walked toward the main street.

Haggadah stepped over a rivulet of sewage streaming downhill to Nor Loch. She looked over her shoulder at her mother, who was coughing again. "Where should we go?" She flattened herself against the wall, allowing a robust woman to pass by.

Freya shook her head. "I don't ken." With only a few coins to their name, she knew they could not afford a room. She reasoned the money would be better spent on food. The ill woman thought of the only place to bide their time until nightfall. "This way." Freya headed north toward Nor Loch with her daughter following.

Haggadah's shoulder was bumped by several people in the narrow passage as she tried to follow closely behind her frail mother.

Freya stopped abruptly, causing her daughter to collide with her back. She grabbed Haggadah's arm, silently encouraging her to do as she did and flatten herself against the stone wall. A hooded figure stopped before them.

Haggadah held her breath as her steel gray eyes stared into the emerald eyes of the old hag staring back at her. She wished the woman with the renowned reputation as a witch would move on. What was seconds seemed like several minutes. Gooseflesh pricked her arms as the old woman stared with intrigue at Haggadah until she satisfied her curiosity. The old woman glanced at Freya, then moved on.

Exhaling, Haggadah turned to her mother. "That was the healing witch, wasn't it?"

Freya nodded. "Aye, Grizel."

"What is she doing in this part of the city?"

"It's none of your concern, nor mine."

Haggadah watched as people in the passage stepped aside, giving a wide berth for Grizel to pass through the narrow lane.

Everyone knew where the town healer lived. All they had to do was look at the night sky and see the billowing green smoke emanating from her chimney as she conjured in her ancient cottage several blocks away.

Haggadah shivered as a chill went up her spine. She hoped to never cross paths with the old hag again.

Chapter 2

The mother and daughter emerged from Niddry's Wynd and wove through the streets to Saint Cuthbert's Kirk on the west end of Nor Loch.

Haggadah wrinkled her nose at the odorous stench from the lake, mostly sewage. "Mum, what are we doing here?"

"I don't ken what else to do. I thought it would be a good idea to seek the advice of a higher authority." She stepped through the iron gate onto the hallowed ground.

Haggadah followed her mother onto the kirk's cobble pathway. She looked up at the unfinished tower that awaited a steeple and scanned the many headstones in the kirkyard. "Are we here to pray?"

"Aye, and ask for help from the priest." Freya pushed open the kirk door and stopped abruptly as several people standing immediately inside turned and stared at her. Freya scanned the interior filled with people.

Haggadah stepped beside her mother, looked at the people standing shoulder to shoulder staring at her, and remained silent.

Freya's heart sank in her chest. "Och, I guess they're all here for the same reason we are." She noted the poorly dressed people around her. "To ask for help."

"Everyone," the priest stood on the altar and extended his arms to signify silence. "Saint Cuthbert's is fully aware of your predicament. However, our poorhouse can only accommodate women with wee children. We can't house all of you. I'm sorry."

Sighing her disappointment, Freya coughed. She inhaled, looked at the floor, and admitted. "We're on our own." The corners of her mouth turned upward as she looked at her daughter. "We'll find a nice, dry close, maybe one with a warming fire, and settle in for the night. Perhaps we'll have better luck tomorrow."

Haggadah knew the situation they faced was dire. She was old enough to work yet had little skills to be anything other than a cleaning woman or maid. "Maybe I can seek employment." She offered but stopped speaking as her mother looked at her with feverish, bloodshot eyes. If Haggadah could secure a job, she would receive housing, only to leave her mother on the street shivering in the cold, something she would never do. The distraught daughter winced as she listened to Freya's rattled cough, a reminder of her mother's ill health.

"Many have done so already. There's not a job to be had." Freya justified.

Nodding, Haggadah knew her mother was correct. The city was overcrowded. Talk of developing housing on the north side of Nor Loch would help reduce the problem. More than likely, the wealthy would live in the new development they called New Town, and the poor would remain in Old Town. For now, the talk did little to help those who were displaced from their homes.

Freya watched as women with small children stepped toward the priest. She was nudged aside as a woman with a child on her hip and others in tow rushed forward. Freya scanned the crowded room, turned, and discovered the entrance blocked by others in the doorway. With a tilt of her head, she indicated it was time for her and her daughter to leave the kirk. They wove their way between the people and out the door.

Freya looked at the cloudy sky. The drizzle was intensifying. "We should search the poor box for warmer clothing. It's going to be cold and damp tonight." They went to the poor box on the side of the building. The lid was open. Freya peered inside. It was empty. "Let's be on our way and claim a place to sleep for the night."

Leaving the kirk and passing through the gate, Haggadah stood beside her mother on the sidewalk and watched the newly homeless, who mindlessly stared into the distance as they walked along the street. Their eyes conveyed hopelessness. Since the city contained over seventy closes, Haggadah wondered which direction to turn. "Mum, which close?"

Freya looked right and left, unsure of what to say. "I don't ken. We must find a place to rest for the night."

The sky seemed to share the disparity of the poor as its droplets increased in size to resemble tears. To Haggadah, it seemed as if they wandered the streets of Edinburgh for hours until they came upon Jackson's Close off Cockburn Street. They followed the narrow passage and settled in the sheltered entrance off High Street. They opened the knapsack and put on the additional garments for warmth, wrapped themselves within the thin blanket, split the stale bread between them, and watched people pass by the opening.

Freya's chest ached. She wheezed with each breath she took. She knew the dampness of the night would only worsen her condition. "I feel I'll not recover from this illness." Her voice was raspy, a mere whisper. "Haggadah, you must find employment."

"I have no experience as a maid and possess little talent for doing anything else. The way I'm dressed, who would employ me?"

The opportunity to teach her daughter the basic skills of housekeeping, mending, and cooking never arose. Their time was spent begging for money or food. "I don't think it takes much to ken how to empty a chamber pot." Her daughter's future looked bleak, yet she wanted the best for Haggadah. "Whatever you do, don't sell your body to a gentleman or believe their empty promises. Many do so and often regret it." She smiled at her daughter.

Haggadah had heard her mother's story many times before. She vowed never to become a victim and strive for a better life. She handed the remainder of her stale bread to her mother, who pushed it away.

"I've no appetite." Freya lied, pulling the blanket beneath her chin. She feared death would soon take her and leave Haggadah alone to fend for herself.

"We'll be fine, Mum. I promise." However, Haggadah doubted their situation would improve. She ate the hard crust of bread and watched as her matriarch closed her eyes and fell asleep.

Haggadah lay near her mother as darkness fell like a blanket upon the city. She prayed that tomorrow would bring brighter possibilities.

~

The weeping sky continued through the night and into the following day. Tavish cracked his eyes open at the sound of the shopkeeper sweeping the sidewalk. The merchant did it every morning to let his customers know the interior of his shop reflected the exterior, neat and tidy.

Tavish leaned away from the cold wall of the close. He stretched his arms skyward and inhaled the crisp, damp air, only to have his nose accosted by the stench of emptied chamber pots dumped from the buildings' windows during the night. Tavish stretched and twisted his neck, hoping to relieve the kink from sleeping awkwardly. He stood, brushed his pants free of dirt, and wrapped his oversized tweed coat, one he had pillaged from Saint Cuthbert's poor box, around his body to stave off the dampness. Brushing his auburn hair with his fingertips to make it presentable before returning his flat cap to his head, he went to the shop owner with high hopes of earning a coin or two. "Morning. Any errands or a letter to post today, Sir?"

The owner stopped sweeping as he looked at the tall and lanky lad, whose chestnut eyes sparkled with eagerness. He admired the homeless young man willing to earn a coin or two to provide for himself. "Aye, Tavish." He leaned the broom against the doorway. "A bit foggy this morning."

"Aye." Tavish waited as the shopkeeper went inside.

"I've three today." The man handed the letters to the lad. He reached into his pocket and dropped several coins into Tavish's palm to pay for the postage. "Keep the change."

"Thank you, Sir." Tavish darted away. He stopped by several other establishments. The shopkeepers were pleased to see the reliable lad, greeted him kindly, and appreciated his honest service.

"Ah, I see the shopkeepers are keeping you busy this morning, Tavish." The clerk greeted him as he accepted the letters, applied the postage, and received the coins from the lad.

"Aye, they are." Tavish's genuine smile was infectious, with dimples on each cheek and perfectly straight teeth.

"Looks like you'll be eating well this morning." The clerk dropped several coins into Tavish's outstretched hand.

"Enough to last me a day or two." Tavish tucked the coins in his pants pocket. "A good day to you." He touched his index finger to the brim of his hat.

"Stay dry. It's a damp one today."

Tavish walked to the bakery, where he knew day-old bread would be for a reasonable price. He planned to stop at the butcher for a few pieces of sliced ham, and if he had enough money, he would treat himself at the sweet shop.

The baker was out of day-old bread but kindly sold Tavish a fresh loaf for the same price. He stepped out of the bakery and stood on the sidewalk to watch the respected Deacon William Brodie on the opposite side of the street. The gentleman, with his walking stick, dressed in a dapper overcoat and tri-fold hat, was renowned for his cabinetmaking. He was the newly appointed head of the woodworkers, giving him a seat on the town council. Tavish knew Brodie lived in an old house in Little's Close on the Lawnmarket and smirked as the councilman paused at the mouth of Libberton Wynd. "Och, leaving mistress Jean and your bairns this morning after spending the night?" He watched as Brodie scanned High Street, the main road in Edinburgh. Tavish recalled seeing the councilman leave another building where it was rumored his other mistress, Ann, lived on Cant's Close. "Your inheritance must give you the means to provide for more than one woman, not to mention the five bairns you have between the two." He watched Brodie continue down the road, his walking stick tapping to the rhythm of his gait. Each step by the councilman projected a tinge of arrogance, or did Brodie strut like a proud rooster to emphasize his elegant walking stick? "You live a complicated life, Councilman."

~

Despite the dreary weather, Brodie was in a grand mood. He entered George Smith's grocery shop to purchase a cigar, his reward for completing another cabinet.

The bell above the door rang, drawing the owner's attention. "Good day to you, Deacon. How may I be of service?" George offered.

Brodie went to the counter and peered down into a glass case. "I would like one of your finest cigars."

"Ah, this brand is particularly nice. Quite smooth to smoke." The grocer took the wooden box from the case and watched the councilman select one. "Excellent. Shall I clip it for you?"

"Aye, thank you." Brodie waited as George returned the box to the glass case and retrieved a knife.

"How's the cabinet business?" The shopkeeper placed the cigar on the counter's edge, cut off its end, and handed it to his customer.

"I'm quite busy. I'm delivering one to a customer today. There's such a demand for my work, it's difficult to keep up."

"When I lived in Berkshire, my trade was a locksmith. If you need a helping hand, I can be of service." He watched as Brodie placed the cigar in his mouth. "Light?"

Brodie's reply was muffled as he pinched the extravagant purchase between his lips. "Aye."

George lit a long splinter of wood in the fireplace and held it before Brodie, who leaned forward and puffed until the cigar set aflame. "Is there anything else I can get you?" The grocer shook the bit of wood until the flame extinguished into a thread of smoke.

"No." Brodie set the money on the counter and held the prize cigar at arm's length. "This is all I need. Good day to you, George."

"Come again soon, and don't forget my offer." George liked the prospect of working part-time with the cabinetmaker. It would give him extra money to pay off a few debts.

"I'll get back to you soon." Brodie blew a plume of smoke into the air as he left the shop.

THE HEALER'S APPRENTICE

~

Deep within the shadowed close, John Brown held his hands near the warming fire. He had been convicted of a crime and put on a ship to sail to an undisclosed location, but managed to escape before it left the dock. The convict recognized the wealthy city councilman as Brodie passed by the close opening and sneered. "Some people have all the luck."

Chapter 3

Haggadah woke from her restless sleep to see the gray sky once again. The cobblestone street was wet. Droplets dripped from the close's sheltered entrance. She looked across the street at the stone building. The lingering fog made it look ghostlike.

As she lay beside her mother's body, Haggadah sensed an intense heat that indicated Freya had a fever. She looked at her mother's peaceful face and placed the palm of her hand on Freya's forehead. It was indeed hot. Haggadah hoped her mother had enough strength to fight off whatever ailed her, but her wheezing and rattled cough foretold a losing battle.

Fully awake, Haggadah rubbed the sleep from her eyes as she sat up, looked out the opening of the close, and saw a young man glance in her direction as he passed by. He appeared homeless, dressed in an oversized tweed coat and eating something. Much to her surprise, he reappeared as he stepped backward, stopped, and stared at her.

"I don't recall seeing you on the street before." Tavish greeted as he entered the close.

Haggadah hesitated in responding. Her first impression of the young man standing before her was that he was quite bold and handsome. Was he flirting with her? Did he always flirt with women so easily? Recalling her mother's warning, Haggadah looked at her for advice, but she was still asleep. Not wanting to appear unfriendly, Haggadah said what was most on her mind. "Mum and I have always managed to keep a roof over our heads. They kicked us out of the tenement building."

He sat across from Haggadah, broke off some bread, and held it with a small slice of shaved ham before her. "Aye, the South Bridge. The streets are crowded with many homeless now."

Haggadah's stomach betrayed her as it grumbled. She stared at the food before looking at Tavish to see if his offer was genuine.

He nodded, encouraging her to accept the meager breakfast.

Hesitating, she looked into his eyes for sincerity before reaching for the food. "Thank you." She stared at the meat, unable to recall the last time she had eaten it. Biting into the ham, Haggadah closed her eyes, savoring the flavor. She set the remainder in her lap, hoping her mother would eat it when she woke. Haggadah bit into the bread and stared at the young man across from her, who appeared to be her same age.

"My name is Tavish." He waited for her to reply, but she remained silent. "Don't be rude now. Your name, Lass."

"Haggadah."

"It's a pleasure to meet you, Haggadah." Tavish continued. "Which building did the two of you live in?"

"The one on Niddry's Wynd." She looked at her mother, who coughed.

Freya opened her eyes a mere crack. She shivered in her dampened clothes, her teeth rattling, before closing her eyes. Her chest wheezed with each breath.

Tavish leaned close to Haggadah and whispered. "Your mum doesn't sound too good. How long has she been sick?"

"For a while now. We've no money for a physician."

"Grizel could help her. She has healed others who have no money to pay for a proper physician." Tavish suggested.

"The witch? Being of the Christian faith, Mum will not approve." Haggadah paused. "Nor will I."

"Grizel is not bad, just misunderstood." He tried to reason. "She's a good healer. In my opinion, better than most physicians."

"Many believe she is Half-Hangit Maggie Dickson, the lady who killed her own bairn, was hanged, and still lived."

Tavish shook his head. "No, Half-Hangit Maggie died many years ago. Grizel would not harm anyone. Like I said, she is a healer."

"People say when green smoke rises from the witch's chimney and into the night sky, she is conjuring a youth potion to hide her true age."

Tavish chuckled. "That's just to keep the curious away and frighten others who dislike her. Don't believe the gossip about Grizel. She's a wise woman."

Haggadah remained silent, unsure if he had told the truth. She had heard too many wicked tales about Maggie. How could the woman have survived a hanging unless she was a witch? Haggadah refused to believe otherwise.

Freya coughed. Her teeth began to chatter again.

Haggadah pulled the thin blanket closer to her mother's chin.

"Have you got any kin to take the two of you in?" Tavish ate his last bit of bread.

Haggadah shook her head.

Tavish looked at the ill woman, whose soul stood on the precipice of death's door. He knew the young lass would be on her own once the woman died. Tavish had seen it before and feared Haggadah's only way to provide for herself would be to sell her body for the pleasure of men willing to pay little for it. He stared into her steel gray eyes, mesmerized by their color. "Stay put. I'll be back soon." He stood and left the close.

Haggadah watched Tavish scurry away. As her mother groaned, she stood, tore a strip of cloth from her skirt, and let the droplets from the close's opening dampen it. "Here, Mum." Haggadah placed the wet cloth on her mother's forehead, hoping to cool her rising fever.

~

Weaving his way through the rain-washed streets, Tavish stood outside the waist-high stone wall, trying to gather his courage to step forward. The decrepit cottage stared back at him, daring him to enter through the rickety gate. He had never called on the town healer for help before but only knew of her abilities from hearsay. Tavish took a deep breath, opened the gate, and walked up the flagstone pathway. He looked about to see if anyone was watching him before he knocked.

Grizel looked toward the wooden door as she wiped her aged, wet hands on a towel. "Another request for a remedy." She tilted her head to the side as she walked toward the door. "No, it's a young man, desperate." Opening the door, she stared into the apprehensive, chestnut eyes of the tall, lanky young man. With a quick glance at his clothing, Grizel knew he was one of the homeless in need of a remedy. She stood staring, as silent as the grave, quite sure she had seen him before.

Out of respect, Tavish jerked his flat cap from his head, revealing his seldomly washed auburn hair. "I'm sorry to trouble you, Grizel, but there is a woman who's quite ill. She and her daughter are bedded down in a close. They were kicked out of their home."

"Ah, the South Bridge." Grizel surmised.

"The woman may not be able to walk. She's quite bad off." Tavish stared in disbelief as the door slammed in his face. He stood transfixed for a moment before determining his request had been denied, returned his cap to his head, and walked away as the steady rain began to fall. Tavish placed his hand on the gate to leave and paused as he heard the cottage door open. He turned and saw the healer dressed in her overcoat carrying a satchel.

Grizel walked with a determined purpose, handed Tavish her bag, and pushed open the gate with such force that it nearly became unhinged. She looked over her shoulder at the lad, who appeared too stunned to move. "Take me to them."

Tavish caught the gate before it could close and stepped beside Grizel, matching the short stride of the elderly woman.

"Do you ken what ails the woman?" She looked at the lad, who shook his head, uncertain what to say.

"She was sleeping when I saw her. Her daughter said she has a cough and may be feverish. I could hear her wheezing with each breath she took."

The pair received inquisitive stares from those they passed and were sidestepped by others. They reached the entrance of the close and entered.

Haggadah peered up into the face of the witch.

"I'm no healer, but I think she is pretty bad off." Tavish knelt by Freya, who was still sleeping.

Grizel looked down at the feverous woman. She had helped her years ago. Freya's aged face indicated time had not treated her kindly since her daughter's birth. The town healer recalled seeing the woman's soul in the parade in April. "I can't help her."

Haggadah's eyes darted from the witch to the kind young man and back.

Tavish's eyes widened at the witch's admission. "You can't make her well? But you're a healer." He insisted, as his heart sank a bit lower in his chest. He wanted to be helpful by retrieving Grizel. Instead, she had made him look foolish. "How do you ken?"

Grizel looked at the young man, unwilling to expose her source. "Her time draws near."

The voices of those around her encouraged Freya to crack open her eyes. Even though her eyelids were heavy, she peered at the faces looking down at her from the shadowed darkness.

Grizel decided to make Freya's remaining time as pleasant as possible. Leaning forward, the town healer stared into her patient's bloodshot eyes. "Freya, you must rise and follow me." Grizel looked at Tavish and Haggadah. "The two of you will help her walk." She took the satchel from the lad to free his hand. "Leave the worthless blanket."

Tavish picked up the carpetbag from the damp ground, slung it over his shoulder, and stepped to one side of Freya. Haggadah disregarded the healer's command and gathered the blanket as she stood on the opposite side of her mother. Together, the pair hoisted the sick patient from the cold dampness of the close and supported her while following Grizel. The rain had slowed to a misty drizzle, sprinkling their clothing with beads of moisture as they walked through the streets, passing the poorest of the poor, who looked at them with pleading eyes.

As they rounded the corner, the healer's ancient house with its protective stone wall stood guard, warning those who approached. Grizel swung open the rickety wooden gate and walked up the flagstone pathway.

Haggadah looked at the old dwelling. She wondered if its pathetic thatched roof leaked. She stared at the stone chimney spewing white smoke before crossing the threshold into the one-roomed house and inhaling the fragrance of spices and flowers.

"Lay her before the fire," Grizel ordered as she closed the door. "Tavish put a log or two on the embers."

The lad looked at Grizel, quite taken by surprise. Even though many in the city knew him, his need to call on Grizel for healing had never occurred. He wondered how she knew his name. He acknowledged the command with a nod and did as the healer ordered.

Not wanting to appear too nosy, Haggadah covered her mother with their blanket. She kept her face downcast while peering beneath her eyebrows at the tiny house's interior. The fireplace had a witch's cauldron hanging over the flames, a single bed against one wall, a large cabinet concealed behind the door when it was open, and a small kitchen with a worktable. The floor was covered with a rag rug, and a round table with four chairs was at its center. Haggadah looked up at the rafters where countless dried herbs hung. She saw a ladder leading up to a loft and assumed the area was used for storage. The wooden beam fireplace mantel was decorated with several unlit candles in wooden holders and a beautiful statue of three women: one young, an expectant mother, and an old crone.

Tavish placed the carpetbag beneath Freya's head as she coughed.

"Swing the kettle over the fire to warm the water for tea," Grizel ordered as she removed her overcoat and hung it on a peg on the wall.

Tavish followed the healer's command. He watched as Grizel opened the apothecary cupboard and pulled jars from the cubbyholes.

Grizel carried an armful of the jars and placed them on the table before retrieving a teapot and teacup from the kitchen cupboard. She removed the lid of each jar, poured a measure of the dried contents into the palm of her hand, and added the herbs to the teapot.

Satisfied the remedy would soothe the woman's passage into the next world, she rotated the iron stand, wrapped her hand with a cloth hanging from a nail on the end of the mantel, and lifted the kettle. She poured steaming water into the teapot and returned the cast iron kettle to its stand.

Grizel looked at her guests. It had been some time since anyone was inside her cottage. To play the role of a proper hostess, she retrieved a tin of biscuits from the cupboard, removed the lid, and offered a tasty treat to her guests.

Tavish helped himself to one. "Thank you."

"You're welcome, Tavish. You've been a great help, so have a second." Grizel waited for the lad to select a second biscuit. She held the tin before Haggadah, who shyly took one biscuit.

Bowing her head, the soon-to-be orphan replied, "Thank you."

The healer nodded, glanced at her patient's closed eyes, and put the tin on the table. "We'll need to wake her when the tea is ready."

"I'll stay to help with the remedy, but then I must go," Tavish announced as he finished eating the first tasty biscuit.

Haggadah stared at Tavish with a look of 'Don't you dare leave me here with this witch.'

The crackling fire played like background music while the three remained silent and waited patiently for the tea to steep.

Grizel looked at her patient as Freya's breathing became labored. She stared at Haggadah, who had yet to meet her gaze. "So, I assume you have been evicted from one of the tenement buildings to make way for the South Bridge?"

Haggadah looked into the emerald eyes of the town healer as she nipped off another bite of the biscuit. She nodded.

Grizel placed the palms of her hands on each side of the teapot and inhaled the aroma emanating from its spout. "It's ready." She poured the remedy into a teacup and nodded toward the patient as she approached Freya. "Up with her now." She instructed Tavish.

As Tavish raised Freya to a semi-seated position, Haggadah knelt beside her mother and placed her palm on her cheek. "Mum, wake up."

Grizel tapped Haggadah on her shoulder and handed her the teacup.

Freya's eyes fluttered open to view her daughter. She tried to grin before the warm liquid was brought to her lips, drank what she could, and then turned her head away, indicating she wanted no more.

Haggadah returned the teacup to the healer, who peered into the vessel.

"Good, she managed to drink half. She should rest easily now." Grizel placed the cup on the table.

Tavish lowered Freya to the floor, ensuring her head rested comfortably on the carpetbag. He looked at Haggadah. "Stay here with your mum. Grizel may need you to help with giving your mum more tea. I'll come by tomorrow to check on you both."

Haggadah watched as he stood, wishing he would stay.

Wanting a moment alone with Tavish, Grizel walked him to the door.

Haggadah looked toward the pair as their whispered conversation reached her ears. Her mother coughed, drawing her attention away from what was being said.

Freya opened her eyes. "Haggadah, lay beside me while I rest." She closed her eyes and grinned as her daughter's arm fell across her chest. It eased Freya's mind to know they were both warm and safe.

After sending the lad on his way, Grizel stood and momentarily watched the mother and daughter. They shared a love that was a void in her life. She often wished to have a child of her own. Someone to care for when they were young and, in return, someone to care for her when she was old. Grizel tilted her head to the side. "Or can I convince the soon-to-be orphan to stay?" She whispered.

Chapter 4

Grizel knew the day would begin with sorrow. After burning sage and various herbs to clear the air of any evil, she sat on a chair near the table and watched the pair sleeping on the floor. She stared at the woman's chest as it rose and fell for the final time. A groan escaped the ill patient's throat, surrendering her soul as it separated from her body. Grizel watched the translucent spirit wrap her arms around her child, tenderly kiss Haggadah on the cheek, and whisper something in her ear before floating upward. The departing soul stared at Grizel as it remained suspended in the air, hovering. It nodded in appreciation and passed the responsibility of caring for Haggadah to the town healer. The healer bowed her head in a silent acceptance and watched as the soul elevated upward, forming a pinpoint where it disappeared through the cottage roof.

Grizel looked at the sleeping orphan lying next to her mother's body. The young lady was blessed with an elegant face and dainty features. When Grizel saw her on Niddry's Wynd and stared into Haggadah's steel-gray eyes, the town healer knew the young lady could become her legacy and a fine healer one day. Yet, convincing her would be a challenge. But now that her mother was dead, Grizel's argument to follow in her footsteps may be more acceptable to Haggadah. The orphan was homeless. At least if she remained with Grizel, she would have a roof over her head, food in her stomach, and be safe.

She heard the creak of the rusty hinges of the front gate, stood, and opened the door before Tavish could knock. "Go and tell Davis and Wiley to ready a pauper's grave. Have them come for the body as soon as they have finished."

Tavish peeked around the healer to see the pair lying on the floor. "What will happen to the lass now?"

"I have decided she will remain with me," Grizel looked over her shoulder at Haggadah and then back at Tavish, "if I can convince her to do so."

Tavish knew the fate of most single homeless women. Many were abused and became pregnant, an ill fate for the child as well. He was determined Haggadah would not succumb to such a horrid fate. "If you can't convince her, then I will."

Grizel sensed the lad's concern. Did he have a fondness for Haggadah? The healer reached into the pocket of her skirt and withdrew three coins. "Go."

With one final glance at Haggadah, he turned and left to do the healer's bidding.

Grizel shut the door. She looked at Haggadah and sighed. There was no potion or remedy she could create to help the young woman overcome the grief she would soon experience.

~

Tavish knew which streets were safe to tread on and which to avoid. He pocketed the coins and hurried to where the kirk had given employment to two homeless young men, Davis and Wiley, both about the same age as himself. They could dig a grave quickly. The wage they earned paid for their room in a boarding house. It was small, but at least they were no longer homeless.

Tavish entered the gate of Saint Cuthbert and quickly located his two friends. The pair was busy filling in a grave. They paused with their shovels in midair as they spotted Tavish walking toward them.

Wiley threw his shovelful of dirt onto the growing mound before putting the tool's tip on the ground to rest. He watched Tavish approach with commanding strides and assumed. "Need a favor?"

"Aye, Grizel needs a grave dug for a woman," Tavish explained as he stopped before the gravediggers. "She asks that you bring a wagon to collect the body from her cottage."

Davis drew his eyebrows together. "Another pauper's grave?"

Tavish nodded. "Any plot will do." He looked down at the mound of dirt. "I don't ken if Grizel has a sheet to wrap the body."

"We have an extra one in the shed. It's not in the best shape, but we'll bring it just in case." Davis assured.

Tavish reached into his pocket and gave a coin to each of them. "Thanks." He nodded in appreciation, left the kirkyard, and returned to the healer's cottage.

~

Haggadah opened her eyes. She sensed something was amiss. She could hear the crackling of the fire and the town healer moving about the room, yet she could no longer hear her mother's wheezing. She looked at Freya's face. It appeared lifeless, like a statue. "Mum?" There was no response. "Mum!" Haggadah shook her mother's shoulder.

"She's gone, Lass. Died as the sun rose." Grizel confirmed. "She sleeps among the angels now."

As her eyes welled with tears, Haggadah stared at the healer who stepped before her. The orphan whispered, her voice barely audible, as she stared into the old woman's emerald eyes. "Tavish said you could heal her." A tear trickled down her cheek.

"I can't do miracles. I saw your mum's soul among those foretold to die this year, so I knew I could not save her." Grizel sighed and sat in a chair. "I'm sorry for your loss."

Haggadah stared at her mother. A tear retraced the rivulet on her cheek. She stared at her matriarch's face, trying to cast the details to her memory, yet fearing the picture would fade over the years. Placing her forehead on her mother's shoulder, she wept in earnest while embracing Freya's lifeless body.

Grizel had witnessed many deaths as the town healer. She had watched their souls depart their bodies and believed they continued to exist somewhere unbeknownst to her. Grizel could offer the grieving orphan little words of comfort. She placed her arthritic hand on Haggadah's back and patted gently. "Grief is a wound that cuts deeply into one's heart. It forms a scar representing the love you will always have for your mum." The healer knew it was best to let Haggadah cry, knowing the only cure for her sorrow was time.

A knock on the door sounded. The healer opened it to see Tavish.

The expression on Grizel's face conveyed the emotion inside the cottage. Haggadah's heart-wrenching sobs drew Tavish's attention. He stepped inside and saw the orphan's shoulders shake as she wept. "Davis and Wiley will be here as soon as the grave is ready. They wanted to ken if you have a sheet to wrap the woman's body."

Grizel shook her head. "No."

"Then they'll use the sheet they'll bring with them." Unable to withstand Haggadah's wailing, he went to her, knelt, and rubbed her back as she continued to cry.

Haggadah failed to notice his comforting touch. She continued to sob, unable to understand how her heart possessed such an achy hollowness. With the feeling of abandonment pressing down on her, she was afraid and uncertain about what to do next.

Grizel busied herself making tea for everyone. Even though the remainder of the day would be difficult for Haggadah, she was determined to ease her mind about the future. When the tea was ready, Grizel poured a cup and placed it on the table. "My dear, come and sit. I made tea for you."

Haggadah ignored the request, unwilling to leave her mother.

Taking matters into his own hands, Tavish whispered into Haggadah's ear, hoping to convince her to drink the offered tea. "Come now, Lass. The tea will do you good." He pulled a chair next to the body before placing his hands beneath her arms and coaxing her to her feet.

Haggadah sat numbly, staring at her mother's lifeless body.

Grizel placed a teacup in Haggadah's lap and helped her wrap her fingers around the warm drink.

Tavish pulled a chair next to Haggadah and sat.

"Drink." Grizel guided the cup to Haggadah's lips and lowered it after several sips. "Good."

Over the next few hours, the trio sat in silence. By midday, Grizel looked toward the door as the clip-clop of hooves sounded on the cobblestone street and halted abruptly. She opened the door to see the gravediggers dismounting from the wagon. "Bring the cloth for the body."

Tears trickled down Haggadah's cheeks as the men wrapped her mother in the soiled cloth and carried it out of the cottage feet first. She placed the teacup on the table as she stood and followed, not ready to say goodbye to her loved one.

Grizel stepped beside Tavish, stopping him before he could follow Haggadah. "Make sure she returns." The healer reached into her pocket and withdrew a coin to pay the lad for doing as she wished.

He looked at the outstretched hand containing the money and shook his head. He knew Haggadah should not be wandering the streets during her time of sorrow. She could easily fall prey to someone unkind. Tavish inhaled a deep, determined breath. "I'll be sure to bring her back." He stepped into the sunlight behind Haggadah.

The grieving orphan walked along the flagstone pathway, unaware of Tavish following her. They watched as the gravediggers loaded the wrapped body into the back of the flatbed wagon. Tavish helped Haggadah sit next to her mother's covered head. He sat on the opposite side of the body, his feet dangling off the end of the wagon. Grizel watched from the doorway, choosing to remain at the cottage.

It was a solemn ride to the kirkyard, with onlookers wondering who had died. When the wagon stopped before the kirkyard gate, Tavish placed his hands on Haggadah's slim waist and lifted her to the street. They stood aside as the gravediggers unloaded the body and carried it to the prepared grave. The young men respectfully lowered the deceased into the awaiting resting place. Wiley recalled several phrases the priest stated at previous funerals and repeated them, hoping to offer Haggadah comfort and cast the woman's soul to Heaven.

Tavish looked at Haggadah from the corner of his eye as he stood beside her. Together, they watched as Davis and Wiley shoveled dirt onto the deceased. Haggadah stood staring. Her bottom lip quivered as tears trickled down her cheeks.

Davis and Wiley finished the task quickly. With their shovels in hand, they paused before Haggadah. "We're sorry for your loss."

Haggadah managed to nod, but remained silent.

Tavish extended his hand. "Thank you, Davis, Wiley." He shook the gravediggers' hands. With their shovels slung over their shoulders, they walked away.

Alone with Haggadah, Tavish stood quietly, searching his mind for something to say. He wanted to give her time to spend with her mother's grave, to come to terms with her death. He decided she needed to redirect her thoughts and not dwell on the loss. "We can return as often as you wish to visit your mum's grave." Tavish encouraged, grasping her hand. "Come, we shall celebrate her life."

She allowed him to lead her away from her mother's resting place. They left the hallowed ground, stopped at the pub, and bought a pint of ale and a meager meal to share. When half of the pint remained, Tavish pushed it toward Haggadah. "You finish it." He hoped the ale would help numb her mind from the day's events.

She looked at Tavish, a thankful expression on her face, and drank.

Even though she remained silent, Tavish understood Haggadah's grief. Like her, he was an orphan and a patient young man who knew she would talk when ready.

He spoke his mind as they walked to the town healer's house. "You are to stay with Grizel."

She stared at him, shaking her head.

"It's the way it's going to be, Haggadah." His voice was firm, unwavering. "I'll come by and visit you as often as I can."

She turned her head away, refusing to look at him.

Tavish sighed. "If you remain on the street, men will take advantage of you. I don't want to see that happen. It's best if you stay with Grizel. She can give you the protection you need, a roof over your head, and food in your belly." He spoke from his heart. "It will ease my mind to ken you are safe and in her care."

With no other place to go, she had little choice in the matter.

Chapter 5

Grizel welcomed the pair as they entered the house.

Haggadah stared at the indent in the carpetbag where her mother's head once rested. The blanket lay in a crumbled heap.

"Haggadah, you'll not need to sleep on the floor." Grizel announced. "There's a bed in the loft. You'll sleep there."

Tavish went to Haggadah's side. "Time for you to settle in. I must go and make a few coins. I can't buy food if I don't work."

Haggadah assumed the worst by staying under the same roof as the witch. She looked at Tavish, her eyes pleading.

He squeezed her hand, ensuring all would be well. Tavish turned to Grizel. "Thank you for all you've done," he paused, "and all you will do." Tavish glanced at Haggadah and grinned to convey she would be fine as he let go of her hand and left the house.

Feeling self-conscious under the witch's stare, Haggadah picked up the carpetbag and blanket and held the items to her chest as if trying to keep what remained of her mother close to her.

Grizel took a candle from the mantel, lit it from the fireplace, and gave it to Haggadah. "You've had a trying day. Go and put your things in the loft while I begin supper."

Haggadah looked at the window framed with curtains and saw the sunlight was fading as the day was nearing its end.

Accepting the lit candle from the healer's gnarled hand, Haggadah climbed the crudely made ladder and stepped on the rough planked floor of the loft. She bumped her head on a beam in the low ceiling. To her left was a wooden chest. She put the carpetbag on it. There was a three-legged stool next to a single bed. She placed the candle on the stool, folded the threadbare blanket reverently, and laid it at the foot of the bed. Haggadah looked down at her footprints left in the dust.

She had slept in worse conditions. At least it was dry, and the cot offered comfort.

She picked up the candle and descended the ladder. Uncertain of what to do next, Haggadah watched the healer add flour from a crock to a bowl and stir it with a wooden spoon.

Grizel looked at the forlorn young woman who stood transfixed. "Blow out the candle and put it on the mantel." She pointed at the doorway leading to the backyard. "Go. Take a basket from the shed ceiling and get a few eggs from the hens. I've no chamber pot, but you can use a cludgie near the coop."

Haggadah did as she was told. She opened the back door and found herself in a shed. It contained several garden tools, a bucket on the floor, and several baskets hanging from the ceiling. As she stepped forward, the floor sounded hollow. She assumed a cellar was beneath. Taking a small basket from a hook, she opened the door to the backyard and stood for a moment as she looked at her surroundings. Before Haggadah was a slumbering garden. She imagined it produced every flower and herb the healer needed, with many dried and hanging from the cottage ceiling. The chicken coop and outhouse were at the opposite end of the fenced yard. She walked along the pathway and saw several plants beginning to push their way up through the soil. Feeling the need, she used the outhouse before collecting eggs from the half-dozen hens. Haggadah returned inside and placed the basket of eggs on the worktable.

"Hang up your overcoat and come wash your hands. I'll have you finish adding flour to the bread." Grizel cleaned off the dough from the spoon and set the utensil aside. She turned toward the dry sink, took a ladle from the bucket of water near the washtub, and pointed at the bar of soap on a chipped dish.

Grabbing the soap, Haggadah washed her hands thoroughly while Grizel drizzled them with water. She returned the soap to the dish. Another dip of the ladle was used to rinse away the suds. Haggadah looked about with her hands raised like a surgeon awaiting sterile gloves.

"The towel is on the hook on the side of the cupboard." Grizel returned to the worktable while Haggadah dried her hands and put the towel back where she found it. The healer sprinkled flour from the crock onto the tabletop, dumped the bread dough in the center, and added flour to the top. "Now, work the flour into the dough. Add more as you go."

Haggadah picked up the wooden spoon from the worktable.

"Use your hands. Like this." Grizel began turning the edge of the dough, pushing it toward the center, and working in the flour. "Have you never made bread before?"

Haggadah shook her head. "We ate bread the baker threw out."

Grizel's hands stilled. More than likely, the bread was too moldy to sell. No wonder her mother was ill. "Well, then, you must learn. Do as I do." She demonstrated. "Now, you do it." The healer watched Haggadah knead the bread, instructed her when more flour was needed, and told her when the dough was the right consistency. "Now, the dough must rise." She put lard on the inside of a cast iron pot and placed the dough inside. "We must ready the fire to bake the bread." Together, they added wood to create embers.

A knock sounded on the door, causing the town healer to look toward it.

Grizel went to the door. She listened to a woman describe her ailments, shut the door, and looked at Haggadah. "Never let an ill person into this house." The healer opened the apothecary, pulled out a concealed board to make a workspace, and selected several herbs.

Curious, Haggadah approached as she scanned the various cubbies of bottles and drawers. She looked at the ceiling of dried herbs, assuming the healer had filled the bottles with them.

"You'll become a great healer someday," Grizel said over her shoulder.

Haggadah stared at the countless bottles again. "I'll never be able to learn everything you ken."

Grizel turned and stared at her young apprentice. "Doubt is the first step toward failure. Never doubt your ability. Come, we'll begin now." Grizel took a small bottle from a drawer. "I'm making a remedy. She is complaining of a sour stomach and chills." Placing a small funnel into the mouth of the bottle, she poured whiskey inside. "This helps to release the herb's benefits." She added several herbs. "Peppermint for her stomach, feverfew for her fever, and white willow bark for a headache, which I assume she has. It will help to relieve any body aches, too." Grizel also added two additional herbs. "Chamomile and lavender to help her rest." She corked the bottle and shook it several times. "She is to take a spoonful three times a day. I don't demand payments for my remedies, but always accept what they offer in exchange." The healer opened the door, gave the woman her remedy, and received a payment in return. Grizel turned to Haggadah with three eggs in her hands. "It looks like we're having eggs with our bread for supper." She grinned at Haggadah before looking at the basket on the worktable.

The comment had given Haggadah a peek at the mysterious woman's sense of humor, yet it did not settle her uneasiness. She watched as Grizel added the eggs to the basket, filling it to the rim.

After an hour or so, Haggadah stood nearby and watched as Grizel used a small shovel hanging near the poker to spread glowing embers on the hearth, nestled the pot of bread within them, and added more embers onto the lid.

"When the bread is done, we will fry the eggs and enjoy supper." Grizel added a log to the fire.

Haggadah stared at the healer as thoughts of wicked rumors echoed in her mind.

"Speak what is on your mind." Grizel encouraged as she added another scoop of embers to the Dutch oven's lid.

"Many suspect you are Maggie Dickson." Haggadah took a hesitant step backward, fearing the woman's reaction to her accusation.

The healer cackled. "Do they now?"

"Aye, Half-Hangit Maggie. They say you killed your illegitimate baby and survived your hanging."

"I would never kill a child, not even an unwanted one. As your Christian religion states, killing is a sin. By killing a bairn, a person deprives themselves of witnessing what the babe could have become. The lad or lass may have influenced and bettered the lives of others." She stilled the shovel as she reasoned a conclusion. "I would think the guilt would haunt the woman until she took her last breath." She added another scoop of glowing embers to the pot's lid, ensuring it remained at the proper temperature. "Have I swayed your opinion of me?" Grizel pointed to a chair at the table, silently indicating Haggadah should sit.

"I don't ken what to think." She followed the unspoken instruction of the healing witch.

Grizel thought of a way to convince her new apprentice of her true self, to gain her trust. "It has been sixty years since Maggie was accused."

"Some believe you have a potion that keeps you young." Haggadah insisted.

"A potion? A magic potion that keeps me young? If I could produce such an elixir, I would be a wealthy woman," Grizel spread her arms wide, "not living in this old hovel." She chuckled as she returned the shovel to its proper place.

Suspicious of the woman's witchy powers, Haggadah pressed. "How did you ken my mother would die, that you could not help her?"

"It was foretold on the Eve of Saint Mark. The time will come when you will understand who you can cure and who you can't. No more questions." Gizel added a bit of lard to a skillet and placed it over the fire. "We can begin the eggs now." She pointed at the basket. Haggadah retrieved it from the worktable and held it before her. Grizel cracked a total of four eggs on the skillet's edge, dumping the contents onto the hot iron to cook. She used the poker to lift the lid off the Dutch oven to check the bread. It was nearly finished, as she assumed. "Go into the cellar and retrieve the crock of butter."

Feeling the need to earn her keep, Haggadah offered. "I have jam if you wish us to eat that instead." She paused and then justified. "We didn't steal it, if that's what you're thinking. It was a gift."

Taken back by her defensiveness, Grizel wished to set the young woman at ease. "Aye, that sounds delicious."

Haggadah retrieved the jar from her mother's carpetbag and placed it on the table while Grizel poured hot water into a teapot and added tea.

"You'll find plates and teacups in the cupboard. The forks and knives are in the drawer for you to set the table." Grizel instructed.

The plates were of different patterns and chipped in several places. They resembled something someone threw away or put in the poor box. Haggadah retrieved the necessary items and placed them before the chairs where they would sit.

Grizel put two eggs on each plate. "Get the cutting board and knife." She pointed to a wooden board hanging on a nail on the wall. As Haggadah placed it on the table, the healer put the hot round loaf on it.

Haggadah gazed at the steaming loaf of bread, jam, and eggs and watched as Grizel poured the freshly brewed tea into the teacups. She inhaled the aroma of the freshly baked bread. "This looks like a feast."

Grizel paused, realizing what little knowledge the young lady had of a true feast. She dared not embarrass her. "I suppose it does."

As they sat down to eat, Haggadah bowed her head and said a prayer of thanks. Grizel cut the bread into wedges and placed one on each plate. She spread jam on her bread while waiting for the young woman's prayer to end.

Haggadah opened her eyes and stared at the bounty on her plate. She looked at the healer sitting across the table, who nodded for her to begin eating.

Grizel's eyes widened as the young woman ate like a ravenous wild animal. "The food isn't going anywhere. Slow down, or I'll need to make a remedy for your stomach."

Haggadah chewed the mouthful of food as if she could not get it into her stomach quick enough.

The healer dipped the crusty edge of her bread into the egg, breaking open the yolk. "I see we'll have to work on your table manners."

Chapter 6

Haggadah dried the last plate and added it to the small stack in the cupboard as Grizel wrapped the uneaten loaf of bread in a towel and placed it on the worktable.

"Add a few logs to the fire to get us through the night." The town healer ordered as she retrieved a bottle of ink, a pen, and paper from the apothecary.

Haggadah took the poker from the hook on the wall, rotated the dying logs, and selected a log from the pile on the hearth. She added it to the fire and closed her eyes, welcoming the warmth. Her mind recalled the countless cold winter nights she and her mother endured in the crowded room they shared with many others. She added a second log to the fire, returned the poker to its place, and turned to see Grizel sitting at the table, staring at her.

"Light a yellow candle and bring it here." The town healer uncorked the ink bottle and dipped the pen into the ebony liquid. She printed Haggadah's name neatly on the paper.

Haggadah chose the yellow candle from the many other colors tied with a ribbon on the mantel. She put it in an empty holder and lit it from the fireplace flames.

Grizel motioned for her apprentice to sit across from her as the candle was placed between them.

"Why the yellow one?" Haggadah wondered.

"To help you with focus, intelligence, and memory." Grizel rotated the paper for Haggadah to see. "Do you ken what this says?"

Haggadah looked at the squiggly etched markings. She shook her head. "No."

"It's your name." She watched as Haggadah's eyes widened with surprise. "We shall learn the letters so you may write it yourself. I need you to repeat what I say." Grizel pointed at the first letter with the opposite end of the pen. "H."

Hesitant, Haggadah looked at Grizel before repeating the sound. "H."

"A."

"A."

The healer continued to recite each letter with Haggadah parroting her.

"You see, you only have four different letters in your name. Many are the same."

Haggadah pointed to the first letter and discovered the last letter in her name was the same. "Aye."

"Again." The town healer and apprentice repeated the lesson.

"Again." This time, Grizel remained silent. Haggadah stumbled on the third letter.

"Let's try this." Grizel demonstrated a clap when saying a consonant and placed her hands on the table when saying a vowel. She nodded at Haggadah to mimic her movements. Slowing the tempo, she ensured her apprentice could follow along. When confident Haggadah was improving, she increased the speed. They both began to smile, which turned into laughter.

"Well done." Grizel dipped the pen into the ink. "Hold the pen like this," she demonstrated, "and write each letter as you say it."

Haggadah accepted the pen. She tried to imitate the grip, hesitated, and looked at Grizel, who helped her adjust her fingers to the proper position. She wrote the letter "H." It looked similar to the one the town healer wrote, but the lines were askew.

"You will improve with practice. Next letter." Grizel encouraged.

Haggadah wrote each letter. After writing the last letter in her name, she looked at Grizel. "Why must I learn to do this? Many others don't ken their letters and can't write."

Grizel answered. "You must learn to read and write to understand what is in an ancient book." She rose from her chair, retrieved a candlestick from the mantel, lit it, and handed it to Haggadah. "Go to the chest in the loft, lift the false bottom, and bring me what you find there."

Haggadah accepted the lit taper, climbed the ladder, and placed the candlestick on the floor near the chest. She discovered a tray filled with strange things inside – a raven's foot, a bundle of colored candles that were partially burned, and a crystal ball. Haggadah set the tray aside and pillaged through old clothing, which included a black cloak. At the bottom, she found a neatly folded, beautiful light blue, pale green, and black tartan with pinstripes of red and yellow. "The tartan? Is it your clan?" Haggadah felt the softness of the wool.

"No. It belongs to another." Grizel confirmed.

Haggadah set the cloth aside and lifted the bottom board. She raised the candle to peer inside. "An old book?"

"Aye, bring it here." Grizel sat and waited.

After putting everything back in the chest and descending the ladder, Haggadah placed the book on the table and pushed it toward Grizel before blowing out the candle and returning it to the mantel.

"This book is filled with knowledge from others, so you must learn to read what has been recorded on its pages."

Haggadah looked at the leather cover engraved with a triskelion and a clasp made of brass. The edges of the paper looked roughly cut, wavy, and tattered.

"This is a grimoire. Some refer to it as the Book of Shadows." Grizel explained. "It has been passed down for several generations with each owner adding notations." She opened the book, filling the air with the fragrance of sandalwood, sage, and lilac.

Inhaling the fragrance, Haggadah looked behind her, quite sure she heard someone whisper.

Grizel pointed to the names written on the inside cover. "As you see, there have been many healers who have signed their names. Margaret Aitken is the first. My name is at the bottom. When you have practiced your name and feel you can write it as best you can, you'll add your name beneath mine."

"But I'm not a healer," Haggadah confessed.

"Yet." Grizel clarified as she turned the page to explain some of the notations. "The Book of Shadows has been written by several, with each keeper adding their own pages. It contains the phases of the moon, Celtic holidays, and illustrations of herbs and their uses." The healer skipped over any remedies, charms, potions, spells, and lethal concoctions, knowing her apprentice would learn them when she could read.

A knock sounded on the door.

Grizel snapped the book shut and glared at Haggadah with intensity, conveying the importance of her following words. "You must never tell anyone or show anyone this book other than the next healer who will take your place."

"Aye." Haggadah watched as Grizel put the book in a compartment in the apothecary before opening the door to a ragged-looking man in need. She listened, made the remedy, and received a hen for her service.

"Put this with the others." She handed the chicken to Haggadah, who left to put the hen in the coop.

Alone for the moment, Grizel added more wood to the fire. She saw promise in her young apprentice, who seemed willing to learn and did so quickly, yet the healer questioned if it was the young woman's correct life path. Grizel looked at the backdoor as Haggadah entered.

"If you don't mind me asking, why were you chosen to be the next to have the Book of Shadows?" Haggadah inquired as she sat on the stool before the fireplace.

"I was told I had a gift for healing, and by being a healer, I could help the less fortunate." She paused. "Even though many fear me, others respect me because they ken what and who I truly am." Grizel stared at her apprentice. "You have a gift, yet you may not be aware of it yet."

Haggadah yawned.

Grizel recognized the burden of the day had weighed heavily upon the young woman's shoulders. "It's time for us to retire." She picked up the lit yellow candle from the table and blew it out. She put it on the mantel, chose another, lit it, and handed it to Haggadah. "Tomorrow, we will begin learning herbs and their properties. You will also practice writing your name and learn other letters." She nodded toward the loft.

Haggadah climbed the ladder, placed the candle on the stool, and blew out the flame. Wishing to be close to her mother, she retrieved the carpetbag from the chest, spread the blanket over her, and laid her head on the satchel as she stretched out onto the cot. Haggadah yawned. It had been a day of sorrow. The thought of her mother caused tears to seep from the corners of her eyes.

Grizel lay in her bed. She glanced up to where her apprentice lay. Even though her grief was silent, the healer knew Haggadah was crying. Tomorrow would be a better day.

Chapter 7

Shuffling feet echoed from the room below, causing Haggadah to open her eyes. In the shadowed darkness of the loft, it took a moment for her to remember where she was. Still dressed in her layered clothing, Haggadah looked at the beams in the ceiling and assumed it would soon be daylight. She lay still, allowing the cobwebs to clear from her mind while listening to the stirring of the ashen embers in the fireplace and logs being placed upon them. Her stomach grumbled, and she needed to use the outhouse.

Grizel glanced up at the loft. She knew Haggadah was awake. The poor child had whimpered throughout the night, but the healer surmised the grieving orphan had experienced an uninterrupted and restful sleep. Grizel left the room to retrieve a small crock of honey from the cellar beneath the shed floor.

Bewildered by the sudden silence, Haggadah got out of bed and peeked over the loft's edge to discover she was alone in the tiny house. She descended the ladder. The kettle hanging over the fire had steam emanating from its spout, and a pair of plates and teacups were on the table. The remaining loaf of bread was on the cutting board, accompanied by a sharp knife.

Grizel opened the backdoor to see Haggadah standing near the table. "Ah, ready to begin your day?" She placed a crock of honey next to the bread. "You slept well?"

"Aye, my sleep was peaceful. Thank you for the warm and dry place to lay my head." She paused momentarily. "Sorry, but I must use the cludgie." She scooted past the healer and went out the backdoor. Once she returned, Haggadah washed her hands to appease Grizel and joined her at the table.

"All I can offer for breakfast is a meager but delicious meal." Grizel drizzled a wedge of bread with a generous amount of honey and placed it on Haggadah's plate. "Eat while I ready the tea." She stood and went to the cupboard to retrieve the tin of black tea, poured a small amount in her hand, and dumped it into each teacup before filling them with boiling water.

Haggadah bit into the bread and closed her eyes as she savored the sweetness of the honey. She had tasted the amber syrup only once before. It was as sweet as she remembered.

The corners of Grizel's mouth turned upward as she stood with the kettle in her hand. "I assume you like the honey?"

Haggadah opened her eyes. "Aye, very much. Thank you. Mum . . ." She became silent, and the grin on her face became a flat line.

Feeling the need to redirect Haggadah's train of thought, the healer stated, "We have a busy day with..."

A knock on the door interrupted Grizel. "There is a horrid grippe going around lately." She put the kettle back on the hook and opened the door a mere crack to see Tavish's smiling face in the morning sunshine. "Tavish, have you had breakfast?"

"No."

"Then, come." Grizel opened the door wide enough for him to enter.

"My thanks." Tavish removed his flat cap as he entered the house. "Morning, Haggadah." He sat in a vacant chair at the table.

Grizel cut the bread, added honey, placed it on her plate, and pushed it before the young man. She slid her teacup before him. "It's quite hot." She went to the cupboard to get another teacup and plate for herself.

"Thanks." He looked at Haggadah. Her hair was disheveled, but otherwise, she looked well-rested and beautiful. He smiled. "Did you sleep well?" He bit into the bread as he awaited her reply.

"Aye." Curious, she inquired. "Where did you sleep?"

"I found a cozy place." He saw the look of concern on her face. "No need to worry about me. I can take care of myself." Tavish ate another bite of bread and watched Grizel pour a cup of tea for herself and sit. "Men have started to take down the tenement buildings. They began before sunrise. As quick as they are working, they should have the buildings down soon." He swallowed his mouthful and looked at Grizel. "I thought Haggadah may want to watch the workmen for a little while today."

Haggadah looked at the healer, knowing she had their day planned.

Grizel took a sip of her tea. Her plans for the day could wait. She looked at Haggadah. "Would you like to go with Tavish?"

Haggadah looked from Grizel to Tavish and back. "Aye. I'd like to see the building one last time before it's taken down."

Grizel nodded, agreeing. She placed her cup on the table. "After the two of you finish eating, then go and watch the men work."

Haggadah ate the last of her honeyed bread and sipped her tea while she waited for Tavish to eat. She grinned as she watched him hold a crust of bread in one hand while licking the honey that had dripped onto his fingers on the other.

A pang of guilt pierced Haggadah's consciousness. It would be unkind for her to leave the cottage without washing the dishes. She stood and lifted her plate and cup from the table.

The healer could sense Haggadah's uneasiness. "Don't trouble yourself with the dishes. I can wash these few. Put them in the washtub," she reassured, "go, be back before supper."

Tavish stuffed the last of his bread into his mouth and drank his tea in one gulp. He imitated Haggadah by carrying his dishes to the washtub.

Grizel stood from the table, walked the pair to the door, and glanced at Haggadah's layered clothing. "We'll have to get you a warmer overcoat." She motioned for the pair to exit through the door she held open and watched them stroll down the pathway in the morning sunshine. "Maybe she won't follow in my footsteps after all." She closed the door as a steeple bell rang in the distance.

Haggadah stopped walking. "Is it Sunday?"

Tavish noticed the kirk's bell then. "No," he thought momentarily, "unless I've lost track of my days. It's a weekday. It's the bell of Saint Cuthbert marking the early hour."

Her eyes widened. "I'm going to the kirk and pray for my mum's soul. She told me it's always open. Och, and I must attend Mass on Sundays, too. Mum said it's a sin if I don't go every week." She began walking toward the kirk, leaving Tavish dumbstruck and staring.

He lunged forward, grasped her arm, and stopped her. "It isn't safe for you to walk alone. I'll go with you. We have time to watch the workmen until the shops open, then I need to do errands."

They walked through Old Town and rounded Nor Loch. Tavish and Haggadah passed through the gate onto the hallow ground. Other than a few birds chirping, it was peacefully quiet. Haggadah went to the kirk and pulled on the wooden door. It would not open.

Tavish gave the door a good yank, but it remained closed. "Locked. I guess your mum was wrong."

Haggadah looked in the direction of her mother's grave. "If you don't mind, I'll only be a moment."

Respecting her privacy, Tavish stepped to the side of the kirk. "I'll wait here." He sat on a stone bench.

"Thank you." Haggadah went to the area of the pauper's graves. There were three rectangular mounds of dirt. She looked about, trying to determine which grave belonged to her mother.

"Hello, Haggadah." Wiley stood behind her with his shovel on his shoulder.

"Hello." She motioned toward the graves. "I can't remember which grave belongs to my mum."

"It's understandable, being the grave is unmarked. Grief can play tricks on one's mind, too."

Haggadah grinned, imagining her state of mind on the day her mother died affected any logical thinking.

Wiley stepped forward and pointed. "She lies safely here, resting peacefully."

Haggadah looked at the grave and then turned back to the gravedigger. "Thank you."

Wiley nodded and went to join Davis, who had started to dig another grave.

Looking at the dirt that had yet to settle, Haggadah knew her mother's soul was in a much better place than her body lying deep within the cold ground. "Tavish insisted I stay with Grizel, who gave me a place to lay my head last night. I hope you will rest easily now that I'm living with her. I like to believe you will always watch over me from above." Haggadah grinned and looked in his direction. "He's kind. I think you would like him." She sighed. "I was foolish to believe the rumors about Grizel. She is not bad; she's just misunderstood. She is teaching me to read and write. I'll do my best to make you proud, Mum." Her eyes began to well. "I miss you." Haggadah wiped a tear from her cheek. She did not want to cry, but her love for her mother was expressed best through tears. "I must go. Tavish is waiting for me. I love you, Mum." She took several deep breaths, wiped the dampness from her face, and joined her escort.

A breeze came off the Nor Loch as they walked up the hill. Haggadah's long strawberry-blonde hair blew across her eyes. She pulled it aside and coughed as she wrinkled her nose. "There is a strong stench from the loch today." She waved her hand before her face as if pushing the pungent air away.

"It always reeks of chamber pots. The smoke from the fireplaces is a bit thick today, too." He looked into the distance. The smoke made the buildings appear draped with a sheer white curtain.

Haggadah and Tavish stood on the edge of High Street and watched workmen dart in and out of the former residential building. Some carried buckets. Others operated a system of pullies lowering large masonry stones to the street below. Some of the larger stones were cut for ease of movement and could be put back together like a puzzle. Others resembled fieldstones gathered by a farmer when clearing his field for plowing.

"They are reusing the stones to make the bridge," Tavish commented.

Haggadah looked at the window where she once lived. "From what my mum told me, they want to fill the gap of the hill to make it easier to get about the city."

"Aye, and shops will be beneath the bridge. It should be grand."

A commotion of jeering and shouting echoed down High Street, drawing their attention to the crown spire of Saint Giles Cathedral and the buildings nearby.

"There must be a hanging today." Tavish looked at the people gathering near the residential building known as Luckenbooths. He wondered how people could live adjacent to the Old Tolbooth, a jail where people were often tortured, and their cries of pain echoed throughout the buildings. Both buildings were in the center of the main street adjoining the cathedral. He assumed it was built there so the guilty could be closer to God before they died.

"They think the killing of someone is entertaining. I don't want to watch." Haggadah looked away and redirected her attention to the workmen.

Tavish pointed at some of the workmen as they disappeared from his sight over the hill. "Let's go and see if they're beginning to make the bridge."

Tavish and Haggadah walked down the hill of Cowgate while keeping their distance from the chaos.

"Aye, they are reusing the stones," Tavish confirmed as he pointed at the outline of the foundation.

"Makes good sense to me." Haggadah stared at the apartment window she often looked out. The clothesline was still in place.

"Aye, the bridge will make it easier to get about town." He nodded.

They watched the workmen lay the stone while others backfilled with dirt to support the wall.

Tavish ventured an assumption. "Water is going to seep between the rocks."

Haggadah looked about. "What water?"

"See how muddy it is at the bottom of the hill. The rain collects there, along with sewage. Once they fill in the sides of the bridge, nothing will stop the water from seeping through the rocks and into the chambers."

"I'm guessing there will still be a way to bring the cattle in for slaughter." She assumed.

"Aye. I overheard someone say there will be an arched passageway at the bottom for the cattle."

"Och, they must ken what they are doing. After all, the men are skilled masons, experts that work with stone." Haggadah reasoned.

Tavish had his doubts. "I think they're rushing and not thinking about the possibility of flooding. I guess time will tell." Tavish reached into his pocket and pulled out a coin. "Care to walk to the market and get something to eat?"

Haggadah stared at the coin he held between his thumb and index finger. "I would hate for you to waste your coin on me."

A scowl appeared on his face. "If there's one thing I've learned from living on the streets, it's to share with others so the good deed will return to me. Besides, it won't be a waste. We'll both have full bellies." He grinned. "Come."

Haggadah relented with a nod.

They walked past the shops on High Street, tempted to spend their coin in a bakery or butcher shop. However, Tavish knew they could haggle for a reasonable price at the market. Since it was a weekday, only a few vendors would be there, far less than on a Saturday. After weighing their options, they purchased two giant dill pickles, some dried beef, and a small loaf of bread. They bit into their pickles with a resounding crunch as they returned to watch the workmen a bit longer.

Tavish handed her a strip of beef.

Haggadah shook her head. "You should keep it for yourself and the bread, too. Truly, the pickle is more than enough for me."

"Just one strip. I have four." He insisted.

Haggadah sighed. She tried to remember the last time she had eaten beef. "Very well." She bit into the rubbery dried morsel, sawed it with her teeth until a piece broke free, and began to chew.

The workmen resembled a busy hill of ants, each knowing their job. To Haggadah, they seemed to be in a hurry, but maybe they were being paid to complete the bridge by a particular date.

Haggadah overheard one of the workmen say to another as they walked by her. "I've heard the oldest person in the city will be the first to cross the bridge."

"Aye, so I've heard. I've heard a big ceremony is being planned." Replied another. "It will be quite an honor with everyone watching."

Tavish looked at the sun, estimating the time of day. "If you don't mind, I'll walk you back now. I must see if I can make a coin or two before the day's out."

Nodding, Haggadah stood. "Och, I've kept you from your job."

"No, it was my decision and one I don't regret." Tavish stood and smiled. "You've been good company and a pleasant break from another humdrum day. Perhaps we can watch the men work another day."

"Aye, that would be nice."

~

The man pressed the house key into the clay. Satisfied, he did the same for the cabinet key. He made a mold of the opposite side of each key. Binding the clay molds together, he melted iron nails over the fire, poured the liquid into the mold, and allowed it to cool. Opening the mold, he grinned as he took the duplicate keys and used a small file to remove any residue. He held both keys up and examined them closely. "These will work nicely."

Chapter 8

Upon arriving at the ancient cottage, Haggadah hesitated before the front door, uncertain if she should knock or just walk in.

"Come in, Haggadah," Grizel called, knowing the young couple was on the other side.

Haggadah opened the door, stepped inside, and turned to see Tavish still standing on the walkway.

"I must go." He smiled.

"Aye. Thank you for the pickle."

He touched his index finger to the brim of his hat and turned away.

She watched him pass through the gate before shutting the door.

"Did you enjoy your day?" Grizel sat at the table with several bundles of dried herbs and bottles before her.

"Aye. I went to Mum's grave for a visit. We watched the workmen take the tenements apart and went to the market, where Tavish bought me a pickle. Och, there was a hanging at the Old Tolbooth, too."

Grizel selected another herb. She reflected on the many times she had watched someone take their last breath. "There's no pleasure in watching someone die. Let alone watch someone do the deadman's jig on the end of a rope." She plucked the dried leaves from a stem and crumbled them over the mouth of a bottle, letting the herb fall inside.

Intrigued, Haggadah sat across from the healer.

It pleased Grizel to see her apprentice eager to learn. "This is mugwort." She rotated the bottle toward Haggadah and pointed a crooked finger at its label.

Haggadah looked at each letter in the word but recognized only one.

"It's added to a remedy for those who ail from stomach issues, those who suffer worrisome fits, and to help with a woman's courses." Grizel handed her a partially filled jar and a different bundle of dried herbs. "I've given you lavender." She pointed to the label before setting the vessel before her apprentice. "It has many uses. It helps someone sleep, raises one's spirit, and relieves headaches. It also calms a crying baby, helps ease a woman with her monthly courses, is good for healing wounds, and is used in hospitals when cleaning surfaces. Crumble the leaves, stem, and tiny blossoms and fill the jar. Place the cork in its top when you have done so."

Haggadah began crumbling the dried blossoms. "It's quite fragrant."

"Aye." Grizel pressed a cork into the jar filled with mugwort, selected another herb, and turned the jar toward Haggadah. She explained the properties of the dried plant while she worked. "We must always keep the apothecary fully stocked."

"I assume you grow the plants in the backyard." Haggadah continued to crumble the dried leaves and let them fall into the vessel.

"Aye. As many who have taken my remedies ken, my herbs are the highest quality and most effective."

After several hours of filling jars, Grizel returned the bottles to the apothecary while Haggadah put the unused herb bundles on the nails in the ceiling beams.

To tidy the table, Grizel brushed the fragments of the various herbs into the palm of her hand and tossed them onto the fire, causing a lovely fragrance to fill the cottage. She peered into the caldron. The thick gravy bubbled and popped. She inhaled the aroma. "Ah, bring me two bowls."

Haggadah took bowls from the cupboard and handed them to Grizel, who ladled stew into each. Grabbing two spoons and the remainder of the loaf of bread, Haggadah placed them on the table before retrieving the teacups and tea and making the hot beverage. Grizel and Haggadah sat, each taking a wedge of bread, which they used like a sponge to soak up the delicious gravy, wasting not a single drop. The healer quizzed her apprentice on the properties of the herbs while they ate.

Haggadah ate the last bite of sodden bread. "Thank you. The stew was delicious."

"You're welcome." Grizel sat back in her chair as her apprentice stood.

"Since you made supper, I'll do the dishes." Haggadah insisted. She cleared the table and began to wash.

Grizel added a log to the fire, lit the yellow candle, and placed it on the table. Haggadah dried and put away the last plate while she watched the healer go to the apothecary, retrieve the Book of Shadows, and place it on the table.

The young apprentice sat and stared at the old book as it was placed before her. She was leery of the enchantments on its pages, yet eager to learn. She promised to hold true to her Christian upbringing in honor of her mother, yet she did not want to insult the woman who allowed her to remain under her roof.

"Some of the women who wrote the pages of this book were tried and found guilty of being a witch." Grizel sat in a chair next to Haggadah. "They were killed needlessly out of fear. Many were nothing more than healers. Their only crime was they possessed the gift to foresee into the future." Grizel looked at Haggadah, suspecting she could do the same. "Others were condemned for hearsay, a birthmark or mole."

"But that was long ago." Haggadah reasoned, unfamiliar with any innocent woman accused and convicted of being a witch during her lifetime.

Grizel went on to explain. "Some still believe in witches and their ability to cast spells, curses, and such."

"Can you cast spells, curses, and such?" Haggadah pried.

Grizel simply looked at her apprentice and grinned slightly. She opened the book, releasing its fragrance, and turned to the page. "Every healer who has owned this book has added their own incantations. This section is titled, Spells."

"Spells?"

"Aye, Spells." Grizel reaffirmed.

"Like curses?"

Not wanting to scare or disappoint Haggadah's impressionable mind, Grizel shrugged her shoulder. "I'm not quite sure. Whether it is a spell or curse, the accused witch who added the incantation to this book thought it powerful. As you can see, they are not written in the letters I have taught you. They are written in Theban Script."

Haggadah stared at the unusual scribbles on the page. "Why did they write them so?"

"To protect their spells. They wrote them in a script that only witches understand." Grizel turned the page to the next encrypted spell.

Haggadah scanned the page. "Do you ken what each spell says?"

"Aye. I'll teach you to read them after you learn to read proficiently." She turned several pages. "As you can see, these pages have sketches of herbs. Each page also lists its name, the herb's properties, and how to use it." She turned to the page of mugwort.

Haggadah leaned closer to the book as she recognized the herb. "Isn't that the herb . . ."

"Aye, the very one I used to refill the jar, mugwort." She turned several pages. "And here is the lavender herb you filled a jar with today."

Haggadah noted the color of the tiny blossoms in the illustration. "The dried blossoms had dulled in color."

"By drying the herb in the darkness of the cottage, its healing properties are preserved." Grizel continued to turn the pages.

"There are a lot of herbs for me to learn. I'm glad there are sketches. It'll help me to ken which herb is which."

Grizel went on to explain the pages containing the moon's phases, the names and properties of crystals and stones, Sabbat rituals, the use of candle color, how to extract the healing properties from herbs, recipes for various teas, and more. As the pages turned, the flame on the yellow candle sputtered and burned well into the night.

~

Tavish joined the men around the warming fire within the sheltered close. He rubbed his hands together and held his palms before the dancing flames, trying to ward off the chill of the night. He watched as a flask of whiskey was passed around by the men, who kept a watchful eye over the women and children huddled together sleeping. Tavish looked at an infant who coughed. Its mother snuggled the baby close to her body and pulled her ragged coat over it for additional warmth.

Feeling a nudge on his arm, Tavish looked at the flask held before him. He took a swig before passing it to the man next to him.

"The days are getting warmer." One of the men commented as he anticipated the change of season.

"Aye, but the dampness never seems to go away," said another as he looked at the opening of the close. A steady drizzle dampened the cobblestone.

Tavish remained silent and listened to the men's comments.

"The tenement buildings are coming down quickly. The men are working from morning until night. I suspect the bridge will be up soon."

"It'll make traveling about the city much easier. One less hill to climb."

"I'm curious to see the shops beneath the bridge, not that I can afford any of what they sell."

Turning away, Tavish went to the entrance of the close and leaned against the wall. The ten o'clock hour had long passed, and silence blanketed the city. He watched a wayward drunk stumble out of the pub from across the street, his foot splashing in the gutter of sewage. The man staggered to the city well, attempting to pump water unsuccessfully before leaning against it for support. The drunk slid down the small stone structure, lethargically tilting to the side before dropping to the ground and passing out.

Shaking his head, Tavish wondered what troubles the man was trying to forget by drowning himself in whiskey.

The silhouette of a man casually strolling through the street caught Tavish's attention. He pushed himself away from the wall and watched the stranger enter a darkened shop. "Must be Mister Dingwall. Maybe he forgot something." Tavish sat against the wall, pulled his hat over his eyes, and tried to sleep.

Chapter 9

In the wee morning hours at a pub within Fleshmarket Close, the owner, Mister Clark, and his wife were busy tidying the bar, sweeping the floor, and snuffing out candles. They were eager to close for the night. Other than the pair of men in the back corner playing poker and the man sitting at the bar with his eyes closed and a whiskey poised in his hand, the establishment was empty.

Brodie threw his losing poker hand down on the table. "Och, it's not in the cards for me tonight," he said to his opponent sitting across from him. With resentment in his eyes, the councilman watched the man pull the money from the center of the table and fill his pockets. Brodie wished he could slap the grin off the man's face. Patting his pockets, he discovered they were empty. He drank his last dram of whiskey, once again overindulging in the drink. "Even though this evening has been entertaining, it is unfortunate that I'm leaving the table empty-handed." He stood and steadied himself by grasping the back of his chair and waited for a wave of dizziness to subside. Shaking his head to clear it, Brodie took his walking stick from the corner of the room and clasped the brim on his beaver top hat. "I bid you goodnight."

"Goodnight, Councilman." The man stuffed the last of his winnings into his pocket and stood from the table. "Better luck next time."

Brodie tried his best to walk to the pub door with dignity in his intoxicated state. Pushing the door open, he was greeted by a sobering wind and drizzle that dampened his face. Not willing to walk the distance to either of his mistress's houses in fear he would end up face down in a rancid gutter, he held his head up as he exited the close and walked a crooked line to his house in Little's Close.

~

Grizel slept longer than usual. She flexed her aged fingers as she awoke. They were stiff and ached. Taking the poker from its hook, she stirred the ashen embers before placing a log to rekindle the fire. Rubbing her fingers to alleviate the pain, she pulled aside the curtain and peered out the window. It was indeed raining, as she suspected. Grizel turned, looked up at the loft, and grinned. Having someone to share her knowledge with and cast away her loneliness was welcomed in her old age.

The pair had stayed up quite late, with Haggadah absorbing as much information as possible. The healer knew her apprentice had a lot to learn, yet was confident she was capable.

Grizel retrieved a small wheel of cheese and used the remaining eggs from the basket to make their breakfast with a side of beans.

The crackle of the fire and the aroma of frying eggs stirred Haggadah from her sleep. She rose from her cot and descended the ladder to the main floor. "I'm sorry for sleeping in late."

"Nonsense. A body needs rest to stay healthy." Grizel carried the cast iron frying pan to the table.

"I should be making breakfast to earn my keep." Haggadah noticed the place settings and cheese on the cutting board on the table. She saw the kettle over the fire with steam emanating from its spout. "I'll make the tea."

"Very well." Grizel cut and placed several cheese slices on each plate and two overcooked eggs; the yolks were hard yet soft to the touch. After adding beans to each plate, she sat. Grizel watched her apprentice make the tea, pleased by Haggadah's willingness to help with the meal. The healer flexed her fingers. "My hands are stiff this morning. It must be the weather. Haggadah, get me the wintergreen salve in a tiny crock and willow bark before you sit down." She pointed at the apothecary.

Haggadah set the steaming cups of tea on the table and went to the oversized cupboard. She opened the doors and scanned the numerous jar labels in the pigeonholes.

Realizing her apprentice had difficulty locating the items, Grizel offered additional instruction. "The crock is small and brown. It's covered with a cloth and should be on the right."

Haggadah found the item, turned, and showed it to the healer to verify she had the correct crock.

"Aye, the bottle that contains willow bark is brown. It has a label that begins with 'W' that looks like an upside-down 'M.' You'll find it near the bottom on the left.

"M, W," Haggadah repeated. She recalled learning the letter 'M' when spelling the word mum. Tilting her head sideways, she imagined the first letter on the brown bottle upside down and pulled it from the shelf. "This one?"

"Aye. Well done. It says, 'willow bark.' It's used for pain, especially headaches."

Placing the items before Grizel, Haggadah sat and ate as she watched the healer apply salve to her hands and add a measure of willow bark to her tea. Inhaling, Haggadah detected the aroma of mint. She reached across the table, picked up the small crock, and inhaled the scent, casting it to her memory. Looking at each letter on the label on the bottle, she recalled the herb's healing properties. "Did you give this herb to my mum to ease her pain?"

"Aye. There were other herbs I used, too." Grizel looked at her apprentice, who seemed deep in thought while she ate silently. "Speak your thoughts."

Haggadah bit into a thick slice of cheese, hesitating before she spoke. "If you aren't against it, my mum and I always attended Mass every Sunday. I would like to continue to do so in her honor."

"As you wish." Grizel cut her egg with the side of her fork, allowing what remained of the golden yolk to spill onto her plate.

"Are we to continue with my lessons today?" Haggadah blew on her tea before taking a tentative sip.

"Later tonight. We'll spend our day visiting the homeless and giving remedies to anyone who is ill. But first, we'll need to make herbal teas and fill bottles with various tinctures." She scooped beans onto her fork. "I have an aromatic salve for those having difficulty breathing and to loosen any cold in their chests." Grizel grinned. "It's good you're well rested, for our day will be long and tiring."

~

The dreary weather had little effect on Tavish. He began his day eager to earn enough money to eat well. He stopped by several shops, hoping the owners needed his service. Unfortunately, none of them did thus far.

Determined to have a positive outlook for the day, Tavish smiled, walked to the next shop, and stepped aside as the door opened and Constable Roger McLeary passed through it. Even though he had never been accused of anything untoward, Tavish knew of others charged with crimes they did not commit. With a nod, he touched the brim of his hat, showing respect to the officer. "Good morning, Constable McLeary."

McLeary was familiar with many of the longtime homeless in the city. He was aware of the lad's popularity and dependable reputation shared by many shop owners. "Good morning, Tavish." McLeary paused and faced the homeless lad. "It's nice to see you in good health."

"Aye, Sir, and you as well."

"Did you sleep nearby last night?"

Tavish pointed in the direction of the close where he bedded down. "Aye, sheltered and warm for the night. I managed to stay dry." He looked skyward. Seeing a blue sky on the horizon, he assumed the rain would stop soon.

"You've always been a reliable source, greatly appreciated, I must add."

"Thank you, Sir." Tavish noticed the gold wedding ring on the constable's left hand as the officer adjusted his hat on his head.

"This shop was robbed last night. However, there is no sign of a break-in. Did you happen to see anyone suspicious near the building last night?"

Tavish initially shook his head, but then he remembered seeing a man. "I saw someone enter the building. It was late. I thought it was Mister Dingwall returning for something he forgot because the man only stood at the door a moment before entering."

"I see. Mister Dingwall tells me he locked the door. Perhaps he forgot, and someone took advantage of his lapse in memory. Thank you. If you think of anything else, please come to the station house and make a report."

"Aye, Sir." Tavish entered the shop to see a distraught Mister Dingwall. "I'm sorry to hear the news of the robbery."

Mister Dingwall ran his hand through his gray hair, pulling it back over his head. "Thank you, Tavish."

"I saw someone enter your store last night. They seemed to walk right in, so I assumed it was you."

Mister Dingwall shook his head. "I must be getting absent-minded in my old age and left the door unlocked." He stared down into the empty cash box. "They took everything in the drawer. Luckily, I set aside some money in my safe, so they didn't take all of my money. Nevertheless, the loss will make a lean week for my family."

Tavish empathized with the kind shopkeeper. Dingwall and his wife had raised two sons who, along with their spouses and children, lived with them. He indeed had to provide for a houseful. "If you have an errand for me to run, it's no charge today." Tavish offered.

"I've just one letter to post." Mister Dingwall reached into his pocket and handed the lad a coin. "This should cover the postage."

"I'll be sure to keep a watchful eye on your store at night. If they think it's an easy target, they may return." He placed the letter and coin in his coat pocket.

"Aye, thank you, Tavish. And I'll double-check the locks each night." He stared down into the empty drawer as he heard the bell above the shop door ring before it closed.

Tavish passed by the deconstruction of the former tenement buildings on his way to his next stop. The workmen moved about like army ants as they removed each stone and transported it down the hill to its new location. Tavish stood for a moment to watch. He overheard two women discussing Mister Dingwall's robbery as they walked by him. Word was spreading quickly of the shopkeeper's misfortune. Not that a theft was new in the city, but the large sum taken was of great concern.

In the distance, he saw the familiar overcoat of the town healer near the opening of a close. Tavish grinned, realizing Haggadah was with Grizel. He elongated his stride to join the pair.

~

Brodie opened his eyes, looked at the sky from his bedroom window, and guessed it was near midday. His stomach grumbled, urging him to rise from bed. He needed to go to his workshop and finish an order for another custom-made cabinet. Brodie swung his legs over the side of the bed, forcing him to sit up. He looked at his feet to discover he was still wearing his shoes, let alone his clothes from the previous day. "Well, no sense changing them just to work on cabinets." Brodie stood and stomped down the staircase, still half-awake.

Hearing Brodie's heavy footfalls, Amelia, his maid, shook her head. She had kept his breakfast warm in the oven and covered by another frying pan, hoping it would not be as dry as week-old bread. She carried the hot plate into the dining room, placed it before the chair where he would sit, and returned to the kitchen to fetch his coffee.

Plopping himself in his chair, Brodie began shoveling food into his mouth as Amelia entered the room. He placed the side of his fork on the sunny-side-up egg to cut it, but it bounced back without leaving a mark. "These eggs are like rubber."

His maid exhaled as she set the coffee on the table and placed her fisted hands on her hips. "Well, if you would come home at a decent hour and get your arse up in the morning, your breakfast would be fresh.

I've been keeping it warm in the oven for hours." She shook a pointed index finger at Brodie. "I've got to adhere to a tight schedule in order to keep this house tidy, especially with all the damn sawdust you drag in here from the workshop. You're lucky I didn't give you a bowl of cold porridge."

Brodie picked up the slice of toast and tapped the stale bread on the side of his plate, causing it to ring.

Amilia's eyes flared. "Maybe you should make your own breakfast so I can get on with my job." She marched back into the kitchen, muttering to herself.

He had no retort to counter her lecture. What she had said was true. From now on, he would remind himself to dust his clothes before entering the house. Shrugging his shoulder, Brodie used his knife to cut his egg and ate the rubbery white. "At least it is still warm."

~

"Good day, ladies." Tavish greeted.

"Ha! Ladies! I've never been addressed as royalty." Grizel chuckled. "Nevertheless, I appreciate the compliment."

Haggadah grinned, pleased to see his smiling face. "Hello, Tavish."

"Doing a bit of charity work today?" He looked skyward and stated the obvious. "At least the rain has stopped." He glanced down at the bottles in the basket that Haggadah carried.

"Aye. Rain or not, Grizel insisted we venture out and try to nip any illness before it can spread further." She gave a bottle to Grizel's outstretched hand and turned her attention back to Tavish. She looked at the letter sticking out of his pocket. "I see you managed to get a job today."

Tavish patted his pocket. "Aye, not enough to eat, I'm afraid. I'm posting it for Mister Dingwall. His store was robbed last night, so I've just enough money to cover the postage."

"It seems to be the gossip on the street. A few people have mentioned the large amount of money the robber took." Haggadah shook her head, feeling sorry for the shopkeeper.

"Word of bad news always travels fast." Tavish confirmed. "Quite strange, really. I saw a man enter the store last night. I thought it was Mister Dingwall since he entered the building quickly. The constable thought he may have forgotten to lock up."

"A pity. I hope Mister Dingwall recovers his loss soon."

"Haggadah." The healer called.

Haggadah turned to see Grizel several paces away from her.

Grizel waved her hand for her apprentice to come to her. "We must keep moving. There are many others to see."

Looking back at Tavish, she grinned as he motioned for her to go as the healer requested. He fell in step beside her. "Is all going well for you?"

"Aye. I'm learning about herbs and remedies and have a warm place to lay my head at night." She thought for a moment. "I've you to thank for it."

"To see you off the streets is thanks enough." Tavish saw a shopkeeper across the street waving for his attention. "I must go."

Haggadah watched him dodge several horse-pulled carts as he crossed the busy main street. She stopped walking as she nearly bumped into the backside of Grizel, who stood before a woman holding a crying baby. The child looked feverish as it coughed.

Grizel retrieved a bottle and a wooden spoon from the basket. "I added a bit of honey to the remedy, so the bairn will be eager to take some. Give the child two to three spoonfuls at least five times a day. If she has not improved, come and see me. I'll create another remedy."

The woman thanked Grizel, who turned to Haggadah. "How many bottles remain?"

Haggadah counted. "Five."

Grizel walked to the next close and scanned for anyone who may be ill, eyeing those huddled near the warming fire. A few recognized her, approached, and received an herbal remedy.

When the healer and her apprentice gave out the last bottle, they began to walk back to the cottage. Grizel stopped before the butcher shop and gazed into the window. "We did well and deserve a treat." She announced before stepping into the shop. Haggadah followed and stood silently as the healer purchased several slices of ham with a few coins in her pocket. She placed the wrapped meat in the empty basket. As they stepped onto the street, a young girl with a tear-streaked face approached her.

"You must come. My mum needs help birthing a bairn." The child boldly placed her hand within Grizel's and pulled in the direction she wished the town healer to go.

"Come." Grizel urged Haggadah. "You must learn."

They followed the little girl, who was not more than seven years of age, through the street and entered a building. Climbing the stairs to an upper floor, they heard the expected woman's cries of pain as she struggled to give birth.

Entering the room crowded with several people, the expectant mother lay in the corner with several women around her.

Grizel went to the woman, knelt gingerly, and felt the swollen abdomen. "The bairn is breech." She looked at Haggadah, who stood several steps behind her. "Come, give me your hand."

Staring at the expectant mother's face masked with pain, Haggadah approached and held out her hand to Grizel, who fanned out her apprentice's fingers and placed them on the swollen belly.

"Feel." She instructed. "The head is here, rump is here. It's in the wrong position. A bairn should be born headfirst. This child will be born bottom first unless it changes its position."

"Change its position?" Haggadah felt the mother's abdomen become hard beneath the palm of her hand. The woman yelled, causing Haggadah to jerk her hand away and wince at the woman's pain. "The bairn will do that?"

"Not always. Sometimes, the bairn must be encouraged to be born as is. I've managed to turn only one before. But we must try to turn this little one for the sake of the bairn and the mum."

Haggadah gasped. "We?"

"Aye." Grizel examined the woman's abdomen again. "It seems to be floating."

"Floating?"

"Aye. The bairn's bottom isn't in position yet." Grizel ordered the women to elevate the expectant mother's pelvis.

The women glanced at one another, questioning the healer's motive, yet too scared to object to whatever witchcraft technique she planned to use on their friend.

Grizel watched as the women placed a stack of blankets beneath the woman's hips. "Place your hands here and here." Grizel instructed Haggadah as she pointed to the woman's abdomen. The healer put her hands in place on the bairn's rump.

Haggadah knelt on the opposite side of the expectant mother. She placed her hands on the bulbous belly.

"Spread your fingers wide and push toward me when I say."

"Will it hurt the bairn?"

"No. We must encourage it to rotate by pushing gently and then increasing pressure."

Haggadah took a deep breath.

As the contraction eased, Grizel ordered. "Now."

They pushed, increasing pressure. Haggadah could feel the child move slightly. The woman yelled as another contraction began. As it subsided, they tried again. The healer and her apprentice continued to work as the women tried to comfort the expectant mother.

Knowing they had done all they could, Grizel felt the baby's position. "The bairn is head down." She ordered the expected mother to be brought upright. Those surrounding her helped her onto her knees. The healer felt the woman's bulbous belly and nodded to Haggadah. "Feel. Do you notice the difference?"

Haggadah sensed the changed baby's position as she used both hands to feel the infant. "Aye."

"We shall see if she can give birth now."

It was several hours before the child was born. The resounding cry announcing his birth was welcomed and brought a smile to Haggadah's face.

As they left the residence, Haggadah was still grinning. "I did not ken childbirth could be so grotesque and beautiful at the same time."

Grizel's eyebrows raised in question. "You and your mum lived in a room filled with many others. Have you not witnessed the birth of a bairn before?"

"No. Mum made me sit on the stairs. It was her way of keeping me from seeing the truth about birthing. I think she wanted me to have bairns someday and feared if I saw the pain I must endure, I would not want them."

"And what do you think now?"

Haggadah grinned. "I watched the mum's face as she looked at her newborn bairn. She seemed to forget about the pain, for I only saw love on her face."

"Aye. A blessing was bestowed upon the bairn and mum. But I must warn you, not all births end happily. Sometimes, the good Lord takes the soul back to be with him."

The healing pair continued their walk to the cottage. After stoking the fire upon their arrival, they enjoyed a delicious late afternoon meal of ham and cheese before continuing with Haggadah's lessons.

Chapter 10

With his ever-present coffee cup within reach, Constable McLeary sat at his desk in the station house and filled out a robbery report in the late afternoon. After a day of investigating the Dingwall robbery, he logically assumed the shop owner had left the door unlocked. As McLeary returned his pen to the inkwell, he closed the file.

He recalled a similar case that inspired him to become a constable. McLeary was a teen in 1768 when a bank was robbed of eight hundred and thirty pounds. It was an unsolved mystery, with no evidence of forced entry.

McLeary searched the file cabinet in the corner of the room and pulled the file. He stared at the label '13

Aug 1768 Johnston and Smith'. Opening it, he read the victims were bankers at the Exchange in Edinburgh. Their statement indicated they thought a false key had been made and used to enter the building, justifying their reasoning because there was no forced entry. The money appeared to have simply disappeared. The criminal got away with the large sum and was never found.

McLeary's eyebrows formed a 'V' as he concentrated on what little facts were known. He finished reading the report, returned it to the cabinet, and picked up the file from his desk. He went to the office of Chief Inspector Niven and knocked on the door.

"Enter." A stern voice on the other side commanded.

McLeary did so and closed the door behind him for a private conversation with his superior. "Sir, I finished the report on the robbery of Dingwall's shop." He put the file on Niven's desk for his review. "He insists he locked the door when leaving the shop at the end of his day, yet there was no evidence of a forced entry. The details are noted in the report."

Niven looked up from the paperwork he was reading. "He probably forgot to lock up." He refocused his attention on the open file before him. "Thank you, McLeary."

Realizing he had been bluntly dismissed, McLeary nodded respectfully and left the office. He hoped the robbery was an isolated incident, but with so many now homeless, he assumed theft in the city would increase. Considering his superior's opinion about the crime, McLeary assumed he was making too much of the incident and returned to his desk. After reviewing and updating papers on another case, he closed the folder at the end of the day and went home to his wife and children to enjoy their company and an evening meal.

~

Brodie added the final brushstroke of varnish to the cabinet, took a step backward, and smiled, quite pleased with what he made.

The door to the workshop opened, and Amelia stepped inside. "Shall I go through the effort of making you a meal this evening?" The maid glared at the sawdust sprinkled about the floor like confetti. The room was warm, heated by a small fireplace, his woodworking tools hung neatly on a wall, and unfinished cabinets on the workbench awaiting the cabinetmaker's final touch. Amelia wrinkled her nose as the scent of varnish permeated her nostrils.

Basking in the golden glow of the lit oil lamps, Brodie enjoyed the solitude of his workshop and detested any intrusion, especially from his maid.

Refusing to stare into Amelia's inquisitive and belligerent eyes, Brodie answered, "No. I'll dine out this evening." He heard the workshop door slam shut. "I must remember to lock the door." He placed his brush in a jar of solvent and again admired his work. "An evening at the pub is indeed in order."

~

As the sun peeked over the horizon, songbirds chirped to announce the start of the day.

A knock roused Brodie from his intoxicated sleep. His vision blurred as he looked at the bedroom door, wondering how he had made it home and managed to get into bed.

"Deacon?" Amelia called. "Deacon? There is a city council meeting within the hour."

Brodie sighed as he closed his eyes and let his head fall to his pillow, wishing to return to sleep.

"Deacon Brodie, get yourself around. You were late for the last meeting. Do you wish to make a mockery of yourself again?" Amelia turned and descended the staircase.

A pain in his head pounded in unison with each beat of his heart as he listened to her retreating footfalls. Brodie assumed Amelia was setting his breakfast on the table. His stomach was in no mood to accept food. However, he thought several cups of strong coffee may help to clear the cobwebs from his mind.

He swung his legs over the side and sat on the edge of the bed. Once again, the councilman was fully dressed in his previous day's clothes, including his shoes. Brodie squeezed his eyes tightly, put his elbows on his thighs, and placed his pounding head within the palms of his hands, hoping to stop the room from spinning.

With the urge to relieve himself, he went to the chamber pot in the corner of the room, placing his left hand on the wall to keep his balance, and peed, caring little to aim correctly. Brodie patted each pocket in search of money. They were empty. He opened the nightstand drawer next to his bed, lifted the false bottom, and grabbed what little money was there. He stuffed it into his pants pocket before stepping into the hallway. With the help of the handrail, Brodie managed to descend to the first floor and sat at the dining room table.

Amelia anticipated his need and poured a cup of strong, black coffee. She wrinkled her nose at the stale stench of alcohol as she placed two well-buttered slices of toast on his plate. "These should help to sop up what's in your gullet from last night. Maybe you should quit burning the candle at both ends." Amelia turned toward the kitchen, unwilling to listen to Brodie's snide retort.

He wrapped his fingers around the cup, appreciating its warmth, and drank. The caffeinated liquid soothed his body and helped to calm the pounding in his head. Brodie took the maid's advice and ate both slices of toast.

Amelia marched back into the room. "Deacon, here's the correspondence you received over the past few days." She placed the stack of letters beside his plate and crossed her arms over her chest.

He returned his cup to the saucer. "Och, quite a few."

"Aye, and if you were home instead of spreading yourself thin between two women and those five bairns of yours, the stack would not be so big and burdensome." She picked up the empty plate and placed her fisted hand on her hip. "More toast?"

Perceiving her snippy mood, Brodie refused to meet the maid's condescending stare. "Aye." He picked up the top letter from the stack and broke the seal. It was a bill from a merchant, one that Jean used often.

"She spends too much money." The following letter was also a bill. This time, it was a merchant's bill for Ann, whose purchase caused him to frown. "These women will be the death of me."

The hallway clock struck half past the hour, reminding Brodie of his city council meeting. He tossed the letters aside, stood, and grabbed the toast from the plate in Amelia's hand as she entered the dining room. On his way out the front door, he picked up his walking stick and tricorne hat on the foyer floor, assuming the task of putting them in their proper place was more than he could handle in his drunken state the previous night. He put on his hat and stood momentarily, waiting for the throbbing in his head to subside. The councilman stepped onto the front stoop, shielding his eyes from the sun, flagged down a coach, and climbed inside.

The clip-clop of the horse's hooves did little for his aching head. Brodie sank into the corner of the seat, where the darkness agreed with his sensitive eyes.

When the coach came to a stop, the coachman opened the door and waited for his passenger to disembark.

Brodie squinted at the bright opening, wishing he were still in bed. He forced himself to leave the coach, paid the driver the customary fee, and entered the

Edinburgh City Chambers. He ignored the noisy conversations throughout the large room and sat in his designated seat. Brodie winced as the gavel sounded like several cracks of a whip, indicating the start of the meeting. He remained silent as whispers of 'robbery' and 'Dingwall' circled around him. Brodie seconded a proposal and voiced his opinion when forced, praying the meeting would end quickly.

As the gavel ended the meeting, he stood and shook hands with a few city council members near him.

"Deacon."

Brodie heard his name called as he exited the building. He turned to see James Wemyss, a goldsmith, step forward and extend his hand.

"If I may have a moment of your time." The jeweler requested.

Brodie nodded and shook the man's hand, hoping the topic of discussion would not involve politics or city matters.

"I need, or shall I say, my wife would like a cabinet built in our shop. Perhaps if she refrained from continuing to add to our inventory, she would not need the additional storage space." James grinned. "She is a woman of great taste and likes the finer things in life," he chuckled, "like me and our clients. It is in my best interest to keep her happy. Since your work is renowned, she insisted you build a cabinet for our shop. Could you find time in your busy schedule to do so?"

Brodie knew the man standing before him was one of the wealthiest in the city, a renowned jeweler who catered to the extraordinarily rich. He planned to overinflate his price and charge a hefty sum for his work. "I have no plans for today. If you wish, I can accompany you next door to your shop and see what I can do to guarantee your wife's happiness." He grinned. "I can measure the area where she wishes to install the cabinet, make several sketches, and then review them with her for approval. Does that seem reasonable?"

James's eyebrows raised, quite pleased with the idea. "Very much so." He motioned for the cabinetmaker to walk the short distance to his shop.

Brodie's eyes were drawn to the insignia shield above the door, indicating the building housed a goldsmith. He often admired the exterior of the high-end shop. It was a well-kept building with windows washed weekly and the sidewalk always swept.

An employee opened the door so Brodie could enter before James. Scanning the interior, he saw several elaborate wooden cases with elegantly carved features and the purest glass to peer inside at the various items for sale.

The employee presented an open hand. "May I take your hat, walking stick, and overcoat, Sir?"

Brodie was deaf to the request as he gazed around the shop.

James scowled as he corrected his middle-aged employee. "Lorna, he is a deacon. This is Deacon William Brodie."

"Deacon William Brodie!" Janette nearly ran from the back room into the display area of the shop. "The renowned cabinetmaker!"

James smiled at his wife, who was nearly a decade younger than himself. She stood patiently for a proper introduction. "Yes, my dear. This is Deacon Brodie. He has agreed to make your cabinet and is here to see how he can design one to fit your needs."

"Oh, I am pleased." Janette grasped Brodie's arm and led him away as she chattered about what she wanted.

"Good heavens." The goldsmith mumbled under his breath as he looked toward the ceiling and followed the pair into the office.

Brodie listened intently as Janette chatted on. He scanned the room, taking note of the elegant wooden desk and chair, floor-to-ceiling cabinets on one wall, and a safe. He took measurements of the walls in the showroom, noted the size she required, and promised to add decorative details to complement the existing display cabinets.

"I'll return with detailed sketches for you to review in a week. I'm confident at least one drawing will meet with your approval." Brodie explained.

Janette grinned. "I look forward to seeing what you have designed."

The couple walked Brodie to the door and bid him a good day as he accepted his overcoat, hat, and walking stick.

Brodie took a deep breath as he stepped onto the sidewalk, pleased with the unexpected opportunity to add to his income. With his mood uplifted and headache subsiding, he walked to Mister Dingwall's shop. "Good day." He greeted, ringing the bell above the door as he entered. "I heard the dreadful news of your robbery circulating at the city council meeting. Such a shame."

A grim expression masked Mister Dingwall's face. "Thank you. I was quite fortunate to have some money kept in my safe. It will provide for my family until I can recover from the loss."

Brodie shook his head. "More than likely, it was someone desperate and homeless. Do the authorities have a suspect?"

"Unfortunately, no. I blame myself. I may have left the door unlocked." Mister Dingwall ran his hand over his gray hair, pulling it away from his eyes. "I guess my mind is slipping in my old age."

"Och, age creeps up on all of us, but it's better than taking an eternal dirt nap. Let's hope the authorities catch the culprit soon. Good day to you." Brodie left the shop and hailed a coach to take him to Libberton's Wynd. He planned to spend enough time with Jean and their children to stay in her good graces before returning home to begin sketching the cabinet for Janette Wemyss. He grinned as he tapped his walking stick on the sidewalk before entering the open coach door. "I'm looking forward to the added income, indeed."

Chapter 11

On a fine Saturday morning, the citizens of Edinburgh awoke to filtered sunshine through puffy clouds dotting the sky. Grizel and Haggadah each carried an empty basket and walked to the market. They passed the workmen busy shuffling rocks from the tenement buildings to the South Bridge, its arches reaching skyward. To Haggadah, it seemed strange to see the former residence of so many people dissolve like a sandcastle in the rain. The single window of the small apartment where she and her mother had lived was no longer there. Haggadah sighed, realizing only her memories of her former home now remained.

Grizel detected her assistant's melancholy mood. "What would you like to get at the market today?"

Haggadah shrugged her shoulder. "I don't have money to purchase anything. Mum and I always went to the market after the vendors closed. We looked for something we could eat that they threw away. Tavish and I went for a short time on a weekday. He said it's much busier on a Saturday, so I don't ken what to expect."

"Aye, it will be crowded today. I think you'll be pleased by what the merchants, craftsmen, and farmers have to offer."

As they entered the market, Haggadah's eyes enlarged as she looked at what each merchant had on display. Delicious bread was stacked high in baskets, with bakers offering several varieties. The fragrance of baked goods and various floral scents enticed Haggadah's nose. She leaned in toward a basket of handmade soap and inhaled its fragrance. One cart had handwoven towels, knitted hats, and woolen blankets. A tartan plaid with bright and vibrant colors drew Haggadah's attention. She ran her hand over the softness of the lovely woolen blanket, unfamiliar with which clan it identified.

The merchant scanned the poor condition of Haggadah's appearance and assumed she had no money to purchase the item. "Off with you now." He jerked his head to one side, indicating she should walk away.

Grizel stepped beside her apprentice and glared at the man.

The merchant recognized the emerald eyes glaring back at him and took a hesitant step backward.

"So, you dare to judge a person by their clothes and appearance. It's a shame you have such a closed mind." She threw down several coins, grabbed the blanket, and marched away.

Haggadah's jaw dropped open as she stared at Grizel's retreating overcoat. She looked at the merchant, who greedily grabbed the coins and shooed her away with his hand as if sweeping dust in the air. Haggadah hurried her steps to catch up with the healer. "Grizel, there's no need to spend your coin on me."

"It's a gift." The healer handed the blanket to her apprentice. "Put this in your basket." She continued to scan the marketplace. "After all, the one you came with is of little use. We can use it to make a keepsake to remember your mum."

Haggadah's eyes welled with tears as she put the blanket in her basket. "It's bonnie. Thank you."

"You're more than welcome." Grizel put flour, sugar, and a tin of biscuits in her basket. She also purchased a spool of thread and a needle, quite sure she no longer had any within the cottage. Grizel next bought a warmer overcoat for Haggadah. "We can sew your mum's blanket into the lining to keep her near you." She then approached a farmer and paid for straw that would be delivered later that day.

~

John kept his chin down with his flat cap shielding his eyes. He walked among the people in the market with his hands in his coat pockets. His stomach grumbled, urging him to find something to fill it.

He spotted a well-dressed woman with her servant standing before a farmer's table containing several cuts of beef. Peering over their shoulders, he saw a stack of smoked pig's feet. The women selected their purchase. While the farmer was wrapping the meat, John threaded his arm between the women and took a pair of feet. He tucked them inside his coat as he walked away and disappeared among the shoppers.

~

"Good day. It's nice to see you both on this fine morning."

Haggadah looked toward the familiar male voice to see Tavish's smiling face. "Good day, Tavish." She grinned ear to ear. "Look what Grizel got for me. Isn't it bonnie?"

"Aye, a MacLean tartan. A good clan."

"Och, I care little what clan it belongs to. The colors are lovely – red, green, blue, yellow, black, and white."

Grizel handed each of them a stick with bits of cooked meat roasted over a fire. "Tavish, I assume you can eat one, perhaps two."

"Aye, thank you, Grizel." Tavish bit into the delicious treat. The juice of the meat dripped down the side of his mouth as he pulled a portion from the stick.

"Mmmmm…" Haggadah ate a bite of the delicious beef, or was it pork? It had been so long since she had eaten roasted meat that she could not distinguish what she was eating.

Grizel also purchased some dried beef and gave it to Tavish to eat later. She grinned as she watched the young man and her apprentice converse easily while they toured the remainder of the merchants' wares.

"Well, I must be on my way." Tavish tossed the empty stick aside. "It's been nice walking with you through the market, Haggadah," he paused before turning to the healer, "and you too, Grizel. Thank you for the meat." He held up the brown paper package containing the gift he would eat later.

Grizel nodded. "Do take care, Tavish."

"Aye, always do." Tavish touched his index finger to the brim of his flat cap before turning away.

"I think we've seen enough. Let's go home," Grizel suggested.

Even though the pair received stares from many as they passed by them, Haggadah refused to let it bother her. Her day had been pleasant, and she would not let anyone's prejudices ruin it for her. She touched the colorful blanket in her basket, knowing it would keep her warm for many years.

Arriving at the cottage, Haggadah offered. "I'll make tea." She stoked the fire and added a log before peering into the iron kettle. She assumed Grizel had filled it earlier since plenty of water was in it.

A knock sounded on the cottage door, but when Grizel opened it, no one was there. She saw an oversized basket filled with straw on the stoop. "Too afraid to stay?" She giggled as she shook her head, imagining a lad running away in fear. "Haggadah, the straw has arrived to give our feathered friends a clean coop." She stepped aside for her apprentice to see the basket on the walkway. "Carry it to the backyard while I finish making tea."

Haggadah went to the door, placed her fisted hands on her hips, and stared at the heaping basket, doubting her ability to carry such a cumbersome quantity of straw. She stooped and lifted the bundle, pleased to discover it was relatively light. After placing it near the coop, she saw Grizel with a pitchfork walking toward her. "Let the hens out. They can scratch in the garden while we drink our tea." She leaned the tool against the coop for later use and returned inside with Haggadah following.

Grizel opened the tin of fresh biscuits and sat at the table while her apprentice poured the tea into each cup. She pushed the tin before Haggadah, who took a biscuit as she sat.

"Thank you." Haggadah dunked the treat into her steaming cup. "And thank you again for the blanket.

"No need to thank me." The healer chuckled. "It was a pleasure to see the shocked look on the man's face when I put the money on the table." She dunked her biscuit. "I ken he's just trying to make a living, but I hope I didn't overpay him."

After enjoying their pleasant tea, they returned to the backyard. The hens were too busy sunning themselves, dusting their feathers in the dirt, and pecking at bugs to notice the women.

Haggadah stood in the coop's doorway with the pitchfork in hand. She wrinkled her nose at the accosting smell. The cleaning was long overdue. She scooped the soiled straw from the floor and worked her way to the back of the coop.

"The hens produce an excellent fertilizer. Sprinkle it over the herbs." Grizel instructed as she retrieved two baskets from the shed. She collected the eggs from the nesting boxes and placed them in one basket, then cut several herbs and placed them in the other.

Tilting the heaping pitchfork side to side, Haggadah spread the chicken manure over the garden. She replaced the straw in the nesting boxes and put the remainder on the coop's clean floor. Haggadah placed a fisted hand on her hip as she stood outside with the pitchfork, peering inside and admiring her work. "I think the hens will be much happier now that they have a clean home." She glanced at the chickens, who ignored her. "How do we get them back inside?"

Grizel placed a cut herb in a basket. "They will go inside by themselves at sundown. We'll close the door once they have put themselves to bed for the night."

Haggadah glanced at the empty basket on the ground next to the coop. "Should I take the basket back to the farmer?"

"We'll return it the next time we go to the market."

With the pitchfork in hand, Haggadah went to the healer and watched as she put the last cut herb in the basket. Grizel handed the knife to Haggadah. "Cut some flowers for the table."

The colorful, dainty petals stared back at Haggadah. A pang of guilt caused her to question the healer's reasoning. "They're too pretty to cut."

"Yet once you do so, we'll place them in a vase, and they'll share their beauty with us. After all, it will only be a matter of time until their blossoms wither and die. Then they will sleep during the winter and return next year to bloom again." Grizel reasoned as she held out her hand to accept the pitchfork from Haggadah.

After cutting a handful of the flowers and placing them in the basket with the herbs, Haggadah carried the baskets inside while Grizel returned the tools to the shed. The vase was nothing more than a chipped ceramic pitcher. It was filled with water, and the arranged bouquet was placed on the table.

Haggadah took a step back, admiring the flowers. "They are rather bonnie." She sighed, knowing their beauty would soon fade.

~

It was midafternoon when Brodie left his mistress and children. He avoided Amelia's condescending comments by going straight to his workshop. Opening the door, the councilman inhaled the fragrance of fresh-cut lumber as he stepped inside. He passed several tables with commissioned projects awaiting a final coat of varnish or the embellishment of a keyhole and lock. Brodie ignored the sawdust and wood shavings on the cobblestone floor as he sat at his drawing table and looked out the window at his woodyard filled with prime-cut lumber. Setting aside his hat and walking stick, he uncorked the inkwell, selected a sheet of paper from a stack, and dipped his pen into the ebony liquid. The natural sunlight allowed him to spend the afternoon sketching several cabinet styles and noting the dimensions. He added alternative drawings of embellishments and hoped Janette Wemyss would be impressed with his artistic ability.

"It's about time you returned home. The day is nearly over." Amelia scolded as she walked into the workshop with her arms crossed over her chest. "I've got a meal warming in the oven for you. A rather late midday one or early supper, whatever you choose. Just so you ken, I'm not cooking another meal for you today."

"Aye." Brodie held each drawing at arm's length.

"Och." The maid slammed the door, leaving the cabinetmaker to continue working.

Brodie looked at the workshop door that bounced off the frame before it settled in place. "I must remember to lock the door."

Over the next few hours, he scanned each drawing while adding details until the fading sunlight indicated he should stop sketching. Holding a drawing at arm's length, he stated, "Perfect." His stomach grumbled, reminding him of the meal warming in the oven. "It will surely be as dry as a bone by now. A meal at the pub and then taking in a cock fight is more in order." He added the drawing to the stack of others. "Luck is sure to be on my side tonight."

With a sense of accomplishment and the promise of adding to his income in the future, Brodie grabbed his hat and walking stick and left his workshop. Taking a deep breath, he placed his hat on his head and walked to the pub with a spring in his step. His walking stick tapped in time with his gait.

"Deacon, good to see you tonight." The barmaid greeted as Brodie entered the pub.

"Aye. I came for my supper." He sat on a stool at the bar.

"And a whisky." She added.

"You ken me well." Brodie leaned his walking stick against the bar.

"Och, you're a regular. It's my job to remember what you like to drink." She grinned and went to the kitchen.

His meal and a dram appeared before him. Men greeted Brodie as they entered the pub for the evening. He nodded his reply as he ate, hoping to get to the cockfight as soon as he finished with his meal.

Brodie pushed his empty plate away, downed his whiskey, and paid for his meal. Before leaving for the gambling festivities, he purchased the remainder of the bottle from the barkeep.

Unfortunately, lady luck was not on his side. "Damn," he said, losing the last of his pocket money as he watched the wagered rooster take its last breath. As if it were a consolation prize, he tipped the bottom of the bottle skyward, only to receive a drop of the amber beverage on his tongue. Brodie threw the empty vessel aside. He walked to Ann's house on Cant's Close, used his key, and entered the apartment well past midnight.

Ann awoke as she was pushed toward the wall, and Brodie fell into bed beside her. "William Brodie, you come and go as if my door is always open. I don't appreciate you waking me at this late hour." She scolded as she raised onto one elbow and looked down at the man beside her. "Are you here for a quick romp, or will you be staying the night?"

His reply was a loud and resounding snore.

"I guess you'll be spending the night." She wrinkled her nose as he exhaled his tainted whiskey breath in her face. Turning her head, she rolled away from him. "At least I don't have to sleep alone." But she wondered if it would be better if she did.

Chapter 12

The morning at the market reminded Haggadah to rise early the following day and attend Mass.

The responsibility of filling the kettle each morning with water, stirring the ashen embers, and rekindling the fire had become hers. Haggadah moved about the cottage, silently doing the tasks while Grizel slept. Haggadah closed the door quietly, left the house, and walked to Saint Cuthbert to attend Mass. She passed through the iron gate as the kirk's bell began to ring, quite pleased to be in time to enjoy every moment of the reverent weekly ceremony. Grinning, she knew her mother would be proud of her dedication. Haggadah discovered the interior crowded with patrons as she entered through the wooden doors. She stood along the back wall, made the sign of the cross on her body, and clasped her hands together. She prayed for her mother's soul and listened to the priest's lecture. When the congregation was dismissed, Haggadah went to her mother's grave and discovered a beautiful white rock marking it. Scanning the paupers' graves, they were void of adornment.

"We found the rock while digging the other day. It was Wiley's idea to put it at the head of your mum's grave so you can find it easily."

Haggadah turned to see Davis standing behind her with a shovel propped on his shoulder. "That's very kind. Thank you." She looked at the stone. "It's bonnie. Such a white stone, pure like my mum's soul."

Several visitors in the kirkyard stared at Haggadah. One man yelled, "Be off with you. You've no place here on the hallowed ground!"

Haggadah looked away from the rude man, praying for the strength to endure the humiliation.

"Hey! That is not very Christian of you. For heaven's sake, you just went to Mass! You should go to confession for judging a person so!"

Recognizing his voice, Haggadah watched as Tavish approached the abusive man with commanding strides and continued to speak firmly. She strained to listen, but what was said was only for the rude man's ears. From Tavish's body language, she assumed he was giving the man a piece of his mind. The high-class stranger glanced at Haggadah, clasped his wife's elbow, and hurried through the iron gate.

Tavish stared at the retreating couple before shaking his head and walking toward her. "Good day, Davis." He nodded at the gravedigger.

"And to you, Tavish." He looked at Haggadah. "Wiley is going to wonder where I've been off to. Good day to you, Haggadah." He grinned before walking away.

Alone with Tavish, Haggadah questioned. "What did you say to that man?"

Tavish smirked. "I told him that you are the witch's apprentice and that he best leave you alone before a curse comes down upon his head."

Haggadah giggled.

Tavish laughed.

"If Grizel knew how to put a curse on someone, I'm certain the man would receive a wicked one." Haggadah turned back to her mother's resting place. "Did you see the lovely stone Davis and Wiley put at the head of my mum's grave?"

As if on cue, a beam of light streamed through the leaves of the trees and illuminated the stone's pearl color veined of pink. "It's lovely." He looked about at the lingering visitors. "I'm sorry I didn't walk you to the kirk, but when you're ready, I'll walk you home."

"There's no reason to apologize. I can find my way on my own." She insisted.

"I ken, but the streets can be a dangerous place. When I'm with you, it eases my mind to ken you're safe."

His kind words warmed Haggadah's heart in a way that was unfamiliar to her. His sentiment was genuine. His caring was honest. "Well, I'm ready to walk home now and would be honored to have you as my escort." She grinned.

He offered his bent arm and returned her smile,

Her stomach somersaulted, and her heart swelled affectionately as she threaded her arm with his. They left the kirkyard.

"It's a splendid day." Tavish commented, looking up at the cloudless sky. "I would like to take a stroll along the waterfront. It's a bit of a walk, but I thought it would be a change of scenery for an afternoon stroll."

"I've only been there a few times. I liked watching the fishermen clean their catch. The seagulls are annoying yet fascinating. Och, and so many cats waiting for a bit of fish to be tossed their way." She smiled at the memory.

Walking along the harbor, they watched as a ship docked. Men threw large hemp ropes from the seaworthy vessel at the awaiting men, who caught and tied the stays around posts resembling large empty spools of thread. Gangplanks were lowered to the dock and secured. Passengers disembarked, and cargo was unloaded.

"Some people look like they're from America." Tavish mentioned.

Haggadah scanned their style of clothing. "They're dressed quite differently."

"Such an accent, too. I wonder what America is like."

They sat on a bench and watched another ship cast off, set its sails, and head out to sea.

Tavish looked toward a man shouting at a string of men and women tied to a rope. The people walked single file as their escorts of authority ordered them toward the gangplank of a ship. "Looks like convicted criminals who will serve as indentured servants in America."

"For how long?" Haggadah stared at a young lad, assuming he had been caught stealing something. She wondered if he was an orphan like herself or had a tearful goodbye with his parents before he was sentenced.

"I think it depends on their crime. Some, indefinitely. I've heard at least seven years for most."

"Seven years? I guess it's better than hanging from a noose." She reasoned.

"Aye."

"It must take a long time to get to America."

"I believe it depends on the weather. The seas can become wicked and show no mercy to those who trespass on them." He watched the criminals board the ship. "They're lucky. Those who have committed grievous crimes are always hung."

Haggadah watched the fishermen reel in their catch. Other men were at tables along the water, descaling and gutting. Seagulls bobbed up and down in the water, and feral cats crowded around each table, hoping for a remnant to fill their stomachs. Haggadah smiled as one cat arched its back and rubbed against the fisherman's leg.

On their walk to the cottage, Tavish bought a meat pie from an old woman on a corner. He broke it in half and gave a portion to Haggadah. They walked to Calton Hill and stood momentarily, overlooking Old Town and odorous Nor Loch.

"I really like you, Haggadah." Tavish confessed.

"I enjoy your company as well." She admitted.

They smiled at each other, pleased by their confessions. When they finished their meager snack, Tavish offered his bent arm.

Haggadah threaded her arm within his and smiled as he placed his hand over hers, which gripped his bicep.

"Time to get you home." He nodded confidently.

~

"Get up! Get up!"

Ann shook her head and chuckled to herself. The children's plea from the bedroom was soon joined by the sound of them jumping on the bed to rouse their father. She had done her best to allow Brodie to sleep, but after all, it was midmorning. Once the children learned he was in the apartment, she could not deny them the joy of waking him. Ann prayed he woke in a pleasant mood.

"He's not waking." The youngest lifted his father's eyelid and peered into his eye. "Are you alive, Daddy?"

Even though his head throbbed, Brodie fought to contain his smile at the child's innocent tactic. However, he lay as if he were still sleeping.

His daughter leaned close to his face. "He's alive." She pointed her finger at his face. "He's starting to smile."

Brodie began to laugh as he opened his eyes and hugged his children. "Go, I'll be there soon."

It was customary for the children to wait for their father to join them at the kitchen table before beginning their breakfast. Knowing so gave Brodie a reason to force himself to rise and start his day.

Letting his children believe they were successful at rousing him, Brodie sat on the edge of the bed and watched the children scamper away. His head throbbed. "I'm never drinking again." He vowed.

Giving himself time to gather his wits, he used the chamber pot, straightened the wrinkled clothes he had slept in, and went to the meager kitchen. It was a lovely apartment, but not one of luxury. Brodie could afford little else. He had overextended himself by providing for two mistresses and five children. His gambling and drinking were draining his pockets dry, too.

He entered the kitchen and sat in his chair at the head of the table. His children, eager to eat, stared at him from their seats.

"I assume you'll be leaving soon." Ann accused as she set a plate containing his breakfast before him.

"Aye. I must finalize some sketches for the goldsmith and his wife." It was a flimsy excuse, but he needed to ensure each sketch was perfect.

Ann paused with two plates in her hands. "The goldsmith and his wife?" She set the meal before her children, who began to eat.

Brodie froze with his forkful of fried potatoes midway to his mouth, realizing his mistake of boasting about the anticipated high commission. "Aye." He ate the fried vegetable to avoid commenting any further.

"I can only imagine how much they will pay for one of your cabinets. How many cabinets do they want? You must overcharge them." Ann dished food onto her plate and joined the family at the table. She picked up her fork and became lost in thought. "I can get a new dress."

"I think the one you have on is quite bonnie." Brodie attempted to dissuade her before continuing to eat his meal.

"When will we see you again? You haven't been by much lately. One would think you have another mistress sharing your bed." She waited for his answer while watching for a sign of guilt to appear on his face.

Brodie ate the last of his eggs. He stood and reached for Ann, pulling her up from her seat and into his arms. "You ken, I'm a busy man, making a living to provide for you and my bairns. My time must be divided between my work, the city council, and you. I'm spread thin. How can you think I would have another mistress?"

"One would wonder." Ann raised an eyebrow, indicating her suspicion.

"Nothing can be further from the truth." He smacked her on the butt and released her from his embrace. Brodie kissed her on the cheek. After hugging and receiving a kiss from each child, he hailed a coach and returned home.

Amelia heard Brodie thank the driver. She stood in the hallway with her fisted hand on her hip, reached for the stack of mail on the hallway table, and presented it to him as he entered the front door. "This pile of mail continues to grow while you're off doing whatever it is that you do. It isn't going to take care of itself." She scolded.

"It's good to see you too, Amelia. Put it on my desk. I'll go through it after I finalize my cabinet sketches for the goldsmith and his wife."

The maid raised an inquisitive eyebrow. "The goldsmith and his wife?"

"Aye, stop lecturing me and let me get to work." Brodie went to his workshop.

Isolated in the peaceful solitude, Brodie examined each drawing, making only minor changes. He laid the stack of sketches on a rectangular piece of leather, rolled them, and secured the drawings by tying a leather strap around the formed cylinder. Brodie went to the study with his sketches in hand, sat at his desk, and wrote a letter to Mister and Missus Wemyss explaining his planned visit tomorrow morning. "Amelia!" he called as he pressed the brass seal into the melted wax, securing the letter for the recipient. He set the sealed missive aside and looked at the stack of mail awaiting his attention.

"Aye." She scowled as she entered the study.

"I need this sent to the goldsmith's shop. See that a lad takes it to them immediately."

The maid picked up the letter from the desk and held out her hand. "I'll be needing a coin to give to the lad."

Exhaling his frustration, he glanced at the ceiling before opening a drawer in his desk, searched amongst the cluster of many items, and located a single coin. "Here." He dropped it into her outstretched palm.

The maid looked down at the coin, scowled at its inexpensive value, and exited the room.

The hallway clock chimed the hour as Brodie relinquished himself to address the stack of mail on the corner of his desk. Knowing it would take more effort than he wished, he stood from his chair, went to a side table, and poured himself a glass of whiskey from the decanter. After several sips, he returned to his seat, opened the first letter, and read it. It was a request for one of his cabinets. He placed it aside and opened the next letter. Another request. When he finished opening all the letters, he had a stack of requests for his service to either construct a cabinet or repair a locking mechanism. Others were bills he had ignored and were now overdue. As expected, some of the letters involved the sender's desire for changes to the city that the council should address, which he tossed into the fireplace. He picked up the letters requesting his skilled service and left his study. "Amelia, I'll be in my workshop." He left the house without waiting for her reply.

Brodie entered his sanctuary, paused, and remembered to lock the door. He put the requests on his drawing table, took his leather apron from the nail on the wall, and turned to the table as he tied the apron around his waist. Selecting a tool, he looked for his mark on the cabinet for the precise installment of the lock. "It's time to finish these so I can pay my debts."

Chapter 13

Brodie rose early the following day, dressed quickly, and entered the dining room for breakfast.

Amelia peeked out of the kitchen doorway, uncertain if she believed her ears. Could he have risen from his bed so early? She carried a pot of coffee and a cup into the dining room to pacify him until she served his breakfast. "You're up quite early." She placed the cup before him and poured the deep amber liquid, filling the cup.

"Good morning, Amelia. Yes, I've got a lot to do today." He picked up the cup and sipped the hot coffee.

"Aye? Such as?" The maid knew the city council meeting was next week.

"I'm meeting with the goldsmith and his wife this morning. Two of my cabinets will be delivered this afternoon, and I'll receive payment."

Amelia shook her head, knowing that much of what he earned would be spent on his mistresses and lost to gambling and drinking. "We'll see how long you hang onto your money." She returned to the kitchen, dished up his meal, and placed it before him.

"Och, it looks delicious." Brodie lifted his fork and shoveled beans into his mouth.

"Just an ordinary Scottish breakfast," the maid wondered if he was half asleep, "but thank you for the compliment." Amelia shook her head and returned to the kitchen.

The cabinetmaker ate his breakfast while daydreaming about how he would spend the large commission from the goldsmith and the finished cabinets.

Pushing himself away from the table, Brodie retrieved the rolled drawings from his desk, grabbed his hat and walking stick, and left the house. He hailed a coach, sat in the seat, and smiled as his heartbeat quickened in anticipation of his boost in income. "Maybe Ann can get the new dress after all."

The coach came to a stop outside of the goldsmith's shop. Brodie adjusted his hat once he stepped onto the sidewalk and was greeted by the couple as they opened the shop's door.

"Deacon, we appreciate you visiting before we open for the day. It gives us time to give you our undivided attention before customers arrive." James stepped aside and allowed the cabinetmaker to enter.

"We've been extremely busy lately." Janette explained as she escorted the cabinetmaker to the couple's office in the back of the store. "With many attending the upcoming ball, they want to find just the right adornment for the evening. Will you be attending the dance tonight?"

"As a city councilman, I must appear, even though I'm not fond of dancing." Brodie confessed as he stepped into the office.

"I see." Janette sat behind the desk. "Well, I'm eager to see the sketches you've brought us." Her husband stood beside her.

"I've brought several with me and hope one will meet with your approval." Brodie untied the leather lace, put the canister on the desk, and let it fall open as if pulling back velvet drapes on a stage. "However, adjustments can be made to meet your taste. I've noticed my clients tend to choose a design that compliments their personality. So, I've sketched several options for embellishments." Brodie explained the features in the first sketch.

Janette sat forward in the chair. "Oh, this one is quite nice."

The cabinetmaker pulled aside the top sheet of paper to reveal the next sketch.

"My, that one is bonnie too."

After presenting all the sketches, Brodie spread them on the desk so his client could see every option.

"Deacon, you're quite talented." Janette looked at her husband. "Which one do you favor?"

James peered over his wife's shoulder. He selected one and held it at arm's length to fully view it. "This one is quite nice."

Janette scowled, selected one from the desk, and tilted her head. "I like this one."

Her husband knew better than to contradict his wife's choice. "Then, that's the one." James tossed the sketch he held onto the desk.

Brodie gathered the drawings and placed their choice on top.

James, a man who kept accurate accounts, was quick to ask. "What will it cost?"

"Only your livelihood." Brodie chuckled before giving the overinflated price.

James inhaled and opened his mouth, hoping to negotiate a better price, when his wife interrupted.

"I think that's a fair price. After all, a cabinet by Deacon William Brodie is acclaimed to have the highest quality." Janette glanced at her husband, who closed his mouth and nodded in agreement. "When will you have it made?"

"Within a month." Brodie tied the leather laces. "I'll inform you of my progress and when it will be installed." He shook the goldsmith's hand. "Good day."

On his way back to his workshop, Brodie hired a flatbed wagon and a pair of strong men. They delivered the finished cabinets to the Miller family and helped to install them. With his debt paid to the men, he had a reasonable sum left in his pocket. He decided to visit Ann and bring his children a treat. Looking up at the silhouette of Smith's Grocery hanging above the shop door, he entered.

"Good day to you, Deacon. How can I be of service?" George offered.

"I thought I would get a pair of pickles from your barrel."

"Very good." The grocer went to the wooden barrel, used a long fork, and selected two giant pickles. He wrapped them in brown paper and tied a string around them. "Business still robust?"

"As always."

"I can always use extra money in my pockets. So, if you need any help, I'm always available."

"Aye, as I recall you saying."

"Is there anything else I can get you?"

"No. That will be all." Brodie set the money on the counter, picked up his package, and left.

~

Within the shadow of the close, John watched the affluent people of the city pass by. They ignored him as if he were invisible. Stepping near the opening, he pulled the brim of his flat cap down, shielding his face as he watched Brodie walk by. Anger boiled within him. His hands tightened into fists. He glared at the man who seemed to have a life so easy, a high societal position, and wealth.

His stomach grumbled as John leaned his shoulder against the wall and watched the package within Brodie's hand move back and forth like a pendulum with each tap of the man's walking stick. He was tempted to snatch the fancy walking stick from Brodie's hand and sell it for a large sum. Would others recognize it as belonging to the councilman? It was worth the risk. He emerged from the close and followed

Brodie, sneering at the man's confidence as he strutted along the sidewalk like a proud rooster with a bevy of hens.

Brodie stopped abruptly before a shop.

John strolled by his victim, looked over his shoulder, and watched as Brodie entered the establishment. Glancing up, he spotted a silhouette outline of a shoe above the shop door. He leaned against the building and waited. "It must be nice to afford the luxury of a custom-made, new pair of shoes."

~

Andrew Ainslie heard the bell above his shop door ring. He put down his cobbler hammer, wiped his hands on a rag, and removed his leather apron. Andrew hung the protective garment on a nail in the workroom and went to see who had entered. He grinned as he saw his favorite customer waiting at the counter. "Hello, Deacon. I've not seen you in a while."

"Aye. You make such a good shoe; it has taken me a while until I've needed a new pair." Brodie jested. "I'm in the market once again."

"Well, let's make sure you are the same fit and determine what style and color you would like."

Brodie sat in a chair while Andrew measured his feet, which remained unchanged. His attention was drawn to the store window as a man with a dingy cap peeked inside several times.

"I assume you're going to the ball tonight?" Andrew inquired.

Brodie looked at the shoemaker. "Aye."

"Then, if you have time, I can polish the pair you have on, assuming you'll be wearing them tonight."

"Aye, thank you." Brodie watched as the vagrant, who peered through the window, did so again.

After deciding on the style and color of his new shoes and his present pair received a polishing, Brodie left the shop and stood outside the doorway. He took a deep breath and glanced at the vagrant, who leaned against the wall. The man's hat was pulled over his eyes, shading his face, making the hackles on the back of Brodie's neck prickle. He turned and walked past the man. Glancing over his shoulder, his assumption was correct. He was being followed. Brodie abruptly turned into a narrow close and readied his walking stick.

Grinning at the ease of overtaking his victim, John rounded the corner and exhaled abruptly as he collided with the end of Brodie's walking stick. He stepped backward, eyes wide, and stared at the cabinetmaker.

"For what reason are you following me?" Brodie demanded.

Placing his hand on his abdomen, John took a moment to catch his breath. "Who says I'm following you?"

"I do. I saw you peeking through the store window, then leaning against the wall as I stepped onto the sidewalk. And now, I catch you following me around the corner. Why? Why are you following me?" Brodie demanded, taking an aggressive step forward. The man before him was no taller than he, and he was sure he could out-muscle him if necessary.

"Curiosity, I guess," John admitted.

Brodie's eyebrows raised. He was intrigued. "How so?"

"It seems odd that a cabinetmaker can rise so high in society." He accused.

"My work is renowned, thus earning me the title of Deacon, head of woodworkers. It has also allowed me a seat on the city council." He divulged.

John shook his head, doubting the man's reply. He took a step forward and stated what he suspected. "No, I've seen you at cock fights. You lose often. I'm also aware you have two mistresses and several bairns. Do your women ken of each other?" He noticed the shocked look on Brodie's face. His words had struck true.

Brodie's heart began to race. He refused to hand over the money in his pocket. After all, the vagrant would only ask for more to keep his mouth shut. "What do you want?"

"I want in. I want whatever you're part of that gets you so wealthy." John demanded.

"My cabinets are my income." Brodie defended.

John raised his eyebrows. "Have it your way." He began to walk away.

Fearing the man would tell his mistresses of each other, he appeased the vagrant. "I may have a job for you. What is your name?"

"John Brown."

"John Brown. How do I get word to you?"

"As I've done today, I'll find you." John turned and walked away.

Brodie stepped onto the sidewalk, stood for a moment, and watched the man as he crossed the street. Brown looked as if he had a solid and able body. Brodie could always pay him to do the heavy work in his woodyard and load finished cabinets into a wagon.

He smiled as a plan registered within his mind, but it would have to wait. He needed to see Ann and his children before going home to dress for the evening's inaugural event.

~

Brodie sat in the coach, holding his walking stick between his legs. Dressed in his finest suit and polished shoes for the ball, he vowed to make a short appearance and return home. "Or spend the night with Jean and the bairns." He told himself.

He preferred to hide with the men in the gambling room and watch them play cards to avoid the flirtatious requests from the women to dance. Brodie left most of his money in his desk drawer to give him the excuse of playing only a few hands.

In the solitude of the coach, he grinned, recalling the joy on his children's faces as he handed them the brown package and watched them chomp on the crispy pickles. Ann was quite pleased when he told her she could have a new dress, but the cost must remain reasonable.

The councilman peered out the coach window at the homeless gathered in a close. They stared back at him. He looked away, eager for the hour to tick by quickly.

~

Coaches lined the streets as attendees, dressed in their finest, climbed into their awaiting transportation.

Tavish and the others watched the parade of the wealthy and well-to-do pass by the close. He glanced at the face of the woman beside him. Did she envy something she would never attend? He looked at the others. Most of the homeless only owned the clothes on their backs. Did they imagine the luxury the guests would enjoy, the elegant house hosting the ball, the delicious food, and endless drinks? He had once hitched a ride on a coach, unbeknownst to the driver, and listened to the music echoing from within the wealthy manor as guests in their fancy clothing climbed the steps and were greeted by servants with trays of drinks in crystal long-stemmed glasses. He witnessed the elegant lifestyle and the higher-ranking society he would never be part of. To him, it seemed fake and pretentious.

He wished he could offer Haggadah a proper home where they could reside, raise their children, and live happily. He vowed to save his coins. Perhaps someday he could offer her his dream of their life together.

Chapter 14

Brodie watched the elegant women ascending the stairs of the majestic mansion as the coach pulled to a halt. The councilman disembarked, followed behind a rather buxom woman up the stairs, and entered through the richly embellished open door. He handed his overcoat, hat, and walking stick to a servant, lifted a stemmed crystal glass from a silver tray, and went directly to the room where the men were gathered.

"Deacon, we've saved a chair for you." One of the men greeted as he puffed on his cigar.

"Not tonight. I've got a busy day ahead of me tomorrow and will only stay for an hour." He looked at his pocket watch, noting the time. Usually a man without discipline, Brodie placed his nearly full glass on a passing servant's tray to keep his wits about him. After observing several hands of the game, he bid the gentlemen goodnight, hailed an awaiting coach, and returned home. Before retiring for the evening, Brodie went to his workshop to ensure everything was ready for tomorrow's delivery.

~

"Haggadah."

The apprentice opened her eyes to darkness. Had her name been called?

"Haggadah, we must go and tend to a birth." Grizel quickly added another herb to a small tin. She would make the tea for the expectant mother once they arrived. It would help her through her labor. She returned the herb to its shelf and closed the apothecary door. "Haggadah."

"Aye." She rubbed the sleep from her eyes, got out of bed, and put on her shoes. Descending the ladder, she watched the healer put a knife, string, a small tin, whiskey, and a few bottles into a satchel.

Grizel glanced at Haggadah. "The night air is cold." She nodded toward her apprentice's overcoat on the hook.

Grabbing the garment, Haggadah pushed her arms through the sleeves and followed Grizel out the door. She saw a young man on the flagstone path. He stopped his worrisome pacing and looked at her, relief masking his face.

The expectant father explained. "I'm sorry for disturbing your evening. Most of the physicians have gone to the ball. I don't ken what else to do. My wife has been in labor for such a long time. I hate seeing her suffer so."

"We'll do our best," Grizel reassured the nervous father.

The woman's cries could be heard through the closed apartment door. Haggadah glanced at the healer's face, which showed little concern for the expectant mother.

They were led into the bedroom. Grizel placed her satchel on the seat of a chair. "Haggadah, look at her face. She wears the mask of labor."

Haggadah noticed the woman struggled to keep her weary eyes open; her face flushed and hair damp.

Grizel approached the woman, placed her arthritic hands upon her swollen belly, and determined the infant's position. She looked over her shoulder at Haggadah. "Come, put your hands as you did before.

Looking at the suffering woman, Haggadah extended her hands with her fingers spread wide and placed them on the bulbous abdomen.

Grizel clasped Haggadah's wrists and placed them so that she may feel the unborn baby. "Here, the bairn's rump. It's in the right position, head down, but I sense it's a large bairn."

Haggadah watched the woman's belly move and felt it grow rigid. She pulled her hands away as the expectant mother screamed. Concerned, Haggadah looked at Grizel. "How long before the bairn is born?"

The healer brushed the damp auburn hair away from her patient's forehead. "Is this your first bairn?"

The woman nodded as she winced in pain.

Grizel turned toward Haggadah. "The first birth is usually the longest, but complications may make it longer." She watched as the expectant mother sighed in relief as the contraction eased. "I'll go and make tea. Try and get her to stand." She pointed at the chair in the corner of the small room. "She can use the back of the chair for support." The town healer motioned for the concerned husband to take her to the kitchen to heat water.

Haggadah's stomach knotted, questioning her ability to help the woman. Even though she had attended another birth with the healer, she mostly stood and watched. Haggadah looked at the woman, near exhaustion, and wondered how she could endure standing.

The apprentice pulled the chair to the side of the bed and took a deep breath. "As the healer said, you must rise." She helped the woman lower her legs to the floor and stand while clasping the back of the wooden chair. "What is your name?" Haggadah hoped to distract the expectant mother from the pain.

"Thayden." She cracked her eyes open to look at the young assistant. "You?"

"Haggadah." Uncertain of what to do, she stood beside the woman and gently wrapped her arm around her patient's back while patting her hand that clutched the chair's back.

Thayden inhaled deeply as another contraction began. She cried out as it increased in intensity.

Haggadah watched the woman's hand tighten on the chair until her knuckles changed from pink to white. She looked at the doorway, thankful to see Grizel enter with tea.

"She may sit and drink this. It will ease her labor."

The contraction subsided. Thayden took a deep breath and sat on the edge of the bed. Grizel handed the cup to Haggadah, who held it to the woman's lips. "Drink, Thayden."

The evening waned with the indigo sky turning a lighter blue. Thayden's worried spouse dared to peek into the bedroom occasionally.

As the baby's head emerged, Grizel looked at her apprentice. "Guide the bairn out when the mother pushes."

Haggadah's eyebrows raised. "Me?"

"Aye, get on the bed. I'll get behind Thayden to prop her up and hold her legs wide to ease the bairn's passage."

Haggadah's heart began to race. She watched as Grizel positioned herself behind Thayden and instructed the woman to bring her knees up where she could thread her hands beneath them.

As another contraction began, the healer nodded at Haggadah. "Thayden, bear down, push your bairn out."

Under the guidance of the experienced healer, Haggadah eased the child into the world. She held the slippery infant and felt his chest expand as he took his first breath. Her eyes widened at the sensation. She looked at Grizel, who nodded her approval. The baby announced his presence with a resounding wail, causing the nervous father to watch as the child was placed on his wife's stomach and covered with a cloth.

"Well done." Grizel congratulated Haggadah. The healer encouraged the new father to enter the room and see his son. With Thayden distracted, the two women worked together to remove the afterbirth and place it in the chamber pot. Haggadah wrinkled her nose, realizing the bucket of excrement would be thrown out the window and into the street.

Grizel helped the new mother nurse her baby and gave instructions on what to expect in the coming days. "Come fetch me if you have any concerns."

Overjoyed by the birth of his son, the new father gave the healer and her assistant several coins in payment for their service.

Haggadah paused in the doorway and looked at the picture-perfect family on the bed before following Grizel out of the room.

The kirk's bell rang five times as they stepped onto the cobblestone street. It was Sunday. Haggadah dared not sleep once she arrived home. She had performed a good deed by bringing a child into the world, but it was no excuse for her to miss attending Mass. She could sleep later.

~

Brodie woke just after sunrise. He was in a splendid mood and entered the dining room humming a tune.

Amelia scowled, suspicious of Brodie's uncharismatic enthusiasm as she served him breakfast.

He ate quickly, knowing the two men and their wagon would arrive soon.

Brodie dabbed his mouth with his cloth napkin, pushed his chair away from the table, and went to his office to write the invoice while waiting for the men to arrive.

Amelia set a loaf of bread to rise. She heard a knock on the front door, wiped her floured hands on her apron, and left the kitchen.

"The cabinetmaker hired us to deliver cabinets for him." The broad-shouldered man stated as he grabbed his flat cap from the top of his head.

Amelia thought for a moment, puzzled. "On a Sunday?"

"Aye. The building is closed, but we're meeting a man who will let us in."

"Drive your wagon to the workshop. I'll tell him you're here." Amelia closed the door. "Deacon! The flatbed is here!" She announced from the foyer before returning to the kitchen.

Brodie ignored his maid, knowing the driver would take a few minutes to go to the workshop. He added the words 'Payment due upon delivery' to the bottom of the invoice, folded it, and put it in his pocket. He grabbed his overcoat, walking stick, and hat from the hallway and went to his workshop, humming the same tune.

"Good day, Deacon." The driver politely tipped his hat. His assistant remained silent and nodded. "You've got cabinets to be delivered?"

"Aye, and a fine one at that."

Between the two men, they loaded the cabinets under the strict guidance of Brodie, who acted like a mother hen watching over her chicks. He ensured the wooden cabinet was well protected as straps were added to secure it to the wagon bed.

Brodie climbed onto the seat of the wagon, joining the two men. With a slap of the reins on the horse's rump, the wagon jolted forward, causing Brodie to look back at the cabinet to ensure it stayed in place.

It was a short ride to the Edinburgh Excise Office in Chessel's Court. The cabinet was unloaded and installed. After presenting his invoice, Brodie was paid. He, in turn, paid the hired men, and they were on their way. It was mid-afternoon when Brodie walked straight to Mister Clark's tavern in the Fleshmarket Close, where he looked forward to a dram of congratulatory whiskey and an evening of gambling.

As he entered the pub, the barmaid grinned. "Deacon, you're looking quite pleased with yourself today. I guess Mass did you well."

"Aye, the Lord will have to forgive me for skipping Mass. I had an important matter to attend to."

"More important than Mass?"

"Aye. I delivered finished cabinets and have been paid quite handsomely, so I'll enjoy a dram or two of your finest whisky."

The barmaid poured a glass to start off the councilman's afternoon. She slid it before him. "Will you be eating too?"

"Aye, Lass. A good meat pie to fill my gullet." Brodie downed the amber liquid and pushed the glass toward the barmaid for a refill.

"So, did you go to the ball last night? From what I hear, it was grand." A tinge of jealousy pulled at the woman's heart.

"Och, as a city councilman, I'm obligated to attend. I hate dancing, so I hid with the men and watched them play cards."

She knew he liked to gamble. "Och, you did not join in? I find that hard to believe."

Brodie held up his hand as if swearing an oath. "Honest, I did not join in." He threw back the second dram and nodded for a third.

Chapter 15

A brisk breeze tossed the colorful leaves across Haggadah's pathway as she stopped before her mother's grave and pulled her strawberry blonde hair away from her eyes. She stared at the rock peeking beneath the dying foliage, crowding around the marker as if huddling for warmth. Haggadah knelt, brushed the leaves away, and sat. "Hello, Mum. It's me again, as every week. I'm doing my best to learn the herbs, and my reading is improving, or so Grizel says. She allows me to make remedies under her watchful eye, of course. I seldom make mistakes, and she is quite pleased with my ability. I've also learned to write. Earlier this week, she referred to me as scholarly, but I think she was just being kind." Haggadah scanned the kirkyard. Even though she was surrounded by the sorrow of death, she smiled. "I delivered a bairn yesterday. I held the wee one in my hands as it began its life. Being the first to touch the babe was both a privilege and a blessing." She took a deep breath and exhaled. "I think you would be very proud of the person I've become; at least, I hope so." She looked at the mounds of soil where several paupers rested peacefully. "Even though they were poor and looked down upon by others, they were good people. I ken you're in good company, Mum."

It was peaceful, sitting among the dead with whispers of leaves tiptoeing across the grass in the breeze. Haggadah sighed, treasuring the quietness, alone with her memories.

Haggadah watched as well-dressed visitors meandered among the graves donned with fancy headstones. They looked at her with upturned noses. "They're no better than us, Mum. It's too bad they think they are." She glanced at Tavish, who was helping Wiley and Davis dig a grave. She stood and looked at her mother's grave. "Goodbye, Mum."

Wiley paused with his shovel's blade on the ground as he saw Haggadah approaching. "Best be on your way, Tavish."

Davis and Tavish turned and looked at Haggadah.

"Thanks for your help. It makes the job go quicker." Davis added.

"You're welcome." Tavish wiped the sweat off his brow with the sleeve of his coat. He pushed his shovel's blade into the pile of dirt, making it stand on its own.

Haggadah threaded her arm through Tavish's as she bid the gravediggers goodbye.

Tavish adjusted his cap upon his head. "Did you have a good visit with your mum?"

"Aye." She grinned. "She had little to say."

A well-to-do couple stepped aside as Tavish and Haggadah passed through the gate.

With the shops closed for the day, Tavish posed a suggestion. "I've nothing to do for the rest of the day. If you don't need to return to the cottage right away, shall we go for a walk?"

Haggadah grinned. "Aye, I'd like that. Especially with you for company."

Tavish looked into her steel gray eyes and smiled. His heart swelled, realizing his growing fondness for the woman who gently clasped his bicep. He had entertained the idea of marriage, but what kind of life could he offer her and any children they may have? Tavish needed to improve his lifestyle before taking her as his wife. He placed his hand protectively over the one clutching his arm.

THE HEALER'S APPRENTICE

~

As the day waned into the night, the streets of Edinburgh quieted. Its citizens gathered in their homes and enjoyed an evening meal. Afterward, they sat in sitting rooms to read, embroider, and puff on a good cigar or pipe while drinking a dram of whiskey before retiring for the night. As lamps were dimmed and candles snuffed out, the windows of the city's buildings became dark as if closing their eyes to sleep. The homeless huddled in a close and gathered around warming fires, envious of those who slept on soft, warm beds. The city seemed to slumber except for a boisterous singing drunk leaving a pub or those who kept to the shadows who were up to no good.

Grizel pulled a bottle from the apothecary, went to the fireplace, and threw a powdery substance on the flickering logs.

Haggadah watched as green smoke rose from the flames and escaped through the chimney. "Why? How?"

The healer grinned, raised her eyebrows up and down several times, and rotated the bottle so her apprentice could read the label. "Sometimes it's fun to pretend you're evil."

The emerald smoke drew a man's attention as he placed a ring of keys wrapped in a protective oilcloth in a hole in the ground. He concealed the hiding place with a rock. He looked skyward as he stood. "The witch conjures."

~

McLeary kissed his wife and hugged his children before leaving their apartment to report to work. He looked at the clouds in the morning sky as he stepped onto the sidewalk. They appeared heavy and threatened rain. As he entered the station house, the constable at the front desk looked up from his paperwork.

"A couple is waiting in an interrogation room to file a statement, a robbery."

"Och, so it begins." McLeary, hoping for a quiet morning, poured himself a cup of steaming coffee before getting the necessary folder, pen, ink, and form for the report. He entered the small room to see two familiar faces. "Mister and Missus Wemyss?"

"Our shop was robbed!" Janette began to sob. "They took everything, everything." She dabbed a handkerchief to her nose.

McLeary glanced at James as he sat on the opposite side of the oak table across from the couple. He placed the paperwork before him, opened the ink bottle, and dipped his pen. "James, Janette, I'm sorry to hear of your loss. After I've written your statement, I'll need to inspect your shop for evidence." He began writing their names and the name of their shop on the report. "Address on Parliament Square?"

James quickly supplied the information.

McLeary dipped his pen in the ink again. "What items are missing?"

"You mean what was stolen." Janette insisted. She dabbed her eyes with her handkerchief.

James patted his wife's arm. "Calm yourself, Janette." He looked at the constable. "We brought our inventory ledger. It's always up to date." James put a leatherbound book on the table. He turned to the appropriate page. "After entering our shop, we noticed several items were absent from the display cases. After a quick inventory of our stock, we discovered the following items gone." He turned the ledger for the constable to see. "As you can see, I've put a checkmark next to each stolen item."

McLeary pulled the journal toward him and examined it thoroughly. He counted the checkmarks and discovered nearly two hundred items had been stolen, which included rings, silverware, various styles of buckles, earrings, and brooches. He began noting the stolen number and a vague description of each in the report.

"It was the strangest thing. We entered the shop early this morning. I hoped to tidy the office before James began to work, but I noticed one of my favorite brooches, his signature piece, was missing from the case. It was then I noticed other pieces missing."

McLeary paused in entering the items. "Was there a sign of a break-in?"

The goldsmith and his wife shook their heads.

"Are you certain you locked the door when you closed the shop?"

"Aye," James confirmed. "Janette insists I turn the knob to make sure it's locked."

"Well, whoever took your items, I assume, may want to sell them." McLeary thought momentarily as he looked down at the long list of stolen merchandise. "I'll need you to put together a description or a drawing of each item, so other shop owners can recognize them as stolen."

Janette's eyes widened. "But what if they go to another city to sell our merchandise?"

McLeary put the lid back on the ink bottle. "We can send the information to other cities. I can't do much more than that. My authority does not go beyond the city limits."

The couple glanced at each other. The constable's words were of little comfort.

Chapter 16

McLeary accompanied the goldsmith and his wife to their shop. He inspected the door and discovered no sign of forced entry.

"As you can see, our cases are empty." Janette pointed to the displays. "Entirely empty." She shook her head, then held her handkerchief to her nose to hide her distraught emotion.

McLeary inspected and noted a locking mechanism on each case. "Were the display cases locked?"

Janette lifted her chin. "Aye. We keep them locked, day and night."

The constable recognized the pride in the woman's reply. "Where do you keep the keys?"

James motioned for the constable to follow him into the office and workshop for inspection. "In the safe. We put our till inside it every night before we close." He opened the safe to reveal a ring of keys on a hook and the untouched cash drawer.

True to the goldsmith's word, McLeary discovered only a few unfinished items on the workbench. He assumed the culprit may have been in a hurry and left the shop without entering the workspace. "I'll update your file and inform others to be leery of anyone wishing to sell any items. Send a messenger with the descriptions and drawings as soon as you finish them."

"Aye. Thank you, Constable." James walked the constable to the door.

~

As November announced its presence with its gusty winds and lower temperatures, the tenement buildings no longer existed, and several arches forming the twin sides of the South Bridge reached skyward with planking supporting the expanse.

McLeary was mystified by a robbery that month. This time, it was a hardware store. Weeks later, he had to file a report for the theft of a tobacco shop. He was called to another hardware store on Christmas Day to take the statement from the owner, who was robbed during the night. In all three cases, there was no evidence of forced entry. It was as if the stolen items and money had simply disappeared.

Concerned about the Wemyss case, McLeary visited several jewelers and sent the list of items to nearby cities, but received no report of them ever surfacing. He could only assume the thief had left Edinburgh.

~

Tavish glanced at the setting sun as he walked up the flagstone path to the cottage carrying a brown paper box bound with a string. His heart raced with excitement as he knocked, adjusted the cap on his head, and waited.

Haggadah grinned and opened the door. "Hello." She motioned for him to enter.

"I brought something for dinner. It's a sweet. Since it's a few days old, the baker sold it to me at a good price." He untied the string and opened the box, eager to show what he had bought.

Haggadah and Grizel gathered around the table and peered into the opened box.

"A cake?" Grizel smiled. "It's been years since I've eaten cake." Grizel's mouth began to water.

Staring at the brown object decorated with nuts, Haggadah thought the cake resembled a hat box she had seen wealthy women carrying. She scrunched her nose. "Cake?"

"Aye, whisky fruit cake." Tavish grinned. "We'll have it as a treat after our meal is finished."

"Och, I've never eaten whisky fruit cake." Haggadah confessed.

"Then you're in for a treat." Grizel added as she picked up the cake and placed it on the worktable for later.

Their tiny feast consisted of beef stew, potatoes, onions, and carrots. Haggadah had made a loaf of bread earlier in the day, which they shared, and topped it with butter. Haggadah glanced at the awaiting treat throughout the meal. Her mouth watered as she imagined its taste.

They sopped up the last of the delicious gravy with their bread. Everyone sighed. With their appetites satisfied by the tasty meal, Grizel placed the cake on the table while Haggadah collected the bowls and put them near the washtub. She retrieved plates and placed them before Grizel, who cut a slice of the cake to reveal the splattering of dried fruit inside. She put the wedge on the top plate. "Who shall get the first piece?" She looked from Haggadah to Tavish as she picked up the plate.

"Since Tavish bought the treat, he should get the first piece." Haggadah suggested.

Tavish shook his head as he looked at the apprentice. "Since you've never had a piece before, you should get it."

Grizel looked at Haggadah for her rebuttal.

"Grizel should have it, so neither of us get it." Haggadah smiled at her cleverness.

The healer placed the plate before her seat and then served Tavish and Haggadah.

Pausing with her fork above her plate, Haggadah watched as Tavish ate a bite. He motioned with his utensil for her to do the same. She cut the cake with the edge of her fork, scooped it, and inhaled its sweetness before putting it in her mouth. She closed her eyes as the flavor tantalized her tongue. "Mmmm..."

Tavish smiled and looked at Grizel, who nodded.

Opening her eyes, she looked at Tavish. "This is delicious. I think I like this cake very much."

Laughter filled the room as they continued to enjoy the scrumptious treat.

Tavish stoked the fire and put on a log while Grizel and Haggadah did the dishes. "Thank you for supper. It's nice to eat in the company of others and share a meal." He grinned at Haggadah as he expressed his gratitude.

Grizel handed the last washed dish to her apprentice. She turned toward Tavish as she dried her hands on Haggadah's towel. "To be in the company of others, as long as it's a good company, is always welcomed. Especially when they bring cake." She smiled as she pulled a chair near the fire and sat.

Haggadah put the dried dish away, hung the towel on the hook, and joined the pair before the fire.

"The people who have asked for remedies over the past month talk of several robberies." Grizel fished for information.

"Aye, it's what I'm hearing too, mostly whispered around the warming fires." Tavish confirmed.

"You've seen nothing strange and untoward?" The healer pressed.

Tavish shook his head. "I'm not looking to find trouble. I keep my head down and mind my own business. You can be accused of something you did not do when you become too nosy."

After a pleasant evening of conversation, Tavish stood to leave. Haggadah walked him to the door. He leaned toward her ear and whispered. "Sleep well."

A growing concern for Tavish's safety caused her stomach to ache. "Please keep a watchful eye. With all these robberies, it seems as if evil is paying a visit to Edinburgh."

~

The winter months were long, cold, and damp, causing Grizel to treat her arthritic hands often. Haggadah learned to read and write proficiently. She added her neatly written name to the bottom of the list in the Book of Shadows. Grizel insisted she memorize every herb and its healing properties. The healer would watch over Haggadah's shoulder as she prepared remedies for those in need and kindly suggested improvements to make the cure more potent. She no longer needed Grizel's supervision to guide a babe into the world.

After attending Mass on a sunny spring day, Haggadah stood before her mother's grave. It was a sad occasion, marking the anniversary of her matriarch's passing. A gentle breeze blew the strand of her hair across her eyes. As she pulled it away to clear her vision, she scanned the branches of a tree, trying to locate the bird that chirped incessantly. Haggadah watched as the scarlet cardinal flew down and perched on the white stone marking her mother's grave. Haggadah grinned. "Hello, Mum. I've always believed you are near me. Sometimes, I thought I could feel your touch. But then again, it may have been my hopeful imagination. Thank you for watching over and guiding me through each day."

Since Wiley and Davis had no demand for a grave to be dug, Tavish sat on the stone bench next to the kirk and waited. He watched Haggadah's lips move, assuming she was saying a prayer or talking to her mother's spirit. He thought the bird may be tame as it stood on the grave's marker.

Haggadah held her palm up and watched in awe as the bird flew to her and landed on the tip of her fingers. It turned its head to look at her with one eye and then the other before flying back to the tree.

Leaning forward, Tavish was intrigued by the bird's boldness before flying away.

Knowing this would be a difficult day for her, Tavish had purchased a few hard candies they could share on their walk back to the cottage. He watched as Haggadah turned toward him to leave for the kirkyard.

He stood, touching his coat pocket to ensure the wrapped candy remained within it.

"That was a bit strange." He commented as he offered his bent arm as an escort.

She threaded her arm with his. "What was strange?"

"The bird. It flew to your hand."

Haggadah grinned. "Aye, it was comforting, though, and made me feel that everything is as it should be. Grizel believes the dead like to send us signs that they are safe and happy wherever they are."

A gust of wind lifted Tavish's hat. "Signs?" He adjusted his cap on his head, setting it firmly in place.

"Aye. I like to believe Grizel is right."

They waved at Davis and Wiley as they left the kirkyard and strolled along the sidewalk. Tavish pulled the wrapped candy from his pocket. "I had an extra coin and bought us a treat to share while we walk to the cottage."

Haggadah unthreaded her arm and watched him open the package to reveal several hard candies. "Oh, such a nice treat." She selected one and put it in her mouth.

Tavish did the same and returned the folded package to his pocket. "With the new season, I've heard talk of the first ball."

"The pageantry would be a sight to behold." Haggadah knew she would never attend a ball in her lifetime. She held no envy or jealousy in her heart, for her life was simple, and she enjoyed her lower social rank.

"Would you like to watch it with me?" Tavish grinned, raising a devilish eyebrow. "We'll spend the evening huddled in a close, see everyone in their fancy clothes climb into coaches, and leave for the ball. I'll walk you home afterward."

"I would like to, but I should ask Grizel if I may." She became lost in thought as concern crept into her mind. "I'm worried about Grizel. She seems very tired as of lately."

Tavish took the candy from his pocket. They each chose a second piece. "She's quite old. Do you think she is ill?"

"She complains of nothing." Haggadah thought for a moment. "With so many calling on her during all-night hours, maybe she just needs rest. I'll insist on answering their nightly pleas for remedies so she can remain in bed."

~

Leading up to the day of the gala ball, dressmakers worked their fingers to the bone to keep up with the demand for new dresses. Women spent hours to ensure they included embellishments of jewelry, gloves, ribbons, and shoes to complement their gowns. They planned to look their best, with every curl of their hair perfectly pinned.

Coaches lined the streets as the daylight surrendered to the moonlit night. Invited guests dressed in their best, anticipating the splendor of the season's first ball. Excitement sparked as prospective young ladies hoped to dance with handsome gentlemen worthy of their attention. If they were lucky, they would turn a young man's head, engage him in conversation, and stroll the well-kept gardens of the mansion arm in arm.

Tavish chose a close where he was sure they could watch the many coaches pass by on their way to the ball. He carried the blanket Grizel had purchased for Haggadah over his arm while she held a small basket. They settled within the close's opening and wrapped the blanket around themselves to keep the chill from the night air at bay. Haggadah opened a towel in the basket to reveal sandwiches made with freshly baked bread smothered with jam. They each took a sandwich and ate as they watched coach after coach passed by them.

Haggadah strained to see the elegant gowns and jewelry each woman had on. "They're a pretentious lot."

"Aye, that they are." Tavish agreed as he finished his sandwich. He placed his arm around Haggadah as she finished eating and watched the pageantry. He grinned as she licked the jam that had dripped onto her fingers and admired her profile. Tavish leaned forward and whispered. "May I kiss you?"

Curious since she had never been kissed, Haggadah nodded.

"Close your eyes." He instructed.

She looked to see if anyone was watching them before closing her eyes.

Tavish placed the palm of his hand on the side of her face, letting his fingertips wrap around the back of her head. He lowered his lips and paused to see if her eyes remained closed before pressing them to hers.

He was gentle. His lips felt like velvet against hers. As their kiss ended, Haggadah looked into his eyes and remained inches from his face.

Tavish whispered. "Do you think you could accept me as your husband someday?"

Haggadah grinned, flattered he would want her as his wife. "Aye, someday."

~

Brodie, still unmarried at age forty-six, put on his overcoat and hat. He wished to detour the coach to the nearest pub as he climbed inside and sat with his walking stick across his lap. The councilman imagined the single women batting their eyes for his attention and hoping to be asked to dance. He groaned.

The coach pulled to a stop before the mansion. He exited and climbed the stairs of the grand estate with his walking stick tapping on each step. Greeted by a footman offering bubbling beverages, he handed his hat, coat, and walking stick to the offered hand of a servant and accepted a fluted glass. Since he had no desire to dance, he avoided the ballroom and headed straight to where the men had gathered to play cards. A hand had just finished, with the loser vacating his chair. The winner raked the mound of money from the center of the table and looked up. "Brodie, come join us." A fellow councilman encouraged.

Eager to try his luck, Brodie downed the liquid in his glass, placed it on a servant's tray, and sat in the chair. He took his money from his pocket and mimicked what the others tossed into the center of the table for the next game. The hands were dealt. Keeping his cards nearly flat on the table, he peeked at them.

"Brodie, when are you going to have my cabinet finished? My wife is hounding me to have you install it before the summer's end."

"I've just finished it. I'll bring it this coming week." He threw in two cards after placing his bet. Brodie was confident he had a winning hand.

~

The clip-clop of horses' hooves on the cobblestone street grew silent.

"That's the last of the coaches." Tavish reasoned. He glanced at the familiar man standing on the opposite side of the close. John was eating a small feast of a half chicken and a meat pie. Tavish wondered how the shady man could afford the meal.

Curious, Haggadah followed Tavish's line of sight and looked at the man eating a drumstick. She looked away and whispered. "Who is he?"

"He says his name is John Brown. Stay clear of him." Tavish watched as the vagrant tossed aside the chicken bones, and a stray dog ran off with the corpse. "It's time I walk you home." He stood and offered his hand to assist Haggadah from the ground. He gathered the blanket.

Haggadah put the basket over her arm. "I suppose the guests won't return from the ball until the sun peeks over the horizon."

"Aye." Tavish glanced at John before placing his hand on the small of Haggadah's back, encouraging her to step forward. He had little trust for the man who stared back at him.

Arm in arm, the couple wove their way through the lit oil lamp streets. Tavish opened the rickety gate to the cottage and escorted Haggadah to the door.

"Before I go," he reached into his pocket, "I want you to put these in a safe place." Tavish dropped two coins into her palm.

Haggadah looked at the pair of coins and then at Tavish. "Coins?"

"Aye, for our future. Keep the coins in a safe place. I'll add more to them when I can." As he kissed her, he felt her arms wrap around his waist. He deepened the kiss by pulling her closer and embracing her. As they parted, Tavish looked into her steel-gray eyes. "Goodnight, Haggadah."

"Goodnight." She opened the door. "Sleep well."

"Aye. You too."

She watched him pass through the gate before closing the door. Haggadah turned to see Grizel sitting before the fire, staring at her.

"It's about time he kissed you." The town healer grinned.

Haggadah could feel the heat rising in her cheeks. She grinned and shrugged her shoulder. "Can you see through the door?"

"No, but I could think of no other reason for the two of you to stand outside of it and stop talking."

Haggadah looked at the pair of coins in her hand. She would add them to her mother's coins in the tin box and hope to soon become Tavish's wife.

Chapter 17

After a night of losing every poker hand he played during the ball, Brodie woke midday to deliver the promised cabinet to his fellow councilman and wife. In truth, he was short of money and needed the income. He regretted telling Ann she could purchase a new dress.

"It's quite bonnie." The woman admired the installed cabinet.

"I took particular care in adding the embellishments." Brodie boasted as he opened the cabinet. "And plenty of dowels, hooks, and a small drawer for all your jewelry."

"Perfect. Perfect." The woman opened the tiny drawer and discovered plenty of room for her numerous brooches.

"Well done, Deacon." The councilman complimented. He led Brodie to his office and paid him.

After being escorted to the door, Brodie withdrew the money from his pocket and counted it to ensure he had been paid the correct amount. He could think of no better way to celebrate the sale of another cabinet than to go to Mister Clark's pub.

~

McLeary was sent on a mid-August morning to investigate the theft of a large quantity of black tea from Mister Carnegie's grocery. He entered the shop at the end of Saint Andrew's Street and discovered, once again, no forced entry. The quantity of tea taken was a large and valuable amount.

As the constable exited the building, he saw several vagrants standing on the opposite side of the street staring at him. McLeary returned their stare, wondering if they had witnessed the robbery. If he approached them, would they confide in him what they saw? Taking the risk, he crossed the street. The homeless scattered like scared rats. He doubted they would provide any information even if he could call out and stop them from running away. "Unless I could offer them something in exchange." He thought out loud. "I ken the baker often has day-old bread. Stale or not, it would matter little to those with empty bellies."

He was able to negotiate a fair price for the dry bread. McLeary broke the loaves into sections as he stood across from the grocery and offered the food to the homeless.

A man with grimy hands took a chunk of bread. "Aye, I saw them. There were three men. Two went inside while the third kept watch by the door."

"Three?" McLeary saw the woman cowering behind the informant with two children and held out another part of a loaf to ensure they all had a bit to eat.

"Aye, all dressed in black, including their faces." The man turned and handed his wife the bread before the family left.

Once the bread was handed out, the witnesses disappeared. McLeary strolled the streets, slowly returning to the station house to file a report. There was a stillness about the city. He assumed it was because some residents were still asleep after arriving home near sunrise from the ball. He saw Tavish from across the way and wondered what the lad may know about the robbery.

Tavish stood in the arch of the close. He wiped the sleep from his eyes and adjusted the cap on his head. With the noise of arriving coaches throughout the night, Tavish managed to doze enough to feel well-rested. He saw McLeary walking toward him with a casual stroll.

Tavish leaned against the wall and looked away from the officer as he spoke. "Good morning."

"Aye, it's a fine day." McLeary pretended to ignore the homeless man as he stood far from him. "There was a robbery last night. Witnesses say it was three men dressed in black."

"After watching the coaches leave for the ball, I walked Haggadah home, then bedded down for the night. Besides the coaches returning with drunken guests until the sun rose, I slept soundly. I didn't see any men dressed in black."

"It seems to be another robbery without evidence of a break-in." McLeary shared.

"Another unlocked door or open window?"

"No, the building was locked, or so Carnegie says."

"The grocery?"

"Aye."

"Maybe someone hid inside at closing. There are lots of hungry people who live on the street nearby. They've no money to buy food."

"Aye. Very well. Thank you, Tavish." McLeary strolled away.

Chapter 18

On Samhain's quiet and dark evening, Grizel lay in bed snoring. Before retiring to her cot in the loft, Haggadah placed a log on the fire to take the chill from the air. She put her foot on the ladder's lowest rung when a knock sounded on the cottage door. The apprentice opened the door to see a frantic child in ragged clothes.

"Mum sent me. My sister is burning with fever."

"A fever, you say? I'll come with you. Give me a moment to gather what I need." Haggadah closed the door, retrieved her carpetbag from the loft, and put the tin with coins under her pillow. Hurrying down the ladder, she opened the apothecary, pulled several bottles, and placed them inside her carpetbag. Putting on her overcoat, she joined the upset boy and followed him through the slumbering city to a dimly lit apartment on the lowest floor of a tenement building.

Haggadah looked at the ill little girl, estimating her age to be three or four. "Hello, my name is Haggadah."

The child was afraid to respond. Her bloodshot eyes looked at her mother for reassurance.

Haggadah placed the palm of her hand on the child's forehead. It was hot to the touch. "She must drink water. Remove the blanket and undress her, except her undergarments. Dampen a cloth and put it on her forehead." Haggadah took several of the bottles from the carpetbag. "How old is she?"

"Five." The worried mother slipped the soiled dress over the child's head.

"Tiny for her age." Haggadah assumed the lack of food may have stunted the child's growth. She searched through her bag for the needed herbs. "I need a bowl."

The lad retrieved one from a shelf. "Here."

"Thank you." She added catnip, white willow bark, and yarrow to the bowl. "Is there not water in the kettle?"

"Aye." The woman replied as she placed a dampened cloth on her daughter's forehead.

Haggadah took a chipped cup from the shelf. She added the blended herbs and hot water to steep. "Until her fever goes down, wash her body with cool water."

"She shivers." The woman looked at the young apprentice, questioning her ability.

"Her fever is rising. The tea will help bring it down once we have her drink some."

Haggadah administered the tea when it was ready. Uncertain of what ailed the child, she would watch over her until the fever broke or she expired.

~

Brodie peeked into the room where his children slept in the same bed.

Ann wrapped her arms around her lover's waist, rose on her toes, and peeked over his shoulder. "What are you looking at?"

Brodie put his hands upon the clasped pair on his abdomen and grinned. "Our bairns. They're bonnie."

"Aye, especially when they're sleeping." She yawned. "Let's go to bed."

~

While the citizens of Edinburgh slept, two men kept to the shadows and quickly passed through the university doors. They followed the given instructions and stood outside the library.

"He said it's in this room, always on display in the same spot." The thief scanned the hallway to ensure they remained undetected, turned the doorknob, and discovered it locked.

Together, the men broke into the library and stood before the symbolic item proudly displayed for all to see. The elegant Mace made locally by craftsmen was a sight to behold with its wood-turned shaft, silver bands, and three-sided adornment at its top. The ceremonial piece presided over every General Council meeting.

The pair took the Mace from its prestigious display and left the building undetected.

~

Fear crept into Haggadah's soul as she looked toward the slightest sound while walking home after the child's fever broke. The dim lighting of the oil street lamps offered little security as she scurried along. She knew Tavish would be displeased to discover she was alone at the late hour. She looked behind her as she rounded the corner of a building.

Haggadah collided with something that knocked her to the ground. Her head landed on the sidewalk with a resounding thud, causing her vision to blacken.

"Leave her!" A man yelled.

As the ebony fog faded from her sight, it revealed two men standing near her. Haggadah planted her hands behind her, sat up, and watched one of the men conceal a decorative stick within his black garments before scampering away and disappearing into the inky night. She blinked to clear the blurriness in her vision, picked herself up from the ground, and touched the growing bump on the back of her head. Haggadah scooped up her carpetbag, went to the next lamp, and felt her painful injury. She examined her fingertips in the dim light. Thankfully, she was not bleeding.

~

Running footfalls caused Tavish to crack open his eyes. Curious, he remained still as he pretended to sleep against the wall of the close. A pair of men dressed in dark clothing ran past him in a blur. He assumed the men were up to no good, but it was not his concern. He heard the kirk bell ring three times, let his eyelids fall, and returned to sleep.

~

Haggadah entered the cottage and put her carpetbag on a chair. She intended to return its contents to the apothecary after sleeping a few hours. She hung her overcoat on a peg, stoked the fire, and lit a candle from the flames wrapping around the dry log. Haggadah felt the aching bump on her head. She assumed the men must have been in quite a hurry to run away and impolitely leave her sitting on the sidewalk.

A snore escaped Grizel. Haggadah looked at her mentor and yawned. With only a few hours of darkness left before daybreak, she climbed the ladder, lay on the bed, and snuggled beneath her blanket as she drifted off to sleep.

Chapter 19

In the morning, word of the university's missing silver Mace spread quickly. Constables swarmed the scene.

McLeary entered the building and was escorted to the library where the sacred item had been kept. He examined the library door and noted the forced entry before asking the logical question. "Was the building locked?"

"Aye, both the front and library door."

"Who has a key?"

"There are many people who have the front door key. For security reasons, only a few have the key to the library."

McLeary examined the broken library door closely. "I'll need a list of everyone with a key to both." His request was twofold. First, someone without a key to the library door would be a suspect. Second, someone with a key to the library may have broken the door to implicate someone else.

"Aye, Constable. It may take a while."

"Send it to the station house when you are finished." Seeing all that needed to be seen, McLeary saw himself out of the building. While walking to the station house, he pondered the robberies that plagued the city over the past few months. The robber or robbers seemed as slippery as eels. It troubled him that thieves enrich themselves on the backs of people who worked hard to earn their living. "I may have to take matters into my own hands."

~

Tavish knocked on the cottage door and was greeted by Grizel.

"Haggadah is still in bed." She whispered and motioned for him to enter.

"Another late-night call for a remedy?" He stepped inside.

"Aye, since she is usually up with the sun, most likely." Closing the door, Grizel went to the cupboard. "Tea?"

"Thank you." He put a log on the fire and rotated the kettle for the water to heat.

Grizel put a pan of water on the fire and added rolled oats. "Some porridge to stick in your stomach should get your day off to a good start." She looked up at the loft and nodded, indicating to Tavish that Haggadah was stirring. "We're having porridge with butter, milk, and bread, Haggadah. Tavish has stopped by for a visit."

A raspy reply came from the loft. "Aye, I heard his voice."

Grizel handed Tavish the bowls to serve the porridge while she put butter, bread, milk, jam, and spoons on the table.

Haggadah descended the ladder, plopped down in a chair, and rubbed the sleep from her eyes.

"What called you away last night?" Grizel held a teapot before Tavish, who filled it from the kettle.

"A feverish bairn." She watched Tavish place a bowl of steaming porridge before her. "Thank you." Haggadah added butter and milk to the bowl. Picking up the spoon, she leaned forward to take a bite. "Och." Her head throbbed. She touched the back of her head and winced as Tavish joined her at the table.

Grizel realized her apprentice was in pain. "Did you hurt your head?"

"Aye, on my way home from caring for the bairn." She began.

The expression on Tavish's face became stern. He stood from his chair and touched the back of Haggadah's head.

"Och." She looked over her shoulder as he pulled his hand away.

"Aye, you have a bump." He separated her hair until he could see it. "It's quite big, no blood." He sat, waiting for an explanation. Even though he did not want Haggadah alone on the street at night, he understood she had no way of getting word to him for his escort.

Haggadah continued. "I came around the corner of a building and collided with something, a man dressed in black. There were two of them. One held a stick and tried to hide it in his clothes before they ran off."

Tavish nearly choked on his porridge. "The university's silver Mace was stolen last night. You crossed paths with the thieves."

Haggadah looked at Grizel and back at Tavish.

"Did you get a good look at them?" He pressed.

"No, their faces were shaded in the light."

Tavish's eyebrows raised in concern. "Did they get a good look at you?"

She shrugged her shoulders. "I don't ken. My vision turned black. One said to leave me be, and then they ran off."

Tavish recalled the men dressed in black running past the close. "You say they were in black? I saw them, too."

"I think both of you must go to the station house and report what you've seen." Grizel insisted.

The witnesses stared at the healer.

"Finish your meal, and then off you go. I'll wash the dishes." Grizel pushed her spoon into her porridge.

~

McLeary returned to the station house to file a report on the stolen Mace.

The constable at the desk said, "There's a pair of witnesses waiting to speak with you."

"Witnesses?" He opened the door to enter the hallway.

"They say they saw who took the university's Mace."

"Did they now?" McLeary grabbed the necessary paperwork, pen, and ink and entered the small interrogation room to see two familiar faces staring back at him. "Ah, Tavish, Haggadah." He sat across from the couple. He readied to take their statement and paused with the pen in midair. "So, shall we start with you, Haggadah. Your last name?"

"Blyth."

"What did you see?"

"I was returning to the cottage after tending to a feverous bairn during the night. When I came around the corner of a building, I ran into a man dressed in black and fell to the ground. I blacked out briefly, but I remember hearing one of the men say, "Leave her." Then they ran off."

"There were two men?"

"Aye. Both were dressed in black. I didn't see their faces, but one had a stick and hid it from me by putting it in his clothes."

"Did you notice their body build? Height? Weight?" McLeary dipped his pen in the ink.

"No, they seemed tall from where I lay on the ground." She thought for a moment. "One was taller than the other. Neither appeared stout or thin, but it was hard to judge with them being dressed in black."

"Tavish?"

"I was sleeping in a close when I heard footsteps. I saw two men dressed in black run past me. I didn't think much of it at the time until I heard Haggadah tell her tale over breakfast."

The constable added the details to the report. "Any idea of the time this occurred."

Tavish thought back. "I heard the kirk's bell ring three times."

"Did you happen to notice their height? Build?"

"No. The men ran past me quickly, and I wasn't very awake."

McLeary finished the entry into the report and closed the folder. "Tavish, I'd like to ask you to keep your eyes and ears open to any talk on the street as to who these two men may be. They may be the same men who robbed Carnegie's."

Haggadah looked at Tavish's profile. The homeless disliked the authorities. She feared his cooperation with McLeary may put him in danger.

Tavish nodded without replying.

"When I'm on patrol, I may stop and discreetly ask if you've learned anything else to help nab the culprits. I ken you are taking a risk by being my informant, but I'll take care so others will be unaware."

It eased Haggadah's mind to hear the officer's reassuring words for Tavish's safety. However, she knew the streets had many eyes and people liked to talk.

Once outside the station house, Haggadah threaded her arm through Tavish's offered elbow. "Since you'll be keeping a watchful eye for the constable, will others be suspicious of you working with McLeary?"

"No need to fear, my love. I'm sure all will be well."

An uneasiness rippled through Haggadah. She sensed something was amiss. A vision flashed in her mind. She shook her head, clearing it from her thoughts.

Tavish looked at her from the corner of his eye. "Is something wrong?" She looked at him with fear in her eyes.

"There's more than two men. They carry flintlock pistols."

He had no reason to doubt what Haggadah sensed. From the expression on her face, he knew she spoke the truth. "Then I'll tell McLeary to arm himself and those under his command."

~

As day turned to night, McLeary put on a tattered overcoat to blend in with the homeless.

"Must you go out in the middle of the night? You've already put in a long day at work." His wife, Maggie, pleaded as she pulled the lapel of a shabby coat close to his neck to ensure he remained warm.

"Don't worry yourself, Mag." McLeary rubbed ash from the ash bucket over his coat and face. He had put on an old, scuffed pair of shoes and clipped the fingers of a torn pair of gloves to expose his fingertips. "The robberies trouble me so. I need to get to the bottom of it." He looked in the direction of the sitting room, where his newborn son began to cry, and his daughter sat on the floor playing with a doll. McLeary kissed his wife on her forehead. "I won't stay out too late."

The constable left his apartment, descended the stairs, stepped onto the quiet street, and went to the main street where most businesses were located. If luck was on his side, McLeary hoped to see a robbery in progress and apprehend the criminals.

He passed several closes with people sleeping or huddled near warming fires. His change of clothing would allow him to fit in with the homeless, confident he would remain unrecognized. He nestled against a wall at the opening of a close and scanned the street for anyone suspiciously lurking about.

Tavish, who slept with one eye open, lifted his hat to see who sat opposite him. He scowled, recognizing the man, but could not immediately place him. He was familiar with most of the homeless in the city. Was this man one of the many displaced by the closing of the tenement buildings?

Tavish studied the vagrant's face. If he was recently evicted or new in the city, it seemed strange that he was alone with no family. Tavish stared at the familiar profile. "Settling in for the night, I see."

The constable replied without looking at the lad. "Aye."

Tavish grinned, confirming his suspicion. "You asked me to do a job for you."

McLeary looked at the lad across from him. "Aye, Tavish, that I did."

"The thief likely has enough money to line his pockets for the time being. Go home to your wife."

McLeary stared at Tavish, tempted to take the lad up on his offer.

"Do you not trust me?" The young man questioned.

McLeary wanted to see the evening through but realized that doing so demonstrated his lack of faith in the lad.

Tavish nodded his head toward the street. "Go. I'll go to the station house to report anything suspicious."

McLeary was sure his wife would appreciate his early return. With a nod, the constable stood. "I prefer you notify me directly. I haven't told my superior I'd be keeping a night watch."

"Aye. If I see anything, I'll ask for you tomorrow morning." Tavish watched as the rookie officer left. He was honored that McLeary trusted him to do as he promised. He doubted the robber would be foolish enough to strike two days in a row.

Tavish recognized the shadow of a tall man darting around the corner of a building. It was John Brown. Why was he lurking about in the night?

Rumors among the homeless men accused John of being a convicted robber who had somehow escaped a penal ship bound for America. John had managed to evade the authorities for a half-dozen years or so. Tavish wondered when John's luck would run out. He hoped it would be soon.

Chapter 20

As the weather turned colder and the passing days inched toward the year's end, the shops closed for the Yule holiday. Tavish went to the healer's cottage to spend the afternoon with Haggadah. His mouth watered in anticipation of the chicken dinner awaiting him. He wished he had the money to purchase a sweet for them both. Even if he did, the baker was closed. Tavish had managed to buy a green ribbon for Haggadah's hair. It was a thoughtful gift, and he hoped she appreciated it since it was all he could afford.

    He walked up the flagstone pathway as Grizel opened the door.

"We've been cooking all day." She boasted, grinning ear to ear.

He stepped over the threshold and inhaled the aroma of spices lingering in the air. "It smells delicious." Tavish took off his hat and coat and hung them on a peg. He went to the fireplace, rubbed his hands together, and held his open palms toward the flames to warm them before stepping to Haggadah. He wrapped his arm around her waist and pressed his lips to hers. "Happy Yule."

She smiled. "Happy Yule."

He looked at the table. The women had covered it with a tablecloth, set out the chipped and unmatched plates, and several sprigs of evergreen with bittersweet in a vase at its center. "It looks lovely." He watched as a fresh loaf of bread was put on the table. "The butcher was quite busy with cooks purchasing their choice of meat for the Yule dinners." Tavish added.

Still concerned for his safety, Haggadah spoke her mind. "Have you seen anything untoward?"

Tavish shook his head. "No, the streets have been quiet, most likely from the cold. One would be out of their right mind to venture out in this wicked weather?"

~

The Yule Ball marked the completion of the season with its pageantry of coaches, elegantly dressed members of society, and the hosting mansion decorated with greenery and illuminated by lit candelabras.

"You're not ready? But the coach is here."

John Tapp, a shopkeeper, looked up from his account books at his wife. She stood before his office desk dressed in her new gown, her hair pinned in place, and satin gloves extending to her elbows. Her face wore a mask of disappointment.

Tapp disliked attending balls, but understood it was his wife's way of visiting with others and catching up on the city's gossip. He had deliberately put off entering several days of sales in the ledger. Tapp planned to use the bookkeeping as his excuse to miss the ball. He thought of smoothing over his decision with a compliment. "I thought I heard you coming down the stairs." His mouth turned up at the corners. "You look bonnie."

She ignored his attempt at flattery. "You ken I've been looking forward to the ball for weeks. Must you work tonight?"

"Aye. Business has been brisk, with no time to record sales. Go ahead. I'll join you shortly." He lied, as he planned on missing the entire evening.

"You'll need to change your clothes before coming. I locked the apartment door and left my key on the hook in the stairway. I don't want to carry it in my purse all evening." She knew her husband had a duplicate key that fit the shop and residence locks. "Please, join me as soon as you can. You ken how I dislike going to balls by myself."

"I will." He dipped his pen in the inkwell and continued with his entries. He heard the bell above the door ring as she left.

As time ticked by, Tapp became absorbed in his work. He heard the bell above the door ring again and assumed his wife had returned. "Did you forget something, Dear?"

"No, but I saw your light and thought you may want to celebrate the Yule with me."

He looked at the doorway of his office to see John Brown, a man who stopped by the shop often. He stood with a bottle of whiskey in his hand.

"Aye," Tapp put his pen in the inkwell, "I can use a dram or two while I finish my entries."

~

After enjoying the delicious meal with Haggadah and Grizel, Tavish huddled near the warming fire in a crowded close. His breath turned to shards of foggy crystals as he exhaled into the frigid evening air. He insisted Haggadah remain in the warmth of the cottage instead of joining him to watch the coaches pass by the close. Tavish pulled a pair of gloves from his coat pocket, a gift Haggadah had given him as a Yule present. He slipped them on, went to the opening of the close, and stared down at the tracks made by the coach wheels in the dusting of snow. Tavish looked in the direction of the guests' destination. He imagined them entering an elegant mansion, the expensive food and drink, and dancing. Their lifestyle was far from the humble living Tavish wanted to share with Haggadah. True to his word, he gave her a coin or two every week, sometimes more, to put in her mother's tin for their future. He hoped to ask for her hand in marriage soon, find an apartment for them, and begin their lives together. Maybe even start a family.

Tavish grinned, recalling how the green ribbon had pleased her so. He hoped to someday shower her with gifts.

A chill went up his spine, causing his body to shudder. With the last of the coaches to pass by, Tavish returned to the warming fire before settling in for a night's sleep.

~

Other than the click of the lock as the key was turned, the men dressed in black entered silently into the darkened residence. They went from room to room, searching for anything of value.

The thief whispered as he looked inside a drawer. "Och, here's some guinea notes and shillings."

"Aye, I found some rings and a silver watch," said the other. Moving about some clothes in a bottom drawer, he discovered a picture frame with a miniature oil of a handsome gentleman. "Maybe the Missus is keeping a secret from the Mister." He turned the frame over and saw the back was made of gold, broke the frame, and took the valuable metal.

The pair tiptoed out of the house, locked the door, and left without being seen.

~

Brown stood as the last drop of whiskey poured from the bottle. "I thought you said you had to go to the ball."

"Aye," Tapp nodded, "my wife is expecting me."

"Then I bid you goodnight and Happy Yule." Brown touched his index finger to his cap.

"Aye, Happy Yule." Tapp closed his ledger. To appease his wife, he locked the shop and went to their apartment to dress.

~

Tavish opened his eyes as voices stirred him from his slumber. He listened as their footsteps drew near. He recognized one of the voices and listened while pretending to sleep.

"Och, what's in the bottle?"

"It's empty." John tossed it aside, shattering the glass on the cobblestone.

"You could have saved some for us."

"Well . . ." John's voice faded as the three men walked past the close.

Tavish opened his eyes and looked to see the trio disappear into the darkness. He assumed the men would be up to no good since John was involved. He would inform McLeary in the morning.

~

After enduring the relentless cries of his infant son throughout the night, McLeary entered the station house. The aroma of coffee greeted him with the promise of clearing the residual fog from his mind. He scanned the chairs along the wall opposite the seated constable. He expected to see people sitting in them. However, the chairs were empty.

The constable at the desk looked at McLeary as he entered through the door to the office. "There's a married couple who need their statement taken. They claim they were robbed last night. I thought their case may be connected to the other robberies you've been investigating, so I've had them wait until you arrived." The constable shook his head. "Another mystery robbery." He grinned.

"Mystery robbery." A tinge of sarcasm in McLeary's comment.

"Aye, no forced entry again."

McLeary shook his head as he helped himself to a cup of coffee before gathering the necessary paperwork. He inhaled deeply, entered the small room, and saw the elegantly dressed couple sitting on the opposite side of the table. "Hello, I'm Constable McLeary. I understand you wish to make a statement about a robbery?" He sat across from what he assumed was a husband and wife.

"While we were at the Yule Ball, someone came into our house and took our belongings." Tapp stated.

"You mean while I was away. You didn't quite make it to the ball."

McLeary watched as the man's wife crossed her arms over her chest. He glanced from one individual to the other, recognizing the tension between the pair.

Tilting his head toward his wife, Tapp avoided her glaring stare as he looked at the constable. "Dear, we don't ken what time the robbery occurred."

McLeary dipped his pen in the inkwell and paused. "Perhaps we should start at the beginning. Your names?"

"John Tapp." He replied and motioned toward his wife to supply her name, who interrupted and spoke for herself.

"I'm his wife, Clara."

Tapp looked at the ceiling, biting his tongue.

"Address?"

Clara gladly answered the question.

"So, you say you were robbed last night?" McLeary began.

Tapp sat back in his chair as Clara continued to speak.

"When I left for the ball, I locked the door to our apartment. We live above our shop. John was in his office, tending to the accounts, so I went to the ball without him. He reassured me he would join me later." She glared at her husband. "Much later, that is. When he arrived, the ball was nearly finished."

"Dear, the ball didn't finish until almost sunrise. I arrived with plenty of time left to dance with you."

McLeary raised his eyebrows and interrupted the argument. "Mister Tapp, did you enter your apartment before going to the ball?"

"Aye, but saw nothing amiss."

"In your intoxicated state, how would you notice?" Clara jibed.

McLeary redirected. "Was your apartment door locked before you entered?"

"Aye, I used my key." Tapp confirmed.

Clara added to her husband's explanation. "The key to the shop also opens our apartment. When I left for the ball, I put my key on a nail at the bottom of the stairs. I didn't want to carry it while at the ball."

McLeary reasoned. "So, could anyone entering your stairway door use the key to enter your apartment?"

Clara looked at her husband. "Aye, but who would do such a thing?"

"Apparently, someone who wished to rob us." Tapp retorted.

"Mister Tapp, can you tell me why you delayed meeting your wife at the ball?"

"Aye, a friend of mine stopped by with a bottle of whisky to celebrate the Yule. I visited with him before locking the shop door, going to our apartment to dress, and then joining my wife."

"Your friend's name?"

"John, like mine. I don't ken his last name. He's a homeless man though, tall, thin, always wears a flat cap."

Even though the description was vague, McLeary scribbled the name in the file. "Did you take the key from the nail at the base of the stairs to the ball?"

"No, I had my own key, so it was where we always keep it." Tapp admitted.

McLeary scribbled the notation. "So, it may be safe to assume the robbery occurred while Missus Tapp was at the ball and you, Mister Tapp, were visiting with your friend, John, in your shop, or it happened while both of you were at the ball?" The constable reasoned.

The couple glanced at one another. Tapp nodded, seeing the constable's logic. "Aye."

"In the future, I suggest you keep your key in hand or find a place to put it so it isn't easily seen." McLeary glanced at the pair to ensure they understood the seriousness of his comment. "After all, those who robbed your apartment ken where the key is and may return." He dipped his pen into the ebony liquid. "I need a list of items that were taken."

Clara blinked her eyes as she thought for a moment. "I'll have to go through our things when we get home. After all, we arrived home at daybreak, noticed our home had been robbed, and came directly here to report it."

McLeary signed the report and filled in the date and time. "We can add the items later. For now, I'll accompany you to your home and inspect your apartment." He closed the folder, tucked it under his arm, and escorted the couple from the room. He handed the file to the constable at the front desk before hailing a coach for their transportation.

As McLeary stepped out of the coach, he followed the couple through the door and noted the key hanging on a nail on the wall at the base of the staircase. He climbed the stairs and stepped inside the residence.

"We left everything as we found it." Missus Tapp explained, and she motioned to the broken picture frame on the floor, and the open drawers with items shuffled haphazardly within it. "Our belongings are kept neat and tidy. I pride myself in doing so." She lifted her chin and grinned slightly. "I thought my husband may have been looking for something before he left for the ball, but he denied doing so."

"If you can put a list together of the stolen items and get it to me quickly, it will allow me to alert others if the thief tries to sell them. Again, put your key in a better place." McLeary had a possible lead. However, having only the first name gave him little to go on.

On his return to the station house, McLeary stopped the coach as he saw Tavish leaving a shop. He assumed the young man was running an errand for the merchant. The constable recognized the perfect opportunity to question him. McLeary dodged horse-drawn wagons and coaches as he crossed the street, deliberately walked in front of Tavish, and tilted his head toward the close.

Apprehensive to follow the officer, Tavish abruptly stopped near the close's opening. He scanned the street to see if anyone was watching him and remained silent.

"There was a robbery last night. Did you happen to see anything? Anyone?"

Tavish thought for a moment. He refrained from making eye contact with the constable. "Aye. Most of the coaches had left for the ball. I was resting my eyes when I heard men talking and footsteps. As always, I pretended to be asleep. I recognized John Brown's voice. He had an empty bottle of whisky with him. Two other men dressed in black wanted a drink, but the bottle was empty. John threw the bottle away. I didn't ken who the men were, but they seemed to ken John."

"What time did you see them?"

"I don't ken the exact time. I'm guessing nine or ten?"

McLeary looked about the street. "Two men with John, you say, around nine or ten?"

"Aye." Tavish confirmed.

"I'm interested in questioning this, John Brown. Do you ken him?"

"Aye, but I suspect he's not who he appears to be. He roams the city, homeless, too. Some say he's a convict who escaped a ship headed toward a penal colony."

"If you see him and I'm about, point him out to me."

"Aye."

"Well, I won't keep you from your work. Thank you, and if you think of anything else, let a constable at the station house know. They'll get word to me."

"Aye." Tavish walked away as McLeary pretended to stroll the street on patrol.

Peering out from the darkness of the close was John Brown. He had remained hidden and listened to the encounter between the officer and the homeless young man. He shook his head as he scowled. "Tavish, what have you gotten yourself into? A spy for the constable, perhaps?" The last thing John wanted was to be apprehended and shipped off to parts unknown.

Chapter 21

Pulling a chair from the table, Tavish joined Haggadah and Grizel for dinner. "The men were up to no good, I say." He reached into his pocket and handed Haggadah two coins for safekeeping. Tavish sliced the loaf of bread, giving each woman a slice before taking one for himself and spreading the butter in a thick layer.

Haggadah's fork stilled in the buttered beans on her plate, and she looked at Tavish. "What men?"

"I don't ken them except for John." He bit into his bread and continued to talk with his mouth full. "I didn't see their faces. They passed by the close where I was sleeping. I peeked out as they walked by and saw two men dressed in black with him."

"John? The man we saw eating chicken on the night of the ball?" Haggadah continued with her inquisition.

Grizel detected her apprentice's concern. She looked from Haggadah to Tavish.

"Aye." He paused chewing and looked at Grizel and Haggadah, both staring at him. "He's no friend of mine. We cross paths once in a while. A mere acquaintance. I didn't trust him when I first met him years ago. I trust him even less now. He's hiding something."

"Stay away from him." Haggadah warned, then loading her fork with beans.

Tavish nodded before glancing at Grizel.

"Aye, she has a way of predicting. I would take her warning seriously." The healer looked at Haggadah, who stared back at her.

So as not to worry either of them, Tavish thought it best to keep his conversation with the constable to himself.

~

On a chilly, overcast January morning, he went for his usual walk through the city after attending Mass. As he had done many times before, the man stopped in front of the shop and examined the lock. He patted his overcoat pocket before peering into the window of Inglis & Horner Silk Merchant Shop. He scanned the exquisite bolts of silk and other high-quality fabrics on the shelves and imagined the vast sum he could obtain. With the shop closed for the day, he pulled the false key from his pocket and looked up and down the street. It was vacant except for a coach coming toward him. Slipping the key back into his pocket, he bided his time by looking in the window until the clip-clop of the horse's hooves became silent.

After glancing at the distant coach, he retrieved the molded key from his pocket and inserted it into the keyhole. He held his breath, hoping the makeshift key could unlock the mechanism for the planned robbery. He rotated it. The lock clicked open. He grinned, pleased with himself. He rotated the key to close the lock, but it failed to latch.

Looking up and down the street, he verified it remained vacant. His heartbeat quickened, and his palms began to sweat. Unless he could relock the device, the shop owner may think the lock was faulty and replace it. He turned the key several times, but each attempt was unsuccessful. He looked about the sidewalk and discovered a twig. Given no other option, he dropped the key into his pocket, picked up the bit of wood, and wedged the arch metal of the padlock into the hole. He exhaled in relief at the temporary fix, knowing he could only hope the owners did not detect the rigging.

Lifting his chin, he strolled away while glancing for any onlookers. He would confess the difficulty at the monthly meeting with his accomplices, describe the problem, and see if a better solution could be found.

~

The wind carried a frigid coldness, causing Tavish to wait just inside the kirk's door while Haggadah visited her mother's grave. Assuming she would not stay long, he pushed the wooden door open a mere crack and saw her walking toward him.

A shiver ran up her spine as Haggadah joined her escort. "It's nippy cold, so I didn't stay long."

Tavish offered his bent arm, and she threaded hers within his.

"Grizel said she was making stew and bread. It should be nearly ready when we arrive; warm our stomachs and take the chill away." Haggadah hugged Tavish's arm to huddle closer to him.

"A cup of tea will taste good, too." Tavish's teeth chattered as a shiver ran up his spine. He pulled his overcoat collar closer to his neck. "I'll be sure to add a log or two to the fire."

The couple hurried their pace, eager to be in the warmth of the aged cottage.

Haggadah shivered. "I hate the thought of you sleeping on the street tonight."

"Och, no worry, my love. I've been doing so for years. I'll just snuggle up to the fire." Tavish grinned and looked into her steel-gray eyes. "But I'd rather be cuddling up beside you." He winked.

Haggadah shook her head and looked skyward, secretly wishing to do the same.

~

As night fell upon the city, a small group of men gathered in the back of a shop. They sat around a table in the candle-lit room, drinking whiskey.

"I stopped by Ingles & Hover during my morning walk. The key I made opened the padlock but didn't close it." The leader announced.

"Och!" A man sat forward in his chair and slapped the palm of his hand on the table. "So, you foretold of our theft?" He accepted a bottle of whiskey from another, tipped it, and filled the glass before him.

The leader shook his head. "I made it look as if it were locked."

"How?" Another downed his dram of whiskey.

"I rigged it with a wee twig, so don't worry yourself." He scowled before downing the glass of whiskey before him.

A man, who had remained silent, brought his glass to his lips and paused. "Did anyone see you?"

"No." The leader informed. "The street remained empty."

Frustrated, one of the men held out the palm of his hand. "Give me your key. I'll make a proper one that works."

The leader pulled the key from his overcoat pocket and tossed it across the table, insulted by the implication of his inadequacy. Pouring another glass, he downed the amber liquid and slammed the empty vessel on the table.

~

Bitter cold and wicked winds remained throughout the week. Tavish hurried from shop to shop, collecting paid errands. The blistering weather conditions caused many shop owners to sympathize with the young man and offer him a generous tip. Tavish happily accepted the money. He would give the extra coins to Haggadah, bringing them one step closer to becoming husband and wife.

With a jingle in his pocket, he walked to the cottage for an evening meal and to warm himself before spending the night in a close.

"Tavish, you are welcome to sleep on the floor near the fire." Grizel offered as she sipped her tea at the finish of the meal.

Tavish shook his head as he glanced at Haggadah. "I don't want wagging tongues telling wicked tales and ruining reputations. I'll do fine, but I appreciate the offer."

"How could my reputation be any more ruined? People think ill of me already." Haggadah defended.

Tavish reached across the table and patted her hand. "No need to give them any more to talk about." He sighed. "I must help keep the warming fire lit all night, especially for the bairns. If the cold becomes more than I can bear, I'll spend a coin to sip a drink in a pub to warm myself." He stood, put on his coat and hat, and withdrew the coins from his pocket.

Haggadah watched as he took one coin and returned it to his pocket before giving her the remainder for safekeeping.

~

Confident they would remain undetected on such a blustery night, the men from various parts of the city, dressed in black, met before the silk shop. The kirk's bell rang three times, announcing the hour.

The acclaimed locksmith pulled the key he made from his pocket and held it proudly before his comrades. "Even though I've yet to examine this padlock, I'm confident this key will open and close it." He inserted the key, rotated it, and grinned slyly as the lock popped open.

"See if it locks before we go inside," the leader said with a jealous tone.

"Aye." Agreed another.

The key maker turned the key and grinned with satisfaction when the lock clicked shut. He looked at the man who had challenged his craftmanship and smirked before reopening the lock.

The men hurried through the open door, fearful of being seen, while one remained outside as the watchman. Within minutes, they carried armfuls of expensive silks and fabrics, including black cambric.

"This must be worth a couple hundred pounds," said one.

"Och, more like seven or eight hundred." Corrected another.

The thieves disappeared into the night while the skilled locksmith turned the key and locked the padlock. Looking up and down the street, he dropped the key into his pocket and stayed within the shadows as he walked to the base of Salisbury Craig. After a quick glance to ensure he was alone, he added the false key to the others on the ring and returned the rock to its place, keeping the secret well hidden.

~

Pulling the collar of his overcoat near his neck to protect him from the bitter wind, McLeary reported to the station house for his shift at daybreak, only to be told by the desk constable that he was needed at Ingles & Hover.

"Another robbery?" McLeary inhaled the aroma of freshly brewed coffee and scowled, knowing he would have to forego his morning ritual of several cups.

"Aye, Chief Inspector Niven wants you to go there immediately. Since word has spread of the robbery, the Procurator-Fiscal has offered a one-hundred-pound reward for identifying the thieves. The government has added another fifty pounds plus a King's Pardon to anyone with past crimes who was involved."

Pivoting on his heel, McLeary walked to the silk shop at the Cross of Edinburgh. As he looked through the shop window, he observed the partners taking inventory.

Inglis looked toward the door as the bell above it rang. "Constable, thank you for coming so promptly." He stepped forward and shook McLeary's hand.

McLeary inhaled the aroma of freshly brewed coffee.

Horner placed his pen in the inkwell and joined them. "Aye, thank you. We've yet to tally the loss, but it may be close to eight hundred pounds."

McLeary shook his head. "There is a reward of one-hundred-fifty pounds for unmasking the culprits. I feel many are tiring of the robberies and want to find them as quickly as possible." He inspected the padlock and toured the interior of the shop. The owners pointed to the vacant shelves and gave their well-rehearsed sales pitch of the fabrics as if selling each bolt to the constable. "It seems the thieves have expensive taste in fabric. Perhaps someone familiar with the fabric's quality." McLeary looked at the empty shelves. "I'll need a list containing what was stolen."

"If you can wait a few moments, we should have a complete list soon." Inglis assured.

Feeling no need to rush back to the station house, McLeary nodded. "Very well."

"Och, I'm forgetting my manners. Let me get you a cup of coffee." Inglis disappeared into an adjacent room and reappeared quickly with a cup of the steaming brew.

"Thank you." McLeary sipped the caffeinated drink as he admired the shop's architectural details of the interior, a reflection of the expensive fabrics.

Within minutes, the list of stolen fabrics was placed in McLeary's hand. He tucked it into his overcoat pocket, gave his empty cup to the shop owner, and left.

Standing on the sidewalk, he wondered if Tavish had seen anything suspicious and walked briskly to where he had encountered the young man before. McLeary scanned the faces inside every close he passed and checked with shop owners, but there was no sign of him. He entered Dingwall's shop, knowing Tavish often ran errands for him. "Good day to you. Has Tavish been by this morning?"

"Aye, he has. Is the lad in trouble?"

"No, I just need to speak to him. Do you ken where he was headed?"

"He was to post a letter for me so you may catch him at the post office."

McLeary nodded. "Thank you."

The constable went straight for the post office only to discover Tavish had left moments ago. He stood outside the building, rubbing his gloved hands together to warm them, and looked up and down the street. "Where are you now, Tavish?"

At that moment, McLeary caught sight of the young man across the street and watched him disappear into a close. Knowing the homeless were not fond of law enforcement, McLeary crossed the street and peeked inside to see Tavish warming his hands at the fire. Hoping to catch the young man's attention, he stood just outside the opening with his hands clasped behind his back. He rocked up onto the balls of his feet as he waited.

An old man held his hands before the warming fire. He looked at the constable, fearing the worst. "The officer must think one of us is guilty of something."

John and Tavish both looked at the opening of the close. John lowered his cap over his eyes and retreated into the darkness.

"I must be on my way," Tavish lied, "there's another shopkeeper I need to see." He left the close, pretending to ignore the constable, and turned left to stay out of sight of those within.

McLeary waited a moment before turning in the direction of his informant.

Keeping a watchful eye on the officer, John raised an eyebrow. He went to the opening and peeked around the corner to see Tavish and the constable talking. Leaning forward, he listened.

"Inglis and Horner Silk Shop was robbed last night. The thieves made away with some expensive stock." McLeary explained.

"Did they, now?" Even though he wore gloves, Tavish tucked his hands into his pockets to keep them warm.

"Like the other robberies, there was no forced entry."

Tavish looked about the street as if ignoring the officer. He thought he saw someone's head disappear into the close.

McLeary went on to explain. "There's a reward of one hundred fifty pounds. Anyone involved in the robbery can receive a King's Pardon for evidence leading to the thieves' capture." The constable looked up and down the street. "I doubt you've done anything that needs a King's Pardon." He grinned and looked at Tavish.

"I didn't see anything. I wasn't in that part of the city. I was feeding a fire in a close for most of the night, then I went to a pub to warm myself and have a draft. I can ask others if they saw something." Tavish looked about the street to see if anyone was watching him.

"Aye, I appreciate you doing so." McLeary walked away.

John peeked around the corner again, not pleased by what he overheard. "A one-hundred-fifty pounds and a King's Pardon, he says. Interesting. It would allow me to start over and wipe my record clean." He left the close and hurried away in the opposite direction.

~

At their established day and time, under the cover of nightfall, the men gathered to plan their next robbery.

"I've weighed our options," the leader began, "the Edinburgh Excise Office will be next."

The others glanced at each other, fearing to express their true feeling about the choice.

A brave one ventured to speak his mind. "That's a bit bold. What makes you think we can pull it off and get away with such a large sum?"

"Aye, it's bold but rewarding and worth the risk. The office closes at eight o'clock. The night watchman goes on duty at ten o'clock. We'll have plenty of time to take what we want and get out undetected."

One man smiled, a twinkle of greed in his eye. "Aye, there's a vast wealth to be had."

"Do you have a key that works?" The key maker goaded.

With a snort, the leader replied, "Aye. I visited the other day. It was hanging on a nail on the wall. I took a mold of it with a bit of clay."

A man turned to another. "What of the snitch you spoke of?" Announced another.

"I've no intention of getting caught." He replied. "I'll make sure there's no trouble for us."

~

Tavish waited inside the kirk door for the Mass to end. He stood with his hat in his hands. It was Haggadah's habit to stand at the back of the nave, so he knew she would be among the first to leave. He spoke to the priest the day before and hoped to delay her from visiting her mother's grave until everyone had left the kirk. Tavish rotated his hat within his hands and shifted his weight from one foot to the other.

"Amen." The priest announced as he made the sign of the cross in the air, blessing the congregation.

Tavish watched the priest as the clergyman greeted a few members while others began leaving the kirk. Haggadah was soon by his side. "If you don't mind, I took a chill earlier. Would you stay inside with me while I warm up a wee bit longer?"

A gust of icy wind came through the open door of the kirk, blowing Haggadah's hair over her eyes. Brushing the strawberry-blonde strands aside, she knew her visit with her mother would be short and reasoned the delay would matter little. She smiled and threaded her arm with his. "I'll wait with you." They stood silently and watched the people exit.

Tavish looked toward the altar where the priest waited. He nodded, indicating he was ready. "Haggadah, there's something I want to ask you." He looked down into her steel-gray eyes as he clasped her hands in his. "Do you love me, Lass?"

She stared at his face, trying to determine why he was questioning her affection for him. "Aye."

"I'm hoping to get an apprenticeship to learn a craft soon. Even though I've given you every coin I can spare, I still need to make a proper wage to provide for us. I pray we're wed and blessed with bairns someday, but I hate the thought of us being homeless, cold and wet at night, with our bairns shivering and hungry. So, I'm asking for your hand, a handfasting, my promise to better myself and wed you properly in a year."

Haggadah's mouth dropped open. "Handfasting?" She noticed the priest waiting at the base of the altar. A smile grew slowly on her face until she could no longer contain the grin.

"Will you be patient? Can you wait a year until I can do what I wish for you, for us?"

"Aye. I can be patient. I'd wait forever, if need be, just to have you as my husband."

He released Haggadah's hands, cupped her face, and gently pressed his lips to hers. "The priest is waiting for us. Shall we commit to each other today, now?"

Haggadah stared into his chestnut eyes. She saw intensity and sincerity within them.

She nodded. "Aye."

"Then will you accept our temporary bondage until better times fall upon us?"

Haggadah chuckled, tears welling in her eyes. "Aye."

Tavish threw his head back and laughed, thrilled by her heartfelt reply. He touched his forehead to hers. "Then let's not keep the priest waiting."

They walked up the aisle as the last person left the nave.

The gravediggers had been sworn to secrecy for several weeks. Now that the day was here, Davis and Wiley slipped inside the kirk and stood quietly to witness their friends' commitment to each other.

Tavish pulled a purple ribbon from his coat pocket and handed it to the priest. He looked at Haggadah, whose eyebrows were raised in question. "It was a gift from the dressmaker."

She assumed Tavish often ran an errand for the woman. It was kind of her to give him the ribbon. "It's bonnie."

Accepting the ribbon from Tavish, the priest began. "The handfasting I'm about to perform is a ceremony where you take an oath to each other. You are committing to be loyal for a year. At the end of the year, you are to return to the kirk and indicate if you wish to remain together for eternity or part ways. Do you understand?"

The couple looked at each other. Haggadah nodded.

"Aye." Agreed Tavish.

The priest went on to explain. "Any child you conceive before you are properly wed will be considered legitimate." He looked at Tavish and Haggadah, who each nodded their understanding.

"Well then, face one another, taking hold of each other's right and left hands, making your arms cross." He waited as they did so, then used the ribbon to gently tie it around their entwined arms. "This ribbon represents your promise to remain loyal, honest, and devoted to each other during your engagement. Do you promise to do so?" The priest looked at the couple to ensure they understood their covenant.

Tavish looked from the priest to the love of his life. "I promise."

Haggadah spoke softly. "Aye, I promise." She grinned.

The priest continued as he made the sign of the cross over the couple's entwined arms. "May the Lord bless and watch over you both in the coming year. Amen." He untied the ribbon and handed it back to Tavish. "May God be with you both."

"Thank you." Tavish accepted the ribbon and shook the clergyman's hand.

Haggadah nodded her appreciation and smiled at her husband-to-be. Even though it was still unclear where they would reside someday, she would hold onto the promise that the issue would be resolved within a year.

The gravediggers congratulated the happy couple before they left the kirk, arm in arm.

Tavish handed the ribbon to his betrothed. "Keep this safe. We can display it in our home someday."

She smiled, tucking it into her overcoat pocket. "Come with me to my mum's grave."

They stood before Freya's resting place, its white stone marking where her head lay.

"Hello, Mum. I've exciting news. Tavish and I were handfasted today. He's a good man, and I ken you would like him."

Tavish was compelled to speak. "Hello. I don't ken if you remember me. I helped you to Grizel's cottage. I've watched over Haggadah since your death and have fallen in love with her. I promise to take good care of your daughter." He smiled at his bride-to-be. "I'm sure you'll watch over us to make sure I do. We will wed in a year. We ken you will be there in spirit for our happy day."

A gust of wind reminded the couple of the frigid weather.

Haggadah shivered. "I think Tavish and I are eager to get in the warmth of the cottage. I love you. Goodbye, Mum."

~

A knock sounded upon the cottage door, drawing Grizel's attention away from the fire she was stoking. She placed a log on the dying embers and went to the door. On the other side was a frantic woman.

"My daughter, she can't breathe. I don't ken what else to do. I need your help."

"How old is the bairn?"

"Three."

"Ah, a wee one." The healer glanced at the young mother's wringing hands before looking at her concerned face. "Wait while I gather my healing herbs." She shut the door, opened the apothecary, and began pulling herbs, salves, and teas. She placed them in her satchel, put on her overcoat, and left the cottage to tend to the ill child. As she stepped into an intersection, she saw Tavish and Haggadah arm in arm in the distance, but continued on her way, knowing the treatment of the child was urgent.

~

Haggadah squinted her eyes as she looked in the distance at Grizel. "I wonder who is sick." She pointed at the healer as she crossed the intersection with another woman.

"Aye. I'm sure Grizel will do her best to cure the person." Tavish watched as the town healer disappeared behind a building.

The happy couple walked briskly, anticipating the warmth of the fire in the cottage.

Once through the gate and inside, Tavish hung his coat and hat on a peg while Haggadah hung her coat beside his. Alone, an awkwardness swelled between them. Now that they were handfasted, the change in their relationship became a reality. Haggadah began to fidget with her fingers, uncertain of what to do.

When she turned to face Tavish, he pulled her near his body and wrapped his arms around her waist.

"If you've got a mind to, I wish to fulfill my commitment." He kissed her forehead and stared into her eyes, hoping she wanted the same.

Haggadah exhaled, hesitant in her reply.

He scowled. "You need not be afraid of me."

She nodded.

"Then tell me what you're thinking?" He waited. "Are you fearing pain?"

Haggadah looked at the fire to compose her thoughts. "I understand the handfasting terms. I fear I may become with bairn, and Grizel will throw me out. We don't have a place to live, and I don't want to end up like my mum."

"You heard the priest. According to the rules of handfasting, if you conceive, the bairn will be legitimate." He reasoned.

"Aye, but we didn't ask Grizel for permission to handfast."

"Do you wish to keep our engagement a secret from her?"

"For now, aye."

Tavish raised a devilish eyebrow. "Then our consummation can be kept a secret, too." He looked about the room. "I won't live here even though I'm entitled to now. How often do you think we'll find ourselves alone in the cottage?"

"Not often."

Tavish pulled her closer to him. "Shall we take advantage of this time then, alone together?" He moved a strand of hair away from her eye.

Haggadah nodded.

"Then, may I kiss you?"

Haggadah grinned. She did not want to appear too bold, yet not shy either, for she wanted to be kissed. "Aye."

Tavish had kissed other women, but not one he cared so deeply about as Haggadah. He removed one hand from her waist, placed his index knuckle under her chin, and elevated her lips to meet his. He hesitated, glancing at her closed eyes. She was willing to accept his advance. Tavish pressed his lips to hers. His eyes closed, savoring the moment, uncertain how often they would share this special time together.

Haggadah's heartbeat quickened. His embrace was warm, and his lips were soft. She wrapped her arms around his waist, hoping the kiss would last longer, but he pulled away before hugging her.

"I promise to not get you with a bairn. I've been told of a way." He led her to the ladder and motioned to the loft.

The corners of her mouth turned upward. She placed her foot on the lowest rung and began to climb.

Chapter 22

After a month of being blissfully engaged to Haggadah, Tavish walked toward his favorite close to bed down for the night. Even though the evening was warm, he went to the fire as he entered and listened to the men converse.

"Spring is coming early this year."

"Aye, it's quite mild for the end of February."

Tavish looked toward the opening of the close as he heard "Gardi loo!" echo from the street. The splash of the chamber pots' contents fell on the cobblestone gutter. But then he heard another odd sound, one of a whimpering female nearby. Concerned, he went to see if he could help, but as he turned to see a woman huddled outside the close entrance, his sight faded to black.

"Well done," a man said to the woman. "Here's a bit of fabric for your troubles." He pulled it from his pocket and tossed it toward his accomplice.

The woman caught the expensive ebony cambric. She smiled as she watched Tavish's hat fall into the sewage-filled gutter and the worn soles of his shoes disappear into the darkness as he was dragged away.

~

Haggadah waited for Tavish to arrive at the cottage and escort her to the kirk for Mass. As time ticked by, she feared she would miss the service. Finally, she walked to the kirk by herself. She assumed Tavish would meet her there. Haggadah scanned the kirkyard for him, then went inside for Mass. When the service ended, the bench he sometimes sat on was empty. Haggadah visited her mother's grave, voicing her concern about Tavish's absence to her and any spirit who would listen. When she finished her visit, Haggadah sought out Davis and Wiley, hoping her husband-to-be was helping them dig a grave.

The gravediggers paused in their work as they saw Haggadah walking toward them.

"Have you seen Tavish?" She glanced at the half-dug hole in the ground.

Wiley shook his head.

"He didn't come with you today?" Davis placed the blade of his shovel on the ground.

"No." Placing her hands in her coat pockets, Haggadah felt something and pulled out the purple handfasting ribbon. She had forgotten to put it in a safe place and stuffed it into the bottom of her pocket. Haggadah scanned the headstones in the kirkyard. A foreboding settled within her heart. She felt a sharp pain on the back of her head and placed the palm of her hand over it. "There's something terribly wrong."

Wiley and Davis looked at each other. They had the feeling Haggadah was right.

~

A groan escaped Tavish's lips as he cracked open his eyes. He placed the palm of his hand on the back of his aching head and felt a bump encrusted with what he assumed was dried blood. His body lethargically rocked back and forth as he lay on a burlap bag filled with something unknown. He listened to the creaking of wood and the sloshing of water that sounded like waves lapping on a shore. Tavish sat up, causing dizziness to blur his vision and his stomach to summersault. He took a deep breath, praying not to vomit, and hoped everything would stop spinning. Widening his eyes to clear the blurriness of his vision, Tavish focused on the golden lines of light shining between the cracks of roughly cut wood. Looking about in the darkness, he saw silhouettes of barrels, crates, and other items around him. He crawled to the widest crack of light, grasped the nearby barrel to help him stand, and peeked through the gap to see a crude staircase on the opposite side of the next room. Feeling along the wall, he discovered a door and pushed it, but it was bolted on the other side. He tried ramming it with his shoulder, but it remained closed. "Hey!" Tavish winced as the volume of his voice caused his head to throb. He balled his hand into a fist and pounded on the door. With no response to his plea, he sank to the floor and leaned against the door to wait for someone to come to his aid.

Hours ticked by. Tavish began to wonder if he would ever be set free. Was it daytime or night? He needed to walk Haggadah to and from Mass. He prayed she would wait until he arrived.

Tavish fell backward as the door was unbarred and opened. He looked up at the round face staring down at him.

"What do we have here?"

Tavish shielded his eyes from the lamp's brightness hanging from a peg beside the door. "Tavish, my name is Tavish. Where am I?"

"On the Lord Stanley. You've been shanghaied, I assume. I'll need to take you to the captain." The cook grasped Tavish's upper arm and helped him walk up the stairs. They ascended several levels before stopping before a beautifully carved wooden door. The cook knocked.

"Enter." Commanded a deep, resinous voice.

The cook opened the door and pushed Tavish before him. "Captain, I found him in storage."

The captain looked up from the navigational chart he was studying on a large table. He scanned the young man from head to toe.

"The lad's been shanghaied." The cook added.

Tavish reached for his hat to respectfully remove it from his head, but it was not there.

"Has he now." He looked from the cook to the young man. "Your name?"

Tavish's vision blurred. He sidestepped as the ship swayed. He looked at the beamed ceiling where a lantern swung back and forth before focusing on the nicely dressed man beneath it. The captain was a stout man of middle age. "Tavish."

"Tavish, you are aboard the Lord Stanley. I'm Captain James White. Against your will, you're accompanying us on our voyage. You look able-bodied. You'll work for your food. Do a good job, and I may pay you for your time."

"I don't ken anything about shipping," Tavish confessed.

"You look bright. I'm confident you'll learn quickly. If you can't get along with the crew or don't do your share of work, I'll sell you as an indentured servant."

"Where are we now?" Tavish managed to ask as he scanned the quarters for a window.

"We cast off from Edinburgh hours ago. The Lord Stanley has been recently sold, but we must fulfill its last contract of dropping off prisoners before picking up cargo and heading to the West Indies and America."

"When do we return to Edinburgh?"

"We?" White chuckled. "After dropping off prisoners, the Lord Stanley will become a cargo ship transporting enslaved people, part of the Triangle Trade. We have no plans to return to Edinburgh."

~

"I'm worried." Haggadah confessed. "He hasn't come by in three days. Do you think something happened to Tavish?"

Grizel suspected foul play was involved. It was not like Tavish to be away from Haggadah for over half a day, let alone three. "Go to Constable McLeary. Maybe he has been in contact with Tavish."

"Aye." Haggadah grabbed her overcoat from the peg, stuffed her arms into the sleeves, and left the cottage. She hurried to the station house as dreadful thoughts of Tavish's demise invaded her mind. Haggadah stepped into the lobby and approached the constable at the desk. Her heart raced as she waited politely for the officer to look up from his paperwork. Her concern for her betrothed caused threatening tears to well in her eyes. Unable to control her worry, she blurted. "My betrothed is missing."

The constable looked at the young woman standing before him, scanned her clothing, and assumed she was homeless. He had dealt with frantic women whose husbands shacked up with prostitutes or passed out in a close after a drunken binge before. Most men eventually returned to their wives when they were good and ready. "For how long?"

"Three days."

"That is not a very long time. Are you certain your betrothed is not in a pub drowning his sorrows?"

"No, Tavish and I were just handfasted a month ago. He would not leave me." Her bottom lip quivered. "I ken something terrible has happened to him."

The constable placed a small piece of paper, pen, and ink before her. "Write his name and a description. Please write your name and where you live. If we find him, we'll contact you."

Haggadah scribbled the description of Tavish. She was tempted to write 'handsome,' but it was her biased opinion. Returning the pen to the inkwell, she reviewed her information before handing it to the officer. "Is Constable McLeary here?"

"Let me check the schedule." The officer left his desk and disappeared down the hallway.

While Haggadah waited, she scanned the people sitting in chairs around the room's perimeter. They stared at her judgmentally. She looked away as she heard approaching footsteps.

The officer returned to his desk. "Lass, he is on duty now."

"On duty? Where?"

"High Street near the South Bridge."

"Thank you." She left the station house and went directly to the intersection, but the constable was not there. "Oh, Tavish, you better have a good excuse for disappearing." She hurried down the street, looking left and right, checking every close and sidewalk before every establishment for the constable. McLeary was nowhere in sight.

"You seem flustered, Lass."

Haggadah turned around to see Constable McLeary standing behind her.

"I am. Tavish is missing. Or at least I think he is. He has been gone for three days. Have you seen him? Do you ken where he is?"

McLeary scratched his chin. He had not seen the young man either. "Let's ask the shop owners if he has been by. They depend on him to run their posts and do other errands. Perhaps they've seen him."

They stopped by several shops, but everyone they asked shook their heads.

"No, I haven't seen him in several days. I had to give my letters to another lad to post them for me." Mister Dingwall explained with a tinge of guilt in his heart. "It's not like Tavish to disappear. He's a dependable and hard-working young man."

Worried more than ever, Haggadah followed the constable out of the shop.

"Oh, I feel it in my bones. Something is terribly wrong." Haggadah's eyes welled with tears as she turned toward the officer.

McLeary looked up and down the sidewalk. "Now, don't think the worst. I'll do some investigating and let you ken what I find." He reassured her.

"Aye, thank you." Haggadah's heart ached as she turned away from the constable. Admitting defeat for now, she stared at the cobbles of the sidewalk and began walking home while scanning each close, hoping to find Tavish.

An object in the sewer-filled gutter caused her to stop abruptly. It was Tavish's flat cap. A tear trickled down her cheek as she lifted the soiled and sodden hat, went to the nearest well, and rinsed it as best she could. She knew Tavish had worked hard to earn the coins to purchase it. He took great pride in his hat and would never part with it unless forced.

Haggadah was convinced that fate had not been kind to her beloved betrothed. Her heart seemed empty, hollow. She knew Tavish would never leave her without saying goodbye. They were to be properly married. They were in love. Other than Grizel, she thought of the only person she could share her concern with and headed there with the dripping hat dangling from her hand.

Chapter 23

People on the sidewalk stepped aside as the determined apprentice rushed to the kirkyard. Haggadah ran through the gate and to her mother's grave, collapsed to her knees, and made the sign of the cross on her body. "God, if you can hear me, please keep Tavish safe, wherever he may be. Mum," sorrow crept into her voice as she pleaded, "if you are able, watch over him. Let him ken that I love him, that I'll keep the promise of our vows, and wait for him until the day he returns."

Davis paused in his digging. "I see Haggadah is here."

Wiley held a shovelful of dirt and looked toward Freya's grave. "Aye, she's praying." He scowled. "She seems troubled."

"Aye, and I aim to find out why." Davis speared his shovel into the ground, welcoming the break in his labor.

Wiley threw the contents of his shovel onto the pile of dirt, pushed the blade of his tool into the ground, and followed.

The pair stood silently and waited until Haggadah rose and turned toward them.

"Are you troubled, Lass?" Davis began.

Haggadah wiped her eyes of dampness. "Aye. Tavish has disappeared. I've not seen him in three days." She looked down at the hat in her hand. "I found it in the gutter."

Wiley adjusted the hat on his head. "Three days, you say."

"Aye."

"It's unlikely a newly handfasted man runs off. Tavish loves you." Davis added.

"Have you seen him?" She glanced from one friend to the other.

The gravediggers shook their heads.

Haggadah bit her bottom lip and shook her head as the loss of her betrothed seemed like shards of glass piercing her heart. "I don't sense him nearby. He's gone."

The gravediggers looked at each other, fearing the same. "We'll send word if . . ." Davis began.

Haggadah glared at the gravedigger, unwilling to hear his unspoken suggestion that Tavish may be dead. She turned and left the kirkyard.

Sensing her apprentice's state of mind as Haggadah entered the cottage and went directly to the washtub, Grizel made tea and retrieved biscuits from the cupboard. She noted Haggadah had yet to take off her overcoat. "Would you like to add hot water to whatever you are washing?"

Haggadah stilled her hands and looked at Grizel.

Seeing her tear-streaked face and bloodshot gray eyes staring back at her, Grizel went to her apprentice's side. "What troubles you?"

Lifting the hat from the clouded water, Haggadah sighed. "I found his cap in the gutter."

Grizel recalled Tavish's hat, always atop his head. "We'll clean it as best we can, put it near the fire to dry, and hang it on a peg for him to have when he returns. First, let me take your overcoat."

Haggadah dried her hands on the towel and slipped off her coat.

Grizel hung the garment on a peg and retrieved the kettle. "This should help get it clean." She added hot water to the washtub.

~

Tavish stared at the sea dancing along the horizon. He knew Haggadah would be worried, but he could do nothing to ease her mind. He was on a course to a place he had never heard of and had no idea when he would return to Edinburgh, if ever.

"Get to work before I get out the cat 'o nine tails and flog you." The Chief Mate threatened.

Dipping the rag mop in the bucket of seawater, Tavish returned to swabbing the deck.

~

The following week, in the dead of night, men dressed in black gathered in Chessel Court.

The leader looked at one of the men. "Well, is there still a concern about tonight?"

"No, there should be no trouble," he said confidently.

"Good." The leader went on to explain. "Let's review the plan. The building will be locked at eight o'clock when the last employee leaves for the night. The nightwatchman arrives at ten. We've only two hours to enter the building, take the money, and leave without being seen." He instructed the others. "You ken what to do." He looked at the man to his right.

"Aye, I'll watch from behind the fence. If someone should approach the office, I'll sound the whistle once. If it becomes an emergency, I'll sound the whistle three times." He watched as the other men nodded to indicate they understood the plan. "If I give the warning of three whistles, then I'll go through the Excise Garden and help those inside through the back window of the hallway." He held up the stick he had been given for his only defense. "And do my best to stop anyone who gets in the way of our escape."

"The three of us will enter through the door with this key." The leader dangled it for the men to see. "As I stated, I visited the Edinburgh Excise Office over the past few months and made a clay impression of the key that hung on the wall near the front door. It's a brilliant likeness." He grinned with pride. "When I was there, I watched a cashier take money from two desk drawers in the office. The two of you will get the money while I stand by the door and watch for anyone approaching or trying to enter." He patted the pair of pistols tucked in his belt. "Do you have your pistols loaded and ready?"

He looked at the men who would join him inside the building. The partners in crime held up their guns.

The kirk's bell rang the eighth hour as the four men walked through the dimly lit streets to the Excise Office. One man took his place behind the fence with his whistle and stick ready.

The leader inserted the handmade key into the lock and rotated it. The lock clicked open. He looked at the others with a conceded grin, pushed the door open, and the three thieves scurried into the darkened office, closing the door behind them.

He stood behind the door and clicked the lock shut while the two men opened the cashier's office door with a pair of curling irons and began looking in the cash drawers. One of the thieves was so pleased by the large sum they would acquire he started to sing in a whisper, "The Beggers Opera."

The man watching from behind the fence saw a familiar gentleman in the distance walking toward the office. "It's James Bonar." He assumed the employee was returning to retrieve something he had forgotten in the office. "Och." He blew the whistle three times, raced to the Excise Garden in the Canongate, threw the stick on the ground, and waited by the window designated for the escape.

Bonar inserted his key in the door, heard the lock click, and pushed it open, forcing the leader behind it to back against the wall.

The thief paused with money in his hand. "Did you hear a door open?"

"It's being watched. Grab what you can." The other ordered, unconcerned by the noise.

As the employee hurried to a stairway, the leader recognized his opportunity to remain undetected and left the building. Once outside, he looked at his pocket watch. It was eight-thirty.

Pulling a second cash drawer open, the thief paused and listened. He whispered. "Do you hear footsteps?"

The other looked at the ceiling as the footfalls sounded overhead. "Aye. Something's amiss." He looked down into the drawer, knowing they managed to only take a small amount of the cash.

"Cock your pistols." He pulled his pair of pistols from his belt while his partner did the same. They left the office and looked toward the footfalls coming down the stairs. Seeing the shadow of a man, the pair hid and waited until the man left the building, locking the door before walking away.

"Apparently, our fearless leader has left us. The door is locked. We've no key," said one as he stood from hiding behind a desk.

"Aye, and the nightwatchman will be here soon. We'll have to break it down." The thieves smashed the front door and disappeared into the night with only sixteen pounds stuffed in their pockets.

Hearing the noise and rapid footfalls on the cobblestone street, the man in the garden hid behind a bush until silence greeted his ears. Tiptoeing from behind the building, he looked about the empty street before emerging into the lamplight and walking away.

With the robbery turning sour, one member recognized the perfect opportunity to exonerate himself. He slowed to a walk, lowered his head, and tucked his hands in his pants pockets. He went straight to the station house.

The constable at the desk looked toward the door as a man dressed in black entered. "May I help you?"

John placed the pair of pistols on the officer's desk. "Aye. I'm here to ask for a King's Pardon."

"Are you now?" The constable picked up the pistols and examined them. "And why would you be wanting a King's Pardon?"

"Because I'm one of the men who was involved in robbing the Edinburgh Excise Office at Chessels Court tonight. I ken who else was involved."

The constable had his doubts as he eyed the vagrant up and down. How could he afford the pistols? He wondered if the confessor had drank too much whiskey. "Very well." He tilted his head toward the hallway door, stood, and placed the weapons in a secure cupboard behind the desk.

John stepped into the hallway and waited for the constable to join him.

"You'll spend the night in a cell until an officer can take your statement in the morning. The constable unlocked the barred door, waited for the confessor to enter, and turned the key to ensure the man remained inside.

John sat on the bench, leaned against the wall, pulled his hat over his eyes, and dozed.

~

Beginning her daily chores, Amelia opened Brodie's bedroom door and stared at the heap of dark clothing puddled on the floor. "Does he think I'm here to cater to his every need? My goodness gracious glory above, do I need to wipe his arse too?" She stooped over and gathered the clothing from the floor. Glancing at the dresser, she exhaled in disgust. "And the man should learn to lock up these pistols. Someone could get hurt." She tossed the soiled clothes on the bed and removed the painting from the wall to reveal a locked cabinet. She used her ring of keys to unlock the secret cupboard, put the pistols inside, and secured it with a twist of her key. After rehanging the oil painting and ensuring it hung straight, she gathered the clothes and left the room.

~

McLeary, on his way to the station house to report for duty, saw several officers in a wagon pass him by at a rapid pace. When he entered the lobby, the constable at the desk stood.

"Niven wants you to meet him at the Excise Office. There has been a robbery. When you return, a man waiting in a cell wants his statement taken. He is asking for a King's Pardon in exchange for information about the same robbery."

With a nod, McLeary forewent his morning coffee, turned, and walked to the Edinburgh Excise Office. He knew it was in his best interest not to keep his superior waiting.

The city was abuzz as word spread of the theft. Nosy bystanders watched the constables inspect the building from top to bottom.

After a quick scan of the area, McLeary reported to his superior.

"McLeary, we aren't certain how the thief got inside, but it's easy to see where he got out." Nevin pointed to the front door, with its frame splintered at the strike plate. "I thought you should be involved." They stepped inside. "The cashier's office door was forced open. The employee, a Mister James Bonar, examined the cash drawers. Only sixteen pounds is missing. He returned to the building after it closed last night but did not notice anything amiss or out of place until he saw the broken door this morning."

"What time did he return to the building?"

"Approximately half past eight. The only other evidence may be a thick stick found in the garden. A crude weapon, perhaps."

"From what I understand, a man is waiting in a cell for their statement to be taken. He's asking for a King's Pardon in exchange for information about this robbery."

"Interesting. Do you think he is credible?"

McLeary shrugged his shoulder. "I'll find out when I take his statement."

"Very well."

McLeary noticed the key hanging on the wall by the door as he left the building. "Another easily accessible key." He muttered to himself. As he began to walk to the station house, he wondered about Tavish. He had not heard if the young man had been found. McLeary had inquired with many of the homeless, but those who knew him merely shook their heads. Out of curiosity, he wandered to the healer's cottage, hoping word of Tavish had reached Haggadah.

The constable walked up the flagstone pathway, took a deep breath, and knocked on the old oak door.

Grizel cracked open the door and peered out. She widened the opening before stating, "Constable McLeary? Are you well?"

"Aye, Grizel. I was wondering if you or Haggadah have received any word of Tavish?"

"No." Grizel looked behind her, ensuring Haggadah was out of earshot. "It's been nearly a week. Haggadah is quite heartbroken and fears the worst has happened to him."

"I've asked many who ken him. If they do ken what happened to him, they're too frightened to talk. Many are puzzled by his disappearance, too. He was well-liked."

Haggadah entered the back door with a basket of eggs over her arm. She looked at the front door and saw the constable. Her heart skipped a beat, hoping he had brought good news about her betrothed. She placed the basket on the worktable and joined Grizel. "Hello, Constable McLeary. Have you heard from Tavish?"

He disliked being the bearer of bad news. "I've yet to find out where he may be. I've asked, but no one seems to ken."

Haggadah nodded and looked down at her hands as she entwined her fingers.

"Don't give up hope, Lass. I ken he had strong feelings for you. If he were able, he would be here."

"Aye." Her eyes began to well with tears. "Thank you."

"I must get to the station house." McLeary touched his index finger to the brim of his hat. "I'll let you ken if I receive any word about him. Good day." He turned to leave.

As he reached the gate, Haggadah followed him. "Constable."

He paused with the gate open and looked at Haggadah as she stopped before him.

She whispered so Grizel, who remained in the cottage doorway, could not hear. "I wanted to tell you that Tavish and I were handfasted just before he disappeared. I ken he would not leave me. He loves me, and I love him."

He glanced at Grizel. "I assume Grizel does not ken."

Haggadah shook her head.

"No worries, Lass. I'll keep your secret." With a nod, he passed through the gate and went directly to the station house.

"I have a note from the night shift for you." The desk constable handed McLeary the scribbled message.

McLeary's eyebrows raised in question as he read the final notation. "Pistols?"

Turning in his chair, the officer retrieved the pistols from the locked cupboard. "Aye." He placed them on the desk.

Picking up each weapon, McLeary examined them before handing the pistols back to the constable. He entered the door into the hallway and paused to watch the officer return the guns to the secure cupboard. "Well, we shall see what he has to confess."

McLeary instructed the guard to release the tattle-tale witness and take him to an inquisition room while he retrieved the necessary paperwork. He nodded to the guard standing outside of the room, silently dismissing him before he entered.

"I'm Constable McLeary. I've been told you wish to ask for a King's Pardon." McLeary began as he sat at the table, opened the folder, and readied a pen to take the man's statement.

"Aye." John replied.

Intrigued, McLeary scanned the man's black clothing and stared the confessor dead in the eye. He recalled the King's Pardon offered for the robbery of the Inglis and Horner Silk Shop and the large reward. McLeary suspected the man across from him might fabricate a story just to collect the hefty sum. However, if this man had any information about who was involved in the fabric shop robbery, he took his time bringing it to the forefront. "What do you need pardoning for?" He tilted his head and waited for a reply.

"Many call me John Brown."

McLeary remembered Tavish mentioning the man's name.

My real name is Humphrey Moore." He watched as the officer's eyebrows raised in recognition.

"Aye, Mister Moore. You've evaded us for quite some time."

Moore grinned. "Aye, that I have."

"I ken of your previous crimes, conviction, and escape from the ship. I assume it's the reason you're asking for the pardon?"

"Aye, it's part of why I'm asking."

"I don't have the authority to grant you a King's Pardon. I can take your statement and present it to my superior, who will determine if it's worth the time of a magistrate." McLeary dipped his pen in the ebony liquid.

Moore sat forward in his chair, placing his fisted hands on the table. "Edinburgh Excise Office was robbed last night." He boasted. "I ken how they got inside the building, why they left with so little cash, and why they made a hasty exit through the front door." He sat back in his chair with an arrogant grin on his face. "I can also tell you who took part in the robbery of the fabric shop and others that have plagued the city over the past two years."

McLeary sat forward in his chair. Doubt crept into his mind as he reasoned the vagrant may have merely observed the robbery from a close. The constable suspected the man would spin a wild tale to win his freedom and the reward. However, any information Moore could give would be helpful. "Now, how would you ken that?"

"I was there. I'm one of the thieves." He waited for his confession to sink in. "There are others. I can name them."

McLeary needed more proof than the thief's word. He sat back in his chair and lifted his chin in a challenge. "Tell me how you got inside each building?"

Humphery smirked. "I can do better. I can show how we did so, but we must go to Salisbury Craigs."

After requesting another constable to accompany them, a coach transported the trio to Salisbury Craigs, where Moore lifted a stone and revealed the ring of duplicate keys.

"I'm not sure if the key to the Excise Office has been added to the ring. One of the other men may still have it. The rest should be here, though." He handed the cache of keys to McLeary. "They're false keys, duplicates. That's how we entered. Except for robbery where we knew the key could be found."

McLeary examined the keys, admiring the flawless craftsmanship. If a key could be matched to a lock where a robbery occurred, the cache would be ironclad evidence. If Moore could provide the robbers' names, he would most likely receive a pardon. With the evidence in hand, McLeary was eager to return to the station house and learn the names of everyone involved and the details of each robbery. Could the convicted criminal divulge all of the information?

Chapter 24

The constable at the desk stood as Chief Inspector Niven entered the station house and passed through the hallway door. "Chief Inspector, McLeary would like you to join him in the inquisition room."

With a nod, he entered the small room to see McLeary seated across from a man.

McLeary returned his pen to the inkwell and stood. "Chief Inspector, this is Humphrey Moore. He claims to have participated in and witnessed the unsolved robberies in the city, including the Excise Office. He surrendered a pair of pistols and revealed where false keys were hidden under a rock at Salisbury Craigs. He is asking for a King's Pardon." McLeary lifted the ring of keys from the table and gave them to his superior. "He has named two other men involved in the robberies."

Niven examined the evidence.

Moore lifted his chin. "Those were made by George Smith. Andrew Ainslie came with us on the robberies."

Niven sought clarification. "There are three of you. Which robberies?"

"There's a key for each one we did, except for the Excise Office. I doubt there was time to add it to the ring." Moore clarified. "Och, and the residence of John Tapp. Why do people leave their keys in plain sight for others to use?" There was a tinge of sarcasm in his voice.

"McLeary, take several men with you and bring Ainslie and Smith in for questioning." Niven redirected his attention to the confessor. "As for you, Mister Moore, you will be placed in a cell for now. If your statement proves true, a magistrate will be presented with what you have revealed and determine if you will receive a King's Pardon." Niven opened the door and called for a constable to escort the witness to a cell.

As Moore was led out of the room, McLeary gathered a group of men and ordered a barred wagon to transport the named suspects. The team of horses pulled the portable jail to the front of the station house, and the officers climbed aboard. A slap of the reins on the horses' rumps sent the wagon toward the grocer's shop in the Cowgate to collect George Smith for questioning.

~

Hearing the bell above the door ring, George looked up from his clipboard, assuming a customer had entered. His grin faded from his face as he saw several constables instead.

McLeary announced. "George Smith, you're to accompany us to the station house for questioning."

A maid, who was shopping, looked from the constables to the grocer, returned the bag of dried barley to a shelf, and scooted out the door.

With the shop empty of customers, George scowled. "Questioning? For what?"

"For robberies within the city over the past few years. Come along now." McLeary insisted.

George took off his apron, hung it on the peg, put on his overcoat and hat, and locked the door of his shop before climbing into the back of the barred wagon.

The constables next visited the shoemaker, Andrew Ainslie. The suspected criminal joined Smith in the wagon.

~

Brodie left Ann's house just before noon and began walking home. He went to Ainslie's shoe shop to pay him a visit and turned the handle on the door, but it was locked. He cupped his hands around his face and peeked through the display window. The shop was indeed empty.

"The constables took him away in a barred wagon."

Brodie turned to see a homeless man leaning against the store. "Took him away? In a barred wagon? When?"

"An hour or so ago. My guess is he's at the station house."

The councilman nodded, confused yet curious. He continued toward home, tapping his walking stick as if announcing his presence. He paused by Smith's grocery store as he overheard two women talking.

"I watched as the constable took Mister Smith and put him in a barred wagon."

Brodie decided to investigate why the pair of men had been hauled away. He flagged down a coach and ordered the driver to go to the station house.

~

McLeary ordered the constables to put Ainslie and Smith in separate rooms for questioning and assigned Sheriff Archibold Cockburn to take Smith's statement. He heard the lobby door open while gathering paperwork. Peeking around the corner, he saw the councilman enter the station house. McLeary stepped behind the seated constable at the desk. "Deacon, how may we help you?"

Brodie tapped his walking stick on the floor as he stopped before the raised dais. "I understand George Smith and Andrew Ainslie are here. I wish to speak with each of them."

"They aren't allowed to have visitors."

The councilman lifted his chin. "May I ask why they are being retained?"

"They are being questioned. If you wish to return later, you may see them then."

"Very well." Brodie tossed his walking stick toward the ceiling, snatched it in his hand, and left the building.

McLeary shook his head. "Word travels fast." He went to his superior's office and knocked.

"Enter."

"Sir, I've Ainslie and Smith in separate rooms. Would you like to sit in on their questioning?"

"Aye, I would." He stopped and grabbed the ring of keys from the secure cupboard, put them in his pocket, and followed McLeary to the first room.

McLeary sat at the table, ready to record Ainslie's statement.

Niven stood behind the constable with his hands clasped behind his back. "Humphrey Moore came to us last night; he has confessed to being involved in the robbery of the Excise Office."

Confusion masked Ainslie's face. "Who?"

"Sir." McLeary pointed at the alias written in the file.

Niven leaned toward the file and read the name. "Och, you may ken him as John Brown."

The officers watched the color drain from the shopkeeper's face.

"He said you were involved with the robbery." McLeary pressed.

Ainsley looked from the constable to Niven. Weighing his options, he thought it best to confess. "I was, but I didn't go inside the building. I kept watch outside behind the fence. The other three entered the building just after eight o'clock. James Bonar, the Deputy Solicitor, came to the building, interrupting our heist."

McLeary scowled at the inconsistency of Moore's confession. "The other three?" Had he misheard Ainslie? "Who else was with you?"

"George was there. He's a fine locksmith. He made the keys from molds, but not all of them."

Niven pulled the ring of keys from his pocket and tossed them on the table. "These keys?"

Ainsley picked up the ring. "Aye, Deacon Brodie made some of the keys from molds, too."

McLeary's pen stilled. His eyebrows raised. "Councilman Deacon William Brodie?"

"Aye, he was the mastermind of it all."

McLeary stood and leaned toward his superior. "Sir, the councilman was just here in the station house asking to see Smith and Ainsley."

Niven glanced at Ainsley. He opened the door and ordered. "I need a prisoner escorted to a cell." Turning back to McLeary. "Go to Smith's room and confirm the councilman's involvement. I'll order the wagon."

McLeary snatched up the file before leaving the room. "Excuse me, Sheriff Cockburn," he apologized as he entered and looked at George Smith. "I'm Constable

McLeary. Mister Ainsley has confessed to the Excise Office robbery. He has implicated you, John Brown, himself, and Deacon William Brodie. Can you confirm the councilman was involved?"

Smith looked from McLeary to Cockburn. "I don't ken what he's talking about."

Cockburn exhaled. "He's tight-lipped."

McLeary clasped Cockburn's shoulder. "Put him in a cell. Perhaps he'll talk later." He met his superior in the hallway. "Smith isn't talking."

"We'll have to assume Ainsley is telling the truth. Go and fetch Brodie." Niven ordered.

McLeary gathered several officers. They climbed onto the wagon. With a slap of the reins on the horses' rumps, they raced through the city and halted their wagon before the councilman's house. McLeary pounded his fist on the door and was greeted by the maid.

Amelia eyed the officers suspiciously. "Aye? May I help you?"

"We must see Deacon Brodie." McLeary insisted.

Amelia scanned the officers standing on the stoop and the awaiting wagon. She knew the Deacon's gallivanting would catch up with him someday. Sighing, she resolved today was the day. "He is not here. He came home last night, changed his clothes, and left. I assume he's at one of his mistress's houses."

"His discarded clothes?" McLeary recalled a detail from the reported sightings of the thieves. "Would they happen to be black?" He pressed.

"Aye, but most of what he wears is black."

McLeary thought quickly. "I'd appreciate it if you would go and fetch them."

The maid raised her eyebrows in question and offered a flimsy excuse. "I haven't had a chance to wash them yet."

"It's evidence. It matters little of the garment's condition."

Shrugging her shoulders, she closed the door, went to the laundry basket she left on the kitchen floor, and retrieved the soiled clothing. "These are them." She handed the clothes to the officer.

"Thank you. What are the names of the councilman's mistresses, and where do they live?"

"I believe one is Jean Watt on Libberton's Wynd, and the other is Ann Grant in Cant's Close."

McLeary touched his index finger to his hat. "Thank you."

People stopped and stared as the barred wagon raced toward Libberton's Wynd.

The robbery of the Edinburgh Excise Office put citizens on alert. Word spread of the men who were taken in for questioning.

After questioning several people about the apartment's location, McLeary stood outside Jean's door. He knocked and listened to several approaching footfalls.

Jean opened the door, her young children at her feet, wide-eyed, stared up at the constables. "May I help you?"

"Is Deacon William Brodie here?" McLeary inquired as he motioned for an officer to search inside the home.

"Here now!" Brodie's mistress pulled her children near her as the officer rudely entered. "What makes you think you can come inside my home?"

"Is he here?" McLeary demanded.

"No, he has not been here in over a week."

The constable returned after a quick search of the home. "Aye, he's not here, Sir."

"If Brodie comes here, please send word to the station house immediately." McLeary glanced at the frightened faces of the children. "Good day." He followed his officers to the wagon.

"Has he done something wrong?" Jean received no answer to her question.

The officers went to Cant's Close. Ann confessed Brodie had spent the night and left over an hour ago. She had not seen him since.

Suspecting Brodie was on the run, McLeary sent an officer to the station house to report to his superior that Brodie may have left the city. He assumed Niven would assign the King's Messenger, George Williamson, to track down the councilman. Meanwhile, he and several men returned to Brodie's residence.

Summoned by a knock on the door, Amelia opened it to see the same constable on the stoop. "You've found no sign of him?"

"No." McLeary looked toward a building near the woodyard. "I need to search the councilman's workshop for evidence in the Excise Office robbery."

The maid glanced at the workshop door. "I've got the key in a cupboard, but the Deacon is forgetful and usually leaves it unlocked. Let me grab it just in case."

Amelia led the way to the workshop with the key in hand and pushed the door open. "Like I said, he's forgetful."

McLeary entered the workshop with his men. "Search for any correspondence, tools, molds, or keys for evidence."

The men worked quickly and confiscated several key molds. McLeary hoped a key on the ring would fit each one.

The men filed out of the workshop with the evidence in hand. McLeary scanned the interior one final time. He turned to the maid, who stood her post at the door. "I need you to lock the door and ensure no one enters. If the councilman returns home, please notify a constable or send a message to the station house immediately."

"Aye." Amelia turned the key in the lock and pushed on the door to ensure it was secure.

~

Haggadah's hands stilled as she stared blindly at nothing in particular.

Grizel sipped her tea while sitting at the table. She perceived the melancholy mood of her apprentice, something she had often recognized since Tavish's disappearance weeks ago. Even though there was enough bread for another meal, the town healer suggested Haggadah make another loaf and watched as she worked. "Do you need to add flour?"

Pulling herself away from her thoughts, Haggadah met Grizel's concerned gaze. "Aye," she said numbly, reaching her hand into the crock and sprinkling the dough with a dusting of white.

The past few weeks had been filled with worry and grief for Haggadah. Tears often threatened to spill when she allowed herself to dwell on Tavish's absence.

On particularly emotional days, Grizel redirected her apprentice's attention to working in the garden, helping restock herbs, and tending to the unhealthy.

Haggadah went to gather eggs while the bread was baking. She paused near the coop and looked in the direction of the harbor. Feeling a strong urge to be near the waterfront, she returned inside and placed the basket of eggs on the worktable. A restlessness settled within her soul, urging her to leave the cottage. After removing the baked bread from the Dutch oven and placing it on a cutting board to cool, she put on her overcoat. "I'm going for a walk."

"The walk will do you good." Grizel poured herself another cup of tea.

The sky was gloomy, but not threatening as Haggadah wandered to the waterfront, sat on a bench, and watched the ships come and go. She questioned how her heart contained an unexplained hollowness yet continued to beat without interruption. She knew Tavish was alive, but sensed he was far away.

She walked to the station house hoping for news about Tavish's whereabouts, but the constable at the desk looked at her as she entered the lobby and shook his head. She turned to leave and sidestepped a man standing behind her. He nodded politely as she walked by him. Haggadah thought he resembled the seaworthy captain. She paused with her hand on the doorknob, purposely delaying her exit from the lobby. She stepped toward the stranger and listened momentarily before sitting in a vacant chair near the door.

"I'm Lewis Geddes. I had a passenger on my ship, the *Endeavour*, named John Dixon. He paid me to drop him off in Flushing, the Netherlands, said he was going to Ostend, and gave me these letters. He asked me to give them to his mistress on Cant's Close. I felt something wasn't right about the gent and thought you should have them." He handed the small stack of letters to the constable.

The officer read the name 'Ann Grant' on the first letter and shuffled through the stack to ensure they were all addressed to the same person. He opened the top letter, read its contents, and noted the vague signature. He looked at the man's weathered face, who awaited his dismissal. "Aye, these are of great interest to us. If you pass through that door, Constable McLeary would like to question you further."

Geddes nodded, complied with the officer's request, and was escorted to a small room.

"Please be seated. I'll notify the constable who is overseeing this case." The officer went to McLeary's desk. "I've put Mister Geddes in a room for questioning."

He placed the stack of letters with the open correspondence before McLeary.

McLeary drank a gulp of coffee, set his mug down, and leaned forward to scan the script. His eyebrows raised as he read the signature. "Och, this may be the lead we've been looking for." He took the letters and case file and went to the inquisition room.

McLeary entered the room. "Mister Geddes?"

The seaman stood from his chair. "Aye."

"I'm Constable McLeary." He announced, motioning Geddes to return to his seat as he sat across from him. He placed the file and letters on the table. "You've brought us some interesting correspondence. Thank you for bringing them to our attention. We've been searching for a gentleman associated with this woman for a few weeks."

"Aye, as I told the officer at the desk, I felt something was amiss. The man was a little too insistent. He said his name was John Dixon. I dropped him off at Flushing, the Netherlands. He was headed to Ostend. He appeared to be a man on the run."

"Can you describe him? Build? Height?" McLeary dipped his pen in the ink and jotted down the man's description. The witness gave a spot-on match to Deacon William Brodie. "Thank you, Mister Geddes, I appreciate you bringing your concern to our attention,"

McLeary added, gathering the file and letters. "If I may retain you a moment longer, I would like to inform my superior."

"Certainly." Geddes sat back in his chair.

Taking commanding strides, McLeary went to Niven's office, knocked, and placed the letters on his superior's desk. "Mister Geddes has presented this evidence of Deacon William Brodie, posing under the name of John Dixon. Brodie was on his ship, paid him to drop him in Flushing, Netherlands, and instructed Geddes to give these letters to his mistress when docking in Edinburgh. Geddes brought the letters to us instead."

Niven scanned the open letter, noting the signature. He looked at McLeary. "And you believe it to be authentic?"

"Aye."

"Then notify Williamson of the lead in the case. Tell him to leave immediately. Let's hope he doesn't lose Brodie's trail this time." He returned the evidence to McLeary, who went to his desk, scribbled down the possible location where Brodie could be found, and went to the lobby desk.

"Send a message to the King's Messenger." He gave the constable the note and saw Haggadah sitting near the door. He went to his desk and grabbed the paper with Tavish's description.

Returning to the inquisition room, McLeary handed Geddes the paper. "Thank you, Mister Geddes. We appreciate you bringing your concern to our attention. You have indeed given us the lead we needed to apprehend Brodie." He presented Haggadah's written description. "We also have a young man missing. Tavish is his name."

Mister Geddes read Haggadah's description and shook his head. "The only way he would get on the ship is if he were shanghaied or hired as a crew member. I've no one by that description or name." He gave the note back to the constable. "A terrible thing to do to someone. Do you ken his age?"

"His betrothed is here." McLeary motioned to the door and escorted the seaman to the lobby.

"Haggadah, this is Mister Geddes. He would like to ken how old Tavish is?"

"He's nineteen." She confirmed as she stood from the chair.

"Lass, I'll be sure to keep an eye out for him. If I find him, I'll bring him home." Geddes reassured.

"Thank you." Haggadah tried to smile.

McLeary shook the man's hand. "Mister Geddes, safe travels."

Haggadah exhaled and looked down at the floor. She had hoped for better. Feeling the officer grasped her forearm, she looked at McLeary's face.

"Chin up. Don't lose hope." The constable encouraged. "We at least have another pair of eyes looking for him."

"Thank you, Constable. My heart believes he is alive, but my hope is dwindling." Haggadah departed for home.

"A message arrived for you, McLeary." The constable at the desk presented the letter.

McLeary took the note, opened it, and read two words – 'Brodie's house.' He tucked the message into his coat pocket, went directly to the councilman's residence, and knocked.

Amelia opened the door and motioned for the officer to enter. "Thank you for coming promptly, Constable McLeary. It dawned on me the other day that I had put away two pistols in the Deacon's wall safe the morning after the robbery. I didn't think much of it since he always leaves his things all over the house. I'm guessing he used them during the heist of the Excise Office." She motioned to the pair of pistols on the hallway table.

"Aye, others involved in the robbery had similar pistols," McLeary confirmed as he picked them up. "Have you received any word from him?"

"No, and if he is guilty, I doubt I will." The maid smirked.

"We've got an idea of where he may be found." McLeary shared. "He should be back in Edinburgh soon."

Chapter 25

Daffodils smiled in the sunshine as the hens were free to roam about the garden, pecking at insects and taking dust baths in the dry soil. Haggadah busily worked the coop's soiled straw into the herb garden ground. She paused to relieve an ache in her back and turned her face toward the welcoming rays on the warm spring day. A haunting ache crept into her consciousness, compelling Haggadah to look where the waterfront was in the distance. She pictured Tavish in her mind, sensing him far away. The corners of her mouth turned upward. "Someday, you will return. I must not think otherwise."

"Daydreaming?" Grizel entered the garden. "I can imagine what your mind is thinking, or shall I say of who?"

Haggadah looked at her mentor. "Aye, you ken me well."

"Good thoughts, I hope." The healer stepped before her apprentice.

"Aye, longing ones, too."

Grizel lifted her chin. The expression on her face radiated pride. "You've become an expert in healing and have exceeded my ability." She winked as she whispered. "But don't tell anyone I said so." She grinned.

As evening approached, Haggadah shut the coop door, securing the hens inside. Weary after a tiring day of gardening, she put her tools away and went into the cottage for the night. The aroma of fresh bread and a stew of smoked ham and potatoes caused Haggadah to inhale deeply. "Smells delicious." She washed her hands while Grizel placed the warm loaf of bread on a plate and added a sharp knife alongside it for cutting.

"You've had a long day, backbreaking work too." The healer admitted.

"Aye." Haggadah sat in her usual chair at the table. Her body ached, her eyelids drooped, and her stomach grumbled. She stood abruptly, realizing tea had not been made, and quickly did so before joining her mentor at the table again.

The crackling fire played like background dinner music as the town healer and her apprentice ate silently. Grizel was aware of Haggadah's early morning walk to the station house and assumed the answer she received remained the same. The healer dared to broach the sensitive subject. "No word from McLeary?"

Haggadah shook her head. "No, but he confided in me, even though he shouldn't have, that he received word that the King's Messenger is in Amsterdam and hoped to have Deacon Brodie in custody soon."

"Ah, still on the run. Well, we'll see if the messenger catches Brodie." Grizel paused with her buttered bread before her mouth. "I think the constable wants the case resolved and the truth to be known."

"He also said two men involved may not be charged, but the magistrate will decide. One may receive the reward of 150 pounds, too. The grocer, George Smith, is being held for trial."

"So, the two men may be given a King's Pardon? They must have given enough evidence to hang the other two."

Haggadah paused with a spoonful of stew above her bowl. "I suppose so."

They finished their meal without further conversation, did the dishes, and gathered near the fire. Grizel gathered her journal, pen, and ink as the hour grew late. She took her pocket watch, a gift she received as payment from a wealthy customer, from the mantel and dropped it into her overcoat pocket before slipping it on.

"Where are you off to at this late hour?" Haggadah grabbed a log to feed the fire.

"It's the Eve of Saint Mark."

"I must have lost track of days." She dropped the log onto the fire. "Would you like me to go with you?"

"No. This is something I must do alone. I'll return in a few hours." Grizel stepped into the darkness of the night, leaving Haggadah staring curiously at the closed door.

The town healer walked to Saint Cuthbert's Kirkyard, where Davis and Wiley anticipated her arrival. As they had done so several times before, the gravediggers waited on the stoop of the kirk with their lit lanterns. They readied themselves to watch the spectacle with the healer.

At the stroke of eleven, Grizel noted the times in her journal when each soul appeared. The trio remained silent and in place until her watch indicated one o'clock.

"I'm sorry, Grizel." Wiley consoled.

"Aye." Davis agreed.

"No need to be sorry. All of our days must come to an end. At least I ken my time will come soon." She closed the pocket watch and gave it to Wiley. "I'm trusting you with this. Once I'm gone, you must tell Haggadah of this night and explain how she will use the parade to ken who she can and cannot make well. I'll put my journal in a drawer in the apothecary. She must record the sightings as I have."

"Why don't you tell her yourself?" Davis inquired as he adjusted the cap on his head and picked up the lantern from the kirk's stoop.

"Because I don't want her to ken I'll die soon. She has lost Tavish. If she knew she'll soon lose me, it would cause her additional worry." Grizel stood. "She can't save me, no matter how hard she tries. It's as it should be." The corners of her mouth turned upward as she scanned the many headstones in the kirkyard. "She will continue to live in my house and be the town healer." Grizel grinned slightly. "Pick out a nice place for me to rest, and thank you, both, for all you've done for me. You have been good and cherished friends, as I assume you will continue to be for Haggadah."

The gravediggers nodded, unable to speak. They watched the town healer gingerly walk through the iron gate and toward home.

Within a month, Haggadah noticed a steep decline in Grizel's health. "I don't understand. I've tried several remedies, yet you're still ill." She gave Grizel a different remedy and placed the palm of her hand on the healer's forehead. It was cool to the touch.

Grizel appeased Haggadah's effort by drinking the concoction and handing the empty vessel to her apprentice. "Och, you worry yourself needlessly. I'm well. Just old and need rest."

Not more than a week later, Haggadah awoke and discovered Grizel had entered an eternal sleep during the night.

As promised, Wiley and Davis kept their word and prepared a lovely spot for the town healer's grave. They carried Grizel's body out of the cottage and put it in the back of the flatbed wagon. Haggadah sat beside her mentor's body while the horses pulled the wagon to the kirk. She looked up at the summer sun, smiling down at her. It added a bit of cheeriness to the solemn day. The gravediggers pulled the wagon to a stop before the iron gates, carried Grizel's body to the awaiting grave, and placed her reverently inside. No words were spoken as the trio stood gazing upon the wrapped body. Haggadah made the sign of the cross on herself and prayed as the gravediggers shoveled the mound of dirt into the hole. Her heart possessed another spot of hollowness, causing it to ache and feel heavy in her chest. She glanced at the white stone marking her mother's resting place as she waited for the last shovelful to be added to the healer's grave.

"Aw, don't be sad. You still have us." Davis tried to console. "You must ken, Grizel foresaw her death."

"How?" Haggadah looked from one gravedigger to the other.

"On the Eve of Saint Mark." Wiley began. "She asked us to tell you that she's put her journal in a drawer in the apothecary. What you need to do on that night is explained in its pages, but we'll be here on the kirk's stoop waiting for you as we were for Grizel. She also wants you to live in her cottage, heal those who can't pay for a physician, and carry on her charitable work."

Davis stepped forward and gripped Haggadah's forearm. "You're a skilled healer. Many will depend on you for help and your remedies."

The gravediggers left Haggadah, giving her time alone with the town healer to say her final goodbye.

Back in the cottage, loneliness surrounded her, consuming Haggadah's heart as she looked about the room. Remembering the journal, she opened the herbal cupboard and searched several drawers until she found the leatherbound book. Holding it reverently, she ran the palm of her hand over its cover. It was the last gift from Grizel. She put a log on the fire, lit a candle, and sat at the table. Taking a deep breath, she exhaled and opened the book to reveal Grizel's secret.

A knock at the door startled Haggadah, who slammed the journal shut. She opened the door to see a woman wringing her hands.

"My daughter, she's so wee and terribly ill." She tried to peek around Haggadah. "Is Grizel not in?"

"She died." Haggadah began. "Last night."

"Dead?"

"Not to worry. I'm able to help. What does your child suffer from?"

After a vague explanation of the child's ailments, Haggadah gathered the necessary items in her carpetbag, blew out the candle, and returned the journal to its proper place before leaving the cottage. In the waning hours of the day, she followed the woman through the streets to a windowless hovel. Haggadah knelt beside the child, who lay on several blankets on the floor, coughing. Haggadah placed her hand on the little girl's forehead. It was hot to the touch. She listened as the wheezing child coughed. Haggadah added aromatic herbs to a small crock of rendered lard and applied the salve to the patient's chest and the bottom of her feet. "Her cough should calm and allow her to sleep."

Haggadah glanced at the fireplace to see a cast iron kettle. "I need hot water to make a tea with herbs."

"Aye." The woman picked up the last crooked stick from the hearth and added it to the fire.

While she waited for the water to heat, Haggadah brushed the blonde hair away from the child's eyes. "How old are you?"

"Five."

"So, you can still count how old you are on one hand." Haggadah grinned as she held up her hand and counted each finger. "When you turn six, you must use a finger from your other hand."

"Or my thumb."

Haggadah chuckled. "Aye, or your thumb. You're a bright girl."

The concerned mother placed a tin pot with steaming water before Haggadah. "Will this do?"

"Aye," Haggadah added several herbs to the water. "The tea must steep for a few minutes. Is there a lid to cover it?"

The woman handed her a dented lid, which Haggadah put on the pot to trap the heat inside.

Throughout the night, Haggadah spoon-fed the child the warm liquid and kept a vigil. The child's fever broke several hours later. Before leaving the first-floor apartment, Haggadah advised the woman to continue giving the child the tea until it was gone. She warned the cough would be persistent, but the continued use of the salve would help it to go away.

The kirk's bell rang five times as she left the apartment. As she walked home, Haggadah watched the sky turn from indigo to light blue. Once inside the familiar walls, she threw a pair of logs onto the dying embers before climbing into the loft and letting sleep overcome her.

She woke several hours later, uncertain how long she had slept. As Haggadah lay in bed, she listened to the silence within the four walls of the cottage. It seemed odd to not hear Grizel shuffling about or tending to the fire.

Feeling the need to begin her day, Haggadah climbed down from the loft and looked at the empty bed. She decided she would no longer sleep in the loft. She busied her day and those after that by thoroughly cleaning the cottage, tending to the herbal garden, and ensuring she made the best remedies for those in need. Haggadah returned the Book of Shadows to the chest beneath the secret bottom for safekeeping. One day a week, she would distribute herbal remedies to the homeless, and on Sundays, she would attend Mass and visit her loved ones, who rested peacefully.

As mid-summer brought warmer temperatures, Haggadah attended the market nearly every Saturday. While at the market one morning, she overheard someone say the South Bridge was finished, and the first to cross the bridge would be the oldest citizen, a judge's wife. It was a great honor indeed.

Haggadah recalled the times she and Tavish watched the dismantling of the tenement buildings and construction of the bridge with its many vaults below. It took several years to construct, but now it would make getting around the city much easier. She wished Tavish could watch the ceremonial opening with her.

A knock sounded on the cottage door one morning as Haggadah lay in bed. She groaned, wishing for a few more moments of sleep after another late-night request for a remedy. She threw the bedcovers aside. Another knock sounded before she could reach the door.

"Och, must be an urgent case." Opening the door, she looked into the eyes of a young lad. Haggadah could hear his wheezed breathing. "Do you have a bad cough, too?"

"Aye, Mum sent me for a remedy."

She felt the lad's forehead. "No fever, good. I'll be just a minute." Haggadah quickly mixed up a salve and remedy. "Rub the salve on your chest and take a spoonful of this three times a day." She explained as she handed the lad both items.

"Thank you." The boy turned to leave, then turned and walked backward. "Have you heard about the judge's wife?"

Haggadah stared as the lad passed through the gate. "The one who will be the first to cross the South Bridge."

"Och! Not the way they planned. She's dead. A wagon will be carrying her across. She'll be in her coffin." He nodded his head and walked away.

Haggadah watched the lad walk along her stone wall and shook her head. "People will be watching the spectacle. Such a superstitious lot they are. I doubt they'll want to use the bridge and follow in the dead woman's footsteps."

Two days later, people gathered to witness the opening of the South Bridge. The gray sky of the overcast August day seemed the perfect setting for the mournful procession. People leaned out of their windows in the tall buildings lining the street to catch a glimpse of the event. Others watched from intersecting streets. No one dared to set foot on the completed structure.

Haggadah stood on the edge of High Street, peering at the end of the South Bridge as men loaded the coffin into the back of a wagon. A bellringer led the way as the solemn procession began. Onlookers remained silent, many with their heads bowed and others making the sign of the cross on their bodies, clasping their hands in prayer. No one dared to follow the deceased across the bridge. The whispered echo of 'cursed' drifted in the air.

As the procession passed her, Haggadah watched the casket continue to the North Bridge, perhaps going to the kirkyard for a proper burial.

A man walked past Haggadah. "Aye, the bridge is cursed."

Haggadah waited and looked at the bridge, yet no one dared to set foot on the new structure. "How idiotic. They'll insist on taking the long way around through the Grassmarket instead of setting foot on a bridge they believe is cursed." She reasoned as she shook her head. "A cursed bridge? Well, enough of this. I may not be an outstanding citizen, but I may be one of the bravest." Haggadah hesitated. She looked at the people on the street, who stopped and stared at her as she stepped on the bridge. Shouting from the tall buildings caused her to look up and see people going to their windows to witness her every step. What did they expect to happen? Did they think she would burst into flames?

Several people pointed at her. "She's cursed."

"A witch, I tell you, she's a witch."

"Oh, the healer's apprentice is a witch."

Haggadah held her head high and continued to the end of the newly built bridge. In a display of stubbornness, she turned around and returned to where she began. She ignored their comments and silly prejudices, risking her reputation to be tainted. At that moment, she inherited the label that would forever follow her for the remainder of her days – the town witch.

Chapter 26

The cost, Haggadah soon learned, was inquisitive stares and whispered conversations as she entered Saint Cuthbert Kirk for Mass. People also gave her a wide birth as she walked the streets to and from the service. At least the homeless knew better, or were they overlooking her new title only to receive her remedies? After visiting her mother's and Grizel's graves, she left the kirkyard and stopped before the South Bridge. It was empty. The superstitious people avoided using the bridge, fearing they would also be cursed.

Activity in the vaults beneath the bridge increased as merchants, eager to make a living in the new space, moved into the one hundred and twenty rooms and set up shop.

On a fine Saturday morning later that month, Haggadah went to the market with a basket in hand. With talk of the vaults circulating around her while she shopped, she decided to purchase what she needed and visit the underground market.

Haggadah stood across the street. The entrance resembled a dark cave more than a doorway. It was as busy as a beehive, with people entering and exiting quickly.

Being avoided by society had its advantages. Haggadah walked to the entrance. The person waiting to enter stepped backward, allowing her to go before him. He waited until she had disappeared into the darkness before entering.

Once inside, Haggadah paused momentarily to allow her eyes to adjust to the darkness. She wrinkled her nose at the smell of fish and musty dampness. She could see oil lamps dimly lighting the passageway and people forming two lines like trained cattle, one entering and the other exiting. She followed in line with the others.

The tin merchant displayed the items of his craft proudly. He demonstrated his skill as he worked on a pot, hoping to entice someone to purchase one of the handmade products.

Room after room was filled with curious people crowding into them. Some rooms were large with tall ceilings, while others were relatively small.

"I feel as if I'm entering the bowels of Hell." Haggadah muttered as she descended to the next level of the vaults. "The air is thin. Not healthy for anyone to breathe." She put the palm of her hand over her nose to avoid the offensive smell of burning fish oil.

She noticed the dampness on the wall and a trickle of water seeping between rocks. Haggadah wondered how long it would be before several chambers became dotted with puddles of water. "Tavish was right."

Haggadah walked through the labyrinth of rooms, taking note of the various merchants. The clang of a hammer echoed from the blacksmith's room as he worked, and the forge's heat made it unbearable to stay in the room for any length of time. Unwilling to tour all one hundred and twenty rooms, Haggadah left the darkness, stepped into the overcast daylight, and inhaled a deep breath of fresh air. As she walked home, she considered the vaults unhealthy conditions – dampness, fish oil, smoke from the smiths, and unemptied chamber pots. "The lamps do little to take away the darkness, making it difficult to see what the merchants offer. We'll see if they can make a go of it."

~

By month's end, Brodie was tracked down in the Netherlands and extradited back to Edinburgh. The courtroom was filled when Haggadah entered on the day of the trial. She went to the rear of the room and flattened herself against the back wall behind the last row of those seated. The town witch peered down into the gallery at Deacon William Brodie and George Smith, both men standing on a spindle-railed platform. Humphrey Moore and Andrew Ainslie stood on a separate platform, gripping the spindled railing, and looked up at the three magistrates on an elevated bench. Haggadah stared at the men dressed in black robes with white collars and perukes made of horsehair on their heads. They projected an intimidating legality and looked down upon the criminal as if judging them guilty without hearing a single word in their defense.

As the gavel sounded to start the hearing, the courtroom became silent. Moore and Ainslie were questioned, evidence was presented, and they were granted a King's Pardon for the evidence they produced. Moore was also given the monetary reward of one hundred and fifty pounds. The pair remained in the courtroom as members of the audience.

A lawyer waited as the prosecutor presented the evidence of Brodie's attempted escape from Edinburgh.

"Deacon William Brodie is being accused of several robberies in the city of Edinburgh, one of which was the robbery of the Excise Office. After his partners in crime were taken in for questioning, Brodie went south to Dover, backtracked to London, then boarded the Leigh ship *Endeavour* using the name of John Dixon. The ship was scheduled to pull into port in Edinburgh, but Brodie paid the captain to drop him in Flushing, Netherlands. He then traveled to Ostend. I would like to call Mister Geddes to the witness stand."

The gentleman took his place in the center of the open floor before the magistrates.

"Please identify yourself and the person upon your ship." The lawyer instructed.

"I'm Lewis Geddes." He pointed at Brodie. "That be him right there. He gave me the letters to take to his mistress on Cant's Close, but I turned them in at the station house."

Jean stood. "Cant's Close! But I live on Libberton's Wynd."

Ann stood. "I live on Cant's Close. The Deacon is the father of my bairns."

"As well as mine." Jean admitted as she glared at the other mistress before looking at Brodie. "They can hang you for all I care." Taking one last hateful look at Ann, Jean stormed out of the courtroom.

"Order! Order!" The magistrate slammed the gavel several times until the room quieted.

Warmth crept into Ann's cheeks as she returned to her seat.

"Continue." The magistrate ordered the prosecutor, who held the letters high for all to see.

"Are these the letters?" The prosecutor held the correspondence before the witness.

"Aye." Geddes confirmed.

"Is there anything else you wish to add, Mister Geddes?"

"No."

"Thank you." The prosecutor waited for the witness to return to his seat. "I would like to submit an invoice written by Deacon William Brodie to verify his handwriting matches that of the letters to his mistress." He placed the evidence on the bench for the magistrates to view. "I'd like to bring forward George Williamson as a witness."

The witness stepped forward.

"Please tell the court your name and occupation and give your testimony."

"My name is George Williamson. I'm the King's Messenger. I tracked Deacon Brodie. After losing his trail near Dover, I returned to Edinburgh. I was allowed to read the letters he wrote to Ann Grant. With the information from the letters and Mister Geddes, I resumed my pursuit and nabbed Brodie in Amsterdam before he could travel to the United States. Brodie was hiding in a cupboard when I found and apprehended him. I brought him back to Edinburgh to stand trial."

"Thank you, Mister Williams." The prosecutor waited for his witness to return to his seat before holding a clay mold high for all to see and explained in detail how the former cabinet maker and locksmith, George Smith, used putty to make impressions of cabinet and door keys, only to return later at night to take what he wanted. He demonstrated how one of the keys on the ring fit perfectly into the mold.

"They have no chance of proving their innocence." Haggadah whispered to herself.

The prosecutor concluded his case and sat.

The center magistrate looked at the accused. "Do you have anything to add to your defense?"

Even though the defense lawyer did his best to discredit the witnesses in his statement, the evidence was stacked against the partners in crime, who remained silent. "I have no witnesses."

The magistrates put their heads together in whispered conversation. As they nodded, the center magistrate announced their ruling. "Deacon William Brodie and Andrew Ainslie, you will be hung until dead on the first of October in the year of our Lord 1888 at the Old Tolbooth before Saint Giles Cathedral. May God rest your souls." The gavel slammed on the circular sound block, finalizing the ruling. The courtroom erupted in conversation as the prisoners were led back to the Tolbooth to await their hanging.

~

As the summer season surrendered its greenery to colorful autumn, Haggadah busied her days with weeding, reseeding, and harvesting the various plants from the garden. Even though she missed her mother, Grizel, and Tavish, she had little time to grieve or feel lonely. There seemed to be a constant need for her ability to help those who could not afford a physician. When she walked through the streets, the citizens continued to ostracize her as if she were a contagious leper. She often heard whispers of 'witch' from those she passed.

During one of her weekly rounds administering remedies to the homeless, she discovered many of the closes were vacant. Hearing a crowd near Saint Giles, she walked to the Tolbooth to see nearly forty thousand people gathered to witness a hanging. She watched as George Smith's lifeless body was taken down from the rope and set aside on the platform. Deacon William Brodie confidently stepped forward.

"No, Daddy."

Haggadah looked to her right at the young girl, not more than ten years old.

"Hush, Cecile. You must be brave."

Haggadah recognized the woman consoling the child as one of Brodie's mistresses.

The bell of Saint Cuthbert's rang.

Haggadah watched as the noose was adjusted three times before Brodie dangled on the rope's end. She thought it odd his body was taken down quickly. The town witch looked at Brodie's daughter, who watched with tears trickling down her cheeks. She thought it was cruel for her mother to allow the child to witness her father's death. Haggadah walked away, disgusted by the enjoyment people sought in the punishment. Maybe they were pleased to see a man of Brodie's social status receive his comeuppance.

Haggadah finished passing out her remedies to the homeless, returned home, and hung up her carpetbag on a peg next to Tavish's hat. Having it where she could see it often made Haggadah feel like he was always near her. She reached into her overcoat pocket and withdrew the handfasting ribbon. Reverently, she hung it with his flat cap before removing her overcoat and putting it on a peg.

Days later, as she stopped before a sweet shop, she overheard two women talking.

"Some say Brodie bribed the hangman to overlook a steel collar and silver tube around his neck. Maybe he hoped to cheat death." The gossipy woman smirked.

"Whatever his plan was, it failed. I'm surprised he was buried in an unmarked grave in Saint Cuthbert's Chapel of Ease." The other confirmed.

"He must have been a generous contributor." The woman looked at Haggadah, grabbed her friend's arm, and the gossipers quickly walked away.

Haggadah assumed Brodie's donation to the kirk must have been quite large. She wondered if the Lord thought it sincere since it was most likely comprised of stolen money.

Chapter 27

The city and its citizens had endured a cold winter. Yule was a lonely time for the town witch. However, Haggadah was busy making remedies for the homeless and receiving requests during all hours of the night.

Haggadah went to the kirk on a blustery January Sunday to attend Mass. It had been one year since she had spoken her vow to become Tavish's wife. With a heavy heart, she waited in an empty pew after the service, hoping her husband-to-be would appear to take their final vows. Entwined in her fingers was the purple ribbon. Tavish's hat lay in her lap.

The priest tidied the altar and snuffed out the candles. He turned to see Haggadah sitting with her hands folded and head bowed. He had known her when she was young, then an orphan, an apprentice to the town healer, and now, the town witch, shunned by many. She possessed a kind and gentle heart and was generous to a fault. Taking pity on her isolation in society, the priest went to her. "Haggadah, how may I help you?"

The town witch looked up at the priest with rivulets of tears cascading down her cheeks. She dared not speak, fearing she would emotionally fall apart.

"Word has reached my ears of Tavish's disappearance." He saw the handfasting ribbon in her lap and recalled the ceremony. Had it been a year already?

"Aye." She wiped her face dry. "I ken he is alive, or at least I feel that he is. If he could, Tavish would be here to say our vows."

The priest searched his mind for the proper words. If she believed Tavish was still alive, so would he. "Tavish is a man of his word. He loves you dearly. Of that, I'm certain." He placed his hand on her forearm. "I'll pray for his return to you. Keep the faith."

"Thank you, Father."

The priest went to the sanctuary, looked back at the town witch, and shook his head. "Such grief for one so young." He entered the room, leaving Haggadah alone with her thoughts and prayers.

She sat for hours in the silence of the church. The solitude was peaceful and calming and made her feel secure. It was here, in the house of the Lord, where she was not judged by anyone other than Him. Haggadah stared at the crucifix on the wall. "Watch over him, God, wherever he may be. Please bring Tavish home to me."

She stood, left the kirk, and went to her mother's grave, where she lay and cried, shedding tears of grief.

Davis picked up a fallen branch from the ground, tucked it in his arm, and paused as he heard a woman's heart-wrenching sobs. He threw the bundle aside and sought out the crying. Soon, he came upon Haggadah, sighed, and shook his head. "There now, come off the cold ground. You'll end up having to heal yourself." He scooped her in his arms and carried her to the stone bench. "What's this blubbering all about?" He retrieved a flask from his inside coat pocket, opened the top, and pushed it before her face. "Drink. It'll warm you."

Haggadah took a rather large swig, causing her to choke. She inhaled to regain her breath and wiped the tears from her cheeks. "I hoped he would be here."

"Tavish?"

"Aye. We were to be wed today."

Davis recalled the handfasting he and Wiley witnessed. "A year already?"

Haggadah nodded. "Aye."

"I'd marry you, but your heart belongs to Tavish." He chuckled. "Och, I doubt you would want to be married to a gravedigger. Besides, Wiley would get lonely." He grinned, hoping to cheer her up.

"It's kind of you to offer, but you're right. My heart belongs to my betrothed." Even though her face was red and puffy and her eyes bloodshot from crying, Haggadah glanced at Davis to convey her gratitude for the offer. She handed the flask back to him. "When others avoid me and label me as the town witch, you and Wiley have remained steadfast by my side, true friends. Thank you."

Davis nodded. "When you get right down to it, we're avoided too. Who wants to chum around with a pair of gravediggers. It's like being friends with death itself." He tucked the flask into his coat. "We must keep believing Tavish will return someday."

Haggadah nodded. "Aye."

~

Tavish stood on the deck. The trees looked odd in this strange land where the sun was hotter than he had ever known. He watched as scantily dressed people with the darkest skin he had ever seen marched single file onto the ship. He saw the exchange of money from his captain to a dark-skinned man. "He's purchasing the people like a sack of flour?" He whispered, speaking his mind.

"Aye," answered the shipmate beside him, "and the captain will sell them for a higher price once we reach port."

"Sell them?"

"There's a lot of money in the sale of a slave. Especially the big, tall men."

Tavish remained silent as he watched the cargo go below deck. A small boy, whose eyes registered fear, clung to his mother. "It doesn't seem right."

Disgusted, he looked in the direction of home, to Haggadah, and hoped she would wait patiently for him to return.

Chapter 28

Over the years, the leaking walls of the vaults were blamed on the curse of the judge's wife. The dampness, insufficient lighting, odorous air, lack of running water, and horrid sanitary conditions forced tenants to eventually leave. Unfortunately, what replaced the merchants were brothels and distilleries, giving the once promising South Bridge Vaults the reputation of a rathole that housed the poorest of the poor.

Haggadah occasionally received a request to venture into the vaults and tend to someone who was ill. It was a place she avoided. However, as a dedicated healer, Haggadah knew her duty was to treat the patient, regardless of the danger or their living conditions.

Still shunned by society twenty years later, the town witch continued to help the homeless, who were grateful for her remedies. Even a few members of affluent families came to her for help when a physician could not be found. No matter her social status, the wealthy patients understood her to be kind and caring, yet they would never acknowledge it among their friends.

Haggadah walked along the sidewalk on a particular spring day with her carpetbag in hand. She stopped before the clocksmith shop and peered in the window at a mantel clock she had long admired. "Today is the day." The town witch entered the shop and purchased the clock with money she had received for treating several patients who lived in New Town.

"I'll have it delivered to your cottage post haste." The owner offered as he accepted her payment. He eyed her suspiciously. "No extra charge."

"Thank you." Haggadah left the shop, stopped at the sweet shop for her favorite candy, and walked home. Within the hour, a knock sounded upon her door. She was pleased to see a lad standing with the boxed clock in his hands. He placed the object in her arms and ran away.

Haggadah carried the wooden box to the table, set it down gently, and opened it to reveal her purchase. She smiled and looked at the crowded mantel. "Och, I guess I'll have to make room." She removed the statue of the three women and the bundle of colorful candles, climbed the ladder to the loft, and added them to the chest. Returning to the table, she proudly placed the mahogany timepiece in the center of the fireplace mantel, stepped back, and admired her purchase.

Haggadah looked toward the cottage door as a knock sounded upon it. Her heart used to skip a beat with each knock, hoping it was Tavish. On the precipice of her forty-first birthday, she no longer hoped. Cast as a cursed witch and spinster by society, she accepted the title long ago and her life of solitude in her cottage.

Opening the old oak door, she stared down into the angelic face of a familiar homeless boy. His twinkling sky-blue eyes stared back at her as the wind disheveled his curly blonde hair. He often called on her, hoping to earn a coin or two by running an errand for her. "Good day, Bryson. I've no errand for you to run today."

"I've news. There is a lass born as cursed. No one in her family will be her godparent. I overheard a woman say, the bairn has a bad case of stomach pains."

"Colic. And you be telling me this why?"

Bryson shifted his weight from one bare foot to the other. His blonde locks moved about like weightless feathers in the breeze. "Talk amongst the people on the street is that you should be her godmother."

Haggadah put her fisted hand on her hip. "Och, that's what they think?"

"Aye." He grinned. "She needs someone to watch over her soul. I ken of no one better than you."

"So, you agree with the others?"

"Aye. You've helped many, cured many, and more than anything, you care for everyone, whether cursed or not. The bairn is going to need a guiding hand." Bryson winked, hoping to convince the town witch. "They're a well-off family. I doubt they want many to ken of their circumstance. It'll be hard to hide it, though. Word has it the wee lass has flaming red hair, and you ken how wagging tongues like to spread gossip."

"Like yourself?" Haggadah raised an eyebrow as she grinned. "In case I'm so inclined, what is the family's name, and where can I find them?"

"It's the Oliver Stewart family in New Town. Thanks, Haggadah. I ken you will do it." Bryson skipped down the flagstone pathway and passed through the rickety gate.

Shortly after the clock on the mantel struck noon, Haggadah could no longer resist the voice inside her head pushing her to do what must be done. Assured the bairn suffered from colic, she made a gentle remedy to ease the wee one's pain. She placed the corked bottle in her carpetbag, put on her overcoat that had become ragged and tattered over the years, and left the cottage.

Haggadah walked through Old Town, which was much of the same. It still reeked of sewage, smoke lingered in the air like ghostly apparitions, and the windows of towering buildings watched over the homeless; many of them had turned to body snatching, selling the dead, to earn enough money to survive.

With Edinburgh's population increasing, construction of New Town continued. The wealthier citizens moved from Old Town to New Town to escape the overcrowding and poor living conditions. Nor Loch, the recipient of emptied chamber pots, was a cesspool of stench on warmer days. It would soon be drained, and a public garden planted in its place. There would be trees, shrubs, flowers, and benches for visitors to rest after a stroll. People no longer feared the curse of the South Bridge and used it to ease their travels about the city. However, the vaults were still a shelter for the poorest of the poor. Haggadah wondered what her mother, Grizel, and Tavish would think of the changes to Edinburgh.

Her attention was drawn to a close as she walked by it. The homeless, with their suspicious eyes, stared back at her as if she were an infectious disease. A woman holding a bairn on her hip nodded, the only sign of respect to the healer. Haggadah recalled giving her a remedy for the child. She nodded in return and continued to walk.

Those along the sidewalk gave the town witch a wide birth. Some knew who she was, while others were simply disgusted by her appearance.

Haggadah crossed the South Bridge and went into New Town. On a well-established, well-to-do street of houses, Haggadah, with her carpetbag in hand, stood out of place on the corner near the crossroads. She took a deep breath and exhaled. If what the lad said was true, she assumed the baby was born the seventh daughter of the seventh daughter. Haggadah was sure no one in the family would step forward to be the cursed child's godparent. Would the family accept her offer as the baby's godmother?

The town witch walked up the few steps to the stoop and knocked. A maid answered the door. Before the woman could speak, Haggadah could hear the painful cries of the baby and announced, "I'm here to claim the bairn as my goddaughter." Uninvited, she stepped into the house.

"What's going on here?" Evelyn Stewart insisted as the strange woman entered the sitting room. "Oliver!" She called her husband.

Haggadah went directly to the bassinet. Setting her carpetbag on the floor, she picked up the crying baby. "There now, I've brought something for your aching belly." The town witch looked at the red-faced babe as she continued to cry and draw up her knees to her abdomen. She reached into her bag, withdrew her remedy, and administered a small portion. The town witch placed the bottle on a side table.

"Evelyn, I'm busy..." Oliver entered the room and stopped abruptly next to his wife. He curled his upper lip as he noticed Haggadah with his daughter in her arms. "Here now. What are you doing with our daughter?"

Haggadah turned toward the couple as she rocked the babe in her arms. "Word has reached my ears of her birth. I'm sorry for your loss of the previous six, but I'm even more sorry to hear she is cursed. So, I'm offering to be the bairn's godmother."

The maid, peeking around the doorway of the sitting room, gasped and then covered her mouth with the palm of her hand.

Oliver stepped forward. An astute businessman, he realized his daughter's dire situation. "Anna's godmother?"

"Oliver, you can't be serious." Evelyn objected.

"Hush, Evelyn." He sternly commanded and watched the child become quiet in the town witch's arms. "Under one condition."

Even though Haggadah held the infant for only a few moments, she loved Anna as if she was her own. To be her godmother would be the closest the town witch would come to experiencing motherhood in her lifetime. Her heart swelled with the thought. She looked from the baby's cherub face and stared at Oliver wearily. "Which is?"

"The ceremony is held privately at the kirk, and you must never come in contact with Anna for the remainder of her life." Oliver held his chin high, waiting for Haggadah to object to his terms.

Her heart deflated like a balloon, expelling its air as Haggadah looked at the baby in her arms, who grinned back at her. The condition Oliver demanded was harsh and cruel but justified. For a wealthy family, associating with the town witch would jeopardize their place in society. Haggadah delayed her reply to enjoy the maternal essence of the babe in her arms.

"Well?" Oliver pressed.

Haggadah's decision was an easy one. Even though she would not be a part of Anna's life, she would still be her guardian. "Aye, I'll keep a watchful eye over her from afar."

"Then I'll arrange the baptism with the priest and send word of the day and time." He watched as the town witch pressed her lips to his daughter's forehead.

Haggadah laid Anna in the bassinet and ran her finger along her goddaughter's soft, chubby cheek. "I'll always be nearby watching over you, little one." She lifted her carpetbag from the floor and pointed to the remedy on the side table. "This will help with the bairn's aching stomach." Haggadah took one last look at Anna and left the house.

Within a week, Haggadah entered the kirk for the baptism and discovered the Stewart family already present. The sacrament was brief but meaningful, especially to the town witch, who accepted her responsibility as godmother to Anna. The Stewart family quickly departed the nave, with Oliver pausing before Haggadah.

"This is the last time you will ever be in my daughter's presence." He warned.

"Aye, as I've promised." Haggadah watched as his retreating figure passed through the kirk doors. She sat in the pew. Even though she had suffered the loss of loved ones, the town witch said a prayer expressing her thankfulness. It was indeed a blessing to be someone's godmother.

As Anna grew, Haggadah often watched her goddaughter play with her younger brother, Lachlan, on warm summer days in the Princes' Street Gardens. "Och, Anna, it's easy to find you amongst the others with your bright, red hair." Unbeknownst to her goddaughter, the town witch attended Mass every Sunday, scanning the congregation to catch a glimpse of Anna.

During one of her nightly calls for a remedy years later, Haggadah stood outside the Stewart house. From across the street, she peered through the picture window to see Anna sitting on a sofa, playing with a doll. "I see Bryson delivered my gift to you. Happy tenth birthday, Anna." Even though she was not welcome within the walls of the Stewart family, it eased her loneliness, knowing the child was part of her life. "Sleep well, my dear." Haggadah turned away and began walking home with a bit of a limp she had developed in her leg. Her hip had taken a turn for the worse lately. "I'll add wintergreen to a salve. Perhaps that will help." Haggadah extended her hand to catch a raindrop as the sky began to weep. "Och, could be why my hip is aching."

Haggadah neared home as she passed through the pitiful streets of Old Town, halted her steps, and listened, quite uncertain of what she heard. "An abandoned bairn?" She looked about. A whimper drew her attention to an entwined ball of fur in the darkness near a set of steps. Staring back at her were a pair of beady eyes. A puppy was cuddled with an ebony kitten, huddling for warmth. The tip of the pup's tail wagged. Even though she had little to offer them, she had a roof over her head and a fire to keep them warm on cold nights.

"A well-dressed man threw the dog out."

Haggadah turned to see a homeless man sitting against the base of a building, tipping a bottle to his lips. She looked back at the furry pair, reached down, and picked up the kitten. She placed it in her carpetbag. The puppy stood with its tail between its hind legs and looked up at her sadly. Haggadah picked up the pup and put it inside her coat. It began to wiggle and lick her chin. "Settle. We'll be home soon." Haggadah could feel his tail thumping against her chest as she held him close and walked the remainder of the way home.

She entered the cottage, placed the puppy on the floor, took the kitten from her carpetbag, and set it next to the puppy. She hung her carpetbag next to Tavish's hat, removed her sodden coat, and put it on a peg.

Haggadah stoked the fire and grabbed the dishtowel from the hook on the wall. She turned and nearly tripped over the puppy, who had followed her. "Come, let me dry you." The puppy followed Haggadah to the chair where she sat, leaned forward, and blotted the cloth on its soaked fur. She looked at the coat of black and brown, its charcoal eyes with brown eyebrows staring at her. The ebony kitten needed little assistance as it sat near the fire, grooming its damp fur.

"I ken it's late, but I think we all need a special treat before going to sleep." Haggadah put the kettle on to warm. She retrieved dried beef from the cellar, crumbled it into two bowls, and added hot water. She retrieved the biscuits from the cupboard and enjoyed a cup of tea while watching her pets eat their meager meal.

She looked at the puppy as he curled on the braided rug before the fire. "Barret sounds like a perfect name for you." The kitten jumped into her lap and lay before closing his eyes and purring. "Nero seems to fit you well." Haggadah sipped her tea and looked from the slumbering puppy to the kitten. They were both warm, content, and happy. So was she.

A Special Preview of

The Cursed Witch

Chapter 1

Edinburgh, Scotland – October 31, 1828

The clip-clop of the horse's hooves on the cobblestone echoed throughout the deserted main street. The driver of the flatbed wagon kept the mare at a slow pace. Sitting next to him was his partner, who scanned every close and window for someone who may be awake at the late bewitching hour of the night.

Flickering candles on windowsills illuminated colorful glass witch balls and hag stones protectively dangling from ribbons, warding off evil spirits. For tonight, the thin veil between the seen and unseen allowed spirits to roam freely amongst the living. At least, the superstitious resurrectionists believed the pagan legend to be true.

"Glad he rented us the horse and wagon. Makes the job easier." Martin encouraged the chestnut mare down a side street and pulled on the reins to bring the horse to a stop.

"Aye, the guard's been paid, right?" John's short legs extended toward the street. He jumped from the seat and grabbed a shovel from the flatbed. He looked up at Martin, who was a head taller, and awaited his reply.

A black cat darted beneath the wagon with a dead rodent dangling limply from her mouth.

Martin looked down as the ebony feline scurried across his boots and disappeared into the shadowed darkness. Slow to react, he took a skittish step backward and kicked his foot toward the feral. "Damn cat!" He made the sign of the cross on his body, praying the feline was not a bad omen. Martin picked up the second shovel from the wagon bed. "Aye, he told us the guard has been bought off. Can't you remember anything, John?" He sighed, lowering the volume of his voice to a whisper. "We should be fine as long as a constable doesn't stroll by the kirkyard." Martin looked up and down the street. "He said this one is young and hasn't been dead long." He flashed his partner a grin of blackened teeth. "We should get near £10 for her."

John's empty stomach grumbled. "Maybe we can get a meat pie for each of us. I do like meat pies. You do too." He patted his abdomen before retrieving the lantern from a hook on the front of the wagon. "Do we need this?" He held the glowing light up for his partner to see.

Martin cringed, waving his arm downward, encouraging John to lower the lantern. He looked at the full moon, another ominous sign. The bright orb shed ample light on the crowded city of Edinburgh, but he feared the young woman's may be overshadowed by a stone wall or another gravestone. "Aye, bring it. Keep it near your body and cover it with the blade of your shovel so its light isn't seen."

Withered leaves swirled in the wind, crossing their pathway as if warning the men of impending danger. They crept along the iron fence of Saint Cuthbert's kirkyard.

John looked at the spear finials topping the barrier and wondered if its purpose was to keep trespassers out or the restless spirits within.

The wind whistled through the nearly bare tree branches, freeing a broken limb. It fell to the ground with a resounding thud. Assuming the noise was a heavy footstep, the men froze and listened.

John's heart pounded like a drum in his chest. His rapid breathing appeared like wispy clouds in the chilly night air. Even though he and Martin were homeless, living within various closes with other poor vagabonds, he knew if they were caught, a speedy trial would ensue. The magistrate may rule to put them on a convict ship with a one-way trip to Australia. On the other hand, if they were accused of murdering the woman, their crime would be considered grievous, and they would be hung in public. He preferred neither option.

The men stopped before the tall iron gate and looked about. Assuming they remained undetected, Martin exhaled, relieved he saw no witnesses. He looked at his superstitious partner, whose previous comment caused doubt to seep into his mind. "Let's hope he is true to his word and the gate is unlocked. Otherwise, we may have to scale the fence."

John held his breath as he watched Martin grasp the latch and lift it cautiously. He cringed, fearing the hinges were rusty and would squeak. He exhaled as it swung open silently.

Pulling the gate wide enough for them to pass, Martin jerked his head toward the opening, signaling John to go before him. Once inside the kirkyard, he closed the gate, leaving it unlatched for their escape. He turned and nearly bumped into John, who hesitated to step on the hallowed ground. Exhaling like an angry bull, Martin stared down at the back of John's head. "She's buried in the northwest corner." He nudged his partner's shoulder, encouraging him forward, but John's feet were planted solidly as he scanned the gravestones within the kirkyard, uncertain of which direction to go.

"You ken I'm not good with compass directions. Which way, left, right, or straight ahead?"

Martin pressed his lips together to control his temper, looked heavenward, and grabbed John by the forearm. He glanced up at a lit window in the tower as they passed by it, ignoring the silhouette looking down at him, and headed toward the grave with his friend in tow.

The guard watched the men, assuming they were the resurrectionists he had expected. Typically, Angus would tour the graveyard, paying careful attention to the recently buried, stopping to listen for the sound of a bell from the dead ringers. He would dig up the survivor saved by the bell if he heard an alarm. His responsibilities included deterring resurrectionists and grave robbers during his long nightly graveyard shift. Tonight, however, he was paid to ignore the men for the few hours it would take them to retrieve a body.

Within the past two days, three bodies had been added to the kirkyard. Two of the deceased were men of wealth. They received a proper burial, including a bell tucked under one hand, before their caskets were sealed. In addition, their families had paid for expensive iron mortsafes to enclose the casket, ensuring their loved ones remained safely in the ground to rest in peace.

The third, a young woman who had yet to reach twenty years of age, had died under mysterious circumstances. She was not given a bell, nor was her casket enclosed in a mortsafe. Many in the city did not want her body buried in the kirkyard, for they knew she was the seventh daughter of the seventh daughter, thus cursing her as a witch. When she was born, those in her immediate family refused to step forward as her godparent. Finally, someone outside the family was kind enough to assume the role. Her godmother, ever-present yet always unseen, guided her goddaughter from afar. She remained hidden in the shadows of the kirkyard during the funeral, loyal to the end.

The haunting call of an owl echoed throughout the kirkyard.

John scanned the treetops, his panic welling within him. "An owl? In the city? It's a sign and a bad one." He was pulled past a gravestone embellished with an hourglass, a skull, and an angel with her wings outstretched. Fixated on the hollow eyes of the sculpture staring back at him, he wondered if the soul within the grave was at rest. He looked from gravestone to gravestone, silent sentinels, as shadows as black as ink danced between them, or was it just his imagination?

As the pair neared the corner of the kirkyard, Martin slowed his pace as he searched the ground for freshly overturned soil. "Here it is." He pointed with the handle of his shovel at the mounded rectangle of dirt.

John set the lantern on the ground and looked at each narrow end of the grave. "No marker. What end do you think they placed her head?"

Martin looked for a nearby grave for comparison, but there were none. The kirk had isolated the woman's body far away from the others. "A good question. They may have buried her in the opposite direction to make sure she never rises from the dead."

"He told us she wasn't given a bell, so the guard won't ken to save her if she wakes, and she can't get out of there, especially not that far down in the ground." John reasoned.

Knowing the townsfolks presumed the girl to be a witch, Martin warned, "Don't be too sure. She may possess the power to do so even in death."

John looked at one end of the grave, then the other. "Let's start at this end," he guessed as he set the tip of his shovel in the loosened soil, "and hope I'm right."

They pushed their shovels into the soil and dropped the dirt in a pile beside the grave. Even in the chilly night air, the men unbuttoned their never-washed overcoats and wiped their brows with the sleeves to sop the dripping sweat from stinging their eyes. They continued digging until Martin's shovel's blade collided with something hollow and wooden. He looked at John and smiled. John grinned in return, displaying his missing front tooth.

They widened the hole, exposing the narrow end of the casket made crudely from repurposed wood.

John retrieved the lantern and held it above the hole. "A few more shovelfuls at each corner should free it enough to bust the end and get her out."

Martin licked his lips as he thrust his shovel into the hole. "I can taste that meat pie already." He dumped a shovelful of dirt onto the pile. "With the colder weather, her body hasn't had a chance to rot much. She'll be a fine one for Knox to cut apart."

The men cleared the casket's end, used the tip of their shovels to pry it open, and saw thick, wavey, scarlet hair lying within.

Martin looked at his partner in crime. "Looks like you guessed right."

John nodded as his chest puffed up like a proud rooster. "Let's get her out." The men tossed aside their shovels.

Martin, being quite muscular and robust, lay on his stomach on the grave and grabbed the corpse's head. Placing his large hands on the cranium, he pulled on the body and exposed the young woman's face. Her eyes were closed as if she was sleeping. He reached into the casket and grasped beneath her arms. "Here she comes." He yanked and thrust the body upward into John's waiting hands.

"Got her." John dragged the body out of the hole as Martin continued to push it upward, stood, and grabbed the ankles as the body was exhumed. They dropped the corpse on the ground. Both men looked at it, breathing heavily and pleased to have the worst of the task done.

"Aye, she's fresh, alright. No stench whatsoever," Martin confirmed.

A gust of wind swayed the treetops. John scanned the kirkyard. A chill ran up his spine as he imagined the restless souls' watchful eyes staring at him, judging him and his partner for their wrongdoing. "Let's grab her and go."

"Don't be daft. We gotta fill the hole first." Martin picked up his shovel. John sighed and retrieved his as well. They each threw a shovelful of dirt back into the hole.

"Ahh-chew!"

"Bless you." The resurrectionists said simultaneously. They looked at each other, pausing with their shovels in their hands.

"I didn't sneeze," John said as he stared at Martin, who stomped the tip of his shovel into the pile of dirt.

Martin pushed his shovel into the pile of dirt and looked at John. "I didn't sneeze either."

The men stood staring at each other as a moan echoed behind them. They looked over their shoulders and watched as the corpse sat up, its head turned, eyes wide, staring at them.

Tales of witches rising from the dead and bestowing curses on those who betrayed them were well known.

John's mouth opened. He became saucer-eyed as he tried to scream, but no sound came.

The color drained from Martin's face, leaving it pasty white. He broke out in a cold sweat.

Transfixed by the living-dead woman, John dropped his shovel and took a blind step forward, falling into the open grave. Abandoning his shovel in the dirt, Martin took a giant step into the loose soil of the grave, twisted his ankle, and tumbled into the hole on top of John, who screamed in terror. Martin used John's shoulder like a stepping stool to climb out of the grave. He turned and grabbed his partner's pleading arms, reaching toward him for help, and yanked John out of the ground. The resurrectionists darted from the kirkyard with their unbuttoned overcoats flapping behind them.

If you enjoyed reading

The Healer's Apprentice

please post your review on Amazon.

For additional information about the author, signings, and her books, please visit.

www.BrendaHasseBooks.com

www.ingramcontent.com/pod-product-compliance
Lightning Source LLC
LaVergne TN
LVHW091704070526
838199LV00050B/2276